"Devlin, wait! There's something I have to show you!"

She reached for her purse. "I have a photo of Livie," Karen explained quickly.

He glanced down at the photograph while she watched his face, waiting for some sign of awareness. There was none. Not yet.

"Her hair wasn't curled for the picture," she said. "It's naturally wavy, and even darker than it looks here. And her eyes—you can't tell in this—but her eyes are a dark blue."

Devlin looked up, catching her gaze. "How old is your daughter?"

"Livie just turned three."

When she thought she couldn't endure another second of his silent scrutiny, he glanced at the picture again. "It isn't possible. We took precautions."

"Yes, and sometimes even the most careful precautions fail."

"And just when," he growled, "were you planning to tell me about her? Or, if I hadn't turned you down just now, would you ever have told me at all?"

Dear Harlequin Intrigue Reader,

We have another outstanding title selection this month chock-full of great romantic suspense, starting with the next installment in our TOP SECRET BABIES promotion. In *The Hunt for Hawke's Daughter* (#605) by Jean Barrett, Devlin Hawke had never expected to see Karen Ramey once she'd left his bed—let alone have her tell him his secret child had been kidnapped by a madman. Whether a blessing or a curse, Devlin was dead set on reclaiming his child—and his woman....

To further turn up the heat, three of your favorite authors take you down to the steamy bayou with *three* of the sexiest bad boys you'll ever meet: Tyler, Nick and Jules—in *one value-packed volume!* A bond of blood tied them to each other since youth, but as men, their boyhood vow is tested. Find out all about *Bayou Blood Brothers* (#606) with Ruth Glick—writing as Rebecca York—Metsy Hingle and Joanna Wayne.

Amanda Stevens concludes our ON THE EDGE promotion with *Nighttime Guardian* (#607), a chilling tale of mystery and monsters set in the simmering South. To round out the month, Sheryl Lynn launches a new series with *To Protect Their Child* (#608). Welcome to McCLINTOCK COUNTRY, a Rocky Mountain town where everyone has a secret and love is for keeps.

More action and excitement you'll be hard-pressed to find. So pick up all four books and keep the midnight oil burning....

Sincerely,

Denise O'Sullivan
Associate Senior Editor
Harlequin Intrigue

THE HUNT FOR HAWKE'S DAUGHTER

JEAN BARRETT

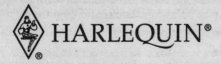

HARLEQUIN®

TORONTO • NEW YORK • LONDON
AMSTERDAM • PARIS • SYDNEY • HAMBURG
STOCKHOLM • ATHENS • TOKYO • MILAN • MADRID
PRAGUE • WARSAW • BUDAPEST • AUCKLAND

ISBN 0-373-22605-5

THE HUNT FOR HAWKE'S DAUGHTER

Copyright © 2001 by Jean Barrett

ABOUT THE AUTHOR

If setting has anything to do with it, Jean Barrett claims she has no reason not to be inspired. She and her husband live on Wisconsin's scenic Door Peninsula in an antique-filled country cottage overlooking Lake Michigan. A teacher for many years, she left the classroom to write full-time. She is the author of a number of romance novels. You can write to Jean at P.O. Box 623, Sister Bay, WI 54234.

Books by Jean Barrett

HARLEQUIN INTRIGUE
308—THE SHELTER OF HER ARMS
351—WHITE WEDDING
384—MAN OF THE MIDNIGHT SUN
475—FUGITIVE FATHER
528—MY LOVER'S SECRET
605—THE HUNT FOR HAWKE'S DAUGHTER

CLASSIFIEDS

HOUSE FOR SALE
3 bdrm, 2 1/2 bath Cape on 1/2 acre in nice family neighborhood. Washer/dryer, frpl, EI Kitchen. Close to schools and shopping.

HANDYMAN
Jack of all trades available to serve your every need!
Need pipes patched?
Walls painted?
VCR hooked up?
Hedges trimmed?
Floors sanded?
Will work cheap!
Call Joe

NEED TO LOSE WEIGHT?
New Ancient Diet Secret from the Orient guarantees that you will lose weight for your big event in just 3 days!
Look good for that
Wedding
Class Reunion
Hot Date
Make everyone sick with jealousy!
We use a combination of natural herbs and stimulants from ancient Asian texts!
Don't miss our introductory offer going on right now!

MEET YOUR PERFECT MATE!
Dating stinks!
Let an old-fashioned matchmaker find your perfect Mr. or Ms. Right!
All our applicants are thoroughly screened and tested. Our members are eligible, gainfully employed and waiting to meet you!

THE HAWKE DETECTIVE AGENCY
Do you yearn to find
a lost loved one from your past?
Do you need protection
from an enemy?
A mystery you
desperately want solved?
All these, and much more, are possible at the family-owned Hawke Detective Agency. Its offices throughout the country are operated by the sons and daughters of the founders of the Hawke Detective Agency. You'll find a branch somewhere near you and a trained investigator eager to serve you. But before you walk through the door with the distinctive golden hawk on it, be aware that danger and romance are waiting on the other side....

PUPPIES FOR ADOPTION!
We have a large assortment of adorable puppies for adoption. All shots and spay and neutering available.
Pugs, Boxers, Poodles,
Golden Retrievers, Labs, Beagles,
Jack Russell Terriers, Yorkies, Poms, and many more.
All waiting for a loving home!
Call now!

CAST OF CHARACTERS

Karen Ramey—She faced a mother's worst nightmare and a temptation she struggled to resist.

Devlin Hawke—The private investigator couldn't refuse the woman from his past, but he feared her effect on him.

Livie—The little girl was a helpless pawn in a game of terror.

Michael Ramey—He guarded a horrifying secret.

Maud Dietrich—She was Karen's friend and business partner, but could she be trusted?

Bonnie Wodeski—Michael's assistant knew the truth, but would she live long enough to tell it?

Scott Wodeski—He was a frightened and unwilling player in his sister's scheme.

Sheriff Neil Holland—He was overwhelmed by the situation.

Veronica Delgado—Her story was a credible one, but was she as innocent as she claimed?

Cassius Bennett—He was a frail old man who didn't seem to know what was happening.

The Hawke family—Would Devlin ever let them matter to him again?

To the Grutzmachers of Passtimes Books
and to Roxanne of Book World.
Bless you for your years of support.
You're the best.

Prologue

"Oh, what a goddess you are!" he whispered eagerly. "Everything a man dreams of, and more!"

Her name was *Antonia,* and she had the sleek, classic lines of a creation so perfect, so thoroughly devoted to pleasure, that she could almost be defined as obscene. He didn't care. She was worth every penny of what it had cost him to possess her.

"You're mine now," he gloated. "Every precious inch of you."

Fletcher Stowe's eyes glowed as they devoured her exquisite, gleaming surfaces. His aging, veiny hand trembled when he leaned forward from his motorized wheelchair to stroke the white leather that sheathed this portion of her elegant body.

Fletcher had told Dennis, his caretaker and bodyguard, to go away. He wanted to be alone with *Antonia,* to savor her at leisure and in private while she was still as fresh and untouched as a virgin. Tomorrow he would share her with the others, introduce her to his young bride, but tonight he wanted *Antonia* to be exclusively his.

Thirty-five million dollars. That's what *Antonia* had cost him. Thirty-five million dollars of pure luxury delivered to him only hours ago. Almost two hundred feet from bow to stern, furnished with every high-tech system imaginable, fitted with exotic woods and precious fixtures, *Antonia* was already the envy of every yachtsman on the West Coast.

The crew would arrive tomorrow to prepare *Antonia* for her maiden voyage to Asia, which would also be Fletcher's honeymoon cruise with his bride. But at this moment he and Dennis were alone on the yacht. Having toured its guest staterooms in his chair, admired the magnificent master suite he would share with Veronica and approved the entertainment room with its mahogany dance floor he would never use, Fletcher had reached the sky lounge.

It was his favorite of the several public rooms with its ceiling, as well as its walls, clad in white leather trimmed in Madagascar ebony and its six-foot-high windows framing views of the majestic San Francisco skyline. He parked his chair in front of one of those windows and gazed out at the winking lights, chuckling to himself.

This night was his triumph. He had fought them and won. They had all been against him, his family, his friends, his employees. They said the car accident had changed him, robbed him of his wits as well as the use of his legs. Said that he was old and foolish, the victim of a conniving young woman interested in nothing but his money.

One of his sons had tried to have him declared incompetent. The other had tried to gain control of his computer software company. They had both failed, along with their army of lawyers. Fletcher Stowe was still in charge of his accumulated millions.

"And I intend to go on spending them," he chortled to the hills outside the window. "The frugal days are over."

There was a six carat blue diamond ring locked away

in the safe of his mansion. He was going to present it to Ronnie at the end of the week when they were married. They were already discussing plans for an extravagant new house. He would build it for her when they returned from their honeymoon. No expenses spared. She made Fletcher happy, which was more than either of his sons or his late wife had ever done for him.

He had survived the car accident. A near-death experience that had taught him his fortune meant nothing if he didn't spend it. So now he was going to live. Starting tonight. Ronnie was waiting for him back at her apartment, and he was suddenly restless, anxious to join her.

Fletcher seized the small, two-way radio hanging from the arm of his chair and pressed the call button. ''All right, Dennis,'' he spoke into the mouthpiece, ''I'm ready to leave.''

He waited a few seconds. There was no response. Irritated by the delay, he repeated his summons. ''Dennis, I want to leave.''

Silence. Damn the fellow! Where was he? Fletcher had told his caretaker to leave him alone, not leave the yacht. If he had disobeyed and gone ashore....

He wasn't used to being kept waiting. Angry now, he tried again. ''Dennis, you'd better be there.''

Still no answer. There had to be a problem. Maybe it was a malfunction with the two-way, because even if Dennis had gone ashore he would have carried the instrument with him clipped to his belt.

No choice about it. Fletcher would have to go looking for him. Muttering his displeasure, he pivoted and headed for the nearest exit, his chair whirring softly. The *Antonia* had been fully equipped on every level for the comfort and convenience of his handicapped condition. The door slid open automatically as he approached it.

Once out on the covered deck, he lifted his head and shouted. "Dennis, I need you!"

There was no reply. Fletcher became aware of the lonely stillness. He wasn't a nervous man, but suddenly he had a case of the jitters. Being bound to a wheelchair like this made him feel vulnerable. And it was late. There was no one down on the dock. He didn't like it.

Nonsense. He wasn't helpless. No reason at all to panic. Dennis had to be somewhere on the yacht. The crew quarters were located forward on the lower level. His caretaker-bodyguard would occupy one of those cabins. Probably he had gone down there to inspect that area. That's where Fletcher would find him.

He rolled along the deck to the nearest of the two elevators. Ah, he was right. The indicator light revealed that the car was rising from the crew deck. Dennis was on his way up.

Fletcher faced the elevator, ready to lecture its occupant. The car arrived, the door whooshed back to reveal the caretaker inside. His brawny figure was sprawled on his back, staring sightlessly at the finely paneled ceiling overhead. Fletcher gazed in horror at the blood that was already caking around the wound in the man's chest.

There was no sound behind him. But Fletcher *knew*. He could sense the danger. Alarmed, he whirled around in his chair. He had no time to cry out and only a second to register the image of a powerful revolver in a gloved hand. Then the weapon, equipped with a silencer, spat at him, drilling him cleanly through the forehead.

THE TWO homicide detectives leaned over the rail of the *Antonia,* watching the morning sun emerging through the mist that cloaked the bay. They were alone now on the yacht. The last of the assorted evidence-gatherers had departed from the crime scene.

"Got a nasty feeling about this one," the heavier of the two men remarked.

"Yeah, I know. No witnesses, no real evidence, and the night watchman out at the gate said he didn't see or hear a thing. Whoever pulled it knew just what they were doing."

"And anyone with a worthwhile motive has a solid alibi."

"The two sons?"

His partner shook his head. "Nope. Both of them conveniently elsewhere. One of them on vacation in Hawaii, the other in L.A. on business."

"Hired killer?"

"Maybe, but try proving it."

"So we go through the motions and hope for a break, which we probably won't get."

"Yeah." He swung his bulk away from the rail and gazed along the impressive length of the luminous white yacht. "Some toy, huh?"

Chapter One

"Good-looking sonofagun!"

Karen, who was having difficulty concentrating on anything but the collapse of her marriage, stared at the young assistant employed by her interior design firm. "Who?"

"This sexy guy I've been telling you about," Robyn explained. "The one who was in here first thing this morning asking for you. He must be awfully anxious to see you because he stopped by again at noon, even though I told him we had no idea when you were arriving from Atlanta. Anyway, I promised him I'd give you his card the minute you walked in the door, which is what I'm trying to do if I can just find where I laid the danged thing...."

Robyn's bright chatter was accompanied by her busy hands searching though the clutter on her desk. Karen was too hot and emotionally drained to be interested.

I should have gone straight home from the airport, she thought. Not come here. But the idea of being alone in the house with her defeat was unbearable. Soon enough to deal with all of that tonight when she faced Michael with her decision.

Besides, she had needed the reassurance that she knew Dream Makers would offer her. Its showroom, with the traditional fabrics and furniture that were a specialty of the interior design firm, told her that at least she could count this part of her life as a success.

Her friend and partner, Maud Dietrich, was on the phone occupied with a client. She had lifted her hand in welcome when Karen stepped through the door of the turn-of-the-century yellow brick building located off Hennepin Avenue. And that, too, was a comfort.

''Here it is!'' Robyn announced triumphantly, handing her a rectangle of cream-colored pasteboard.

Karen, who had impatiently started to edge away from Robyn's desk, accepted the card and glanced at it casually. The prominent logo of a golden hawk on its face leaped up at her. Clutching the card, she could suddenly hear the blood pounding in her ears.

''I'm having trouble imagining that this P.I. has come looking for you to redecorate his office,'' Robyn said, too busy closing drawers she had opened in her search to notice her employer's distress. ''Not when that office is way out in Denver, anyway. Hey, maybe you're a missing heir he's trying to—'' The sight of Karen's face finally stopped her. ''Are you okay, Mrs. Ramey? You look kind of flushed.''

Karen snatched at an excuse. ''It's the heat out there.''

True enough. The Twin Cities were wilting under a blast of summer heat, and it had been a long walk with heavy luggage to where her car had been parked at the air terminal.

Robyn nodded, but she continued to eye her with curiosity.

I must look as shaken as I feel, Karen thought, gazing again at the business card. The Hawke Detective Agency, it said. She had never told anyone about Devlin Hawke, neither Maud nor Michael, and she had no intention of trying to explain him now, and certainly not to Robyn.

"I have no idea why this P.I. wants to see me," she said.

But Karen had a fearful suspicion of exactly why Devlin Hawke was here in the Twin Cities. His arrival, with what she already had to contend with regarding her marriage, couldn't have happened at a worse time.

"Is he planning to show up here again today?" she asked Robyn.

The young woman shook her head. "He didn't say. He sure looked like he had questions on his mind, though. I'm just glad he didn't try asking them, because it would have been awfully hard not giving him whatever answers he wanted to hear."

Yes, Karen thought, she knew all about Devlin Hawke's rugged appeal and what it could obtain. But she didn't want to remember that. Nor did she want to deal just now with his sudden reappearance in her life. Her mind and heart were already too heavy with the burden of her failed marriage.

She was tucking the business card in her purse, trying to bury it along with the image of the man it represented, when Maud got off the phone. The tall, attractive blonde rose from her desk and came forward to greet Karen.

"Sissy Baldwin," she said, explaining the call with the slight trace of the accent she still bore, though she hadn't lived in Germany since her childhood. "She was trying to reschedule that canceled visit you were going to pay her in Savannah after the trade show. I told her we'd have to let her know."

Sissy Baldwin was a good client, Karen thought, but she could be a problem.

Head tipped to one side, Maud considered her. "So, how was the trade show?"

"Well, you know how exhausting they can be, and Atlanta was no exception."

Maud didn't press her for an explanation, but Karen knew that she had to be aware of her anguish. Her face always seemed to betray her emotions, even in moments when she was convinced she registered the look of a perfect stoic.

Maud deserved to know that she had used the trade show as an opportunity to get away on her own for some serious thinking, and that the tough decision she had reached had brought her home ahead of schedule. Karen would tell her everything, but not until after she faced Michael tonight.

"You do look beat," Maud observed sympathetically. "Why don't you just collect Livie from her sitter's and go on home?"

Her partner's suggestion was a strong temptation. She would have liked nothing better than to be with her daughter, but she resisted. "She's scheduled right about now to go down for her nap, and I don't want her routine upset." This whole thing was going to be hard enough on Livie as it was.

Maud nodded understandingly, but Karen knew that her friend thought she was overprotective. Well, Maud wasn't a mother, and even though Livie hadn't suffered an asthma attack in months, Karen needed to be careful with her.

"Besides," she added, "I have all these dealer quotes from the show that I want to log into the computer." It was another excuse. She needed to keep busy.

The phone rang. Robyn answered it. "It's the salvage outlet about that Victorian fireplace mantel," she said.

Maud went to take the call. Karen used the opportunity

to flee into the office off the rear of the showroom. Despite the air-conditioning, her face still felt warm. She didn't know whether to blame it on shock or the sweltering weather.

Slipping into the bathroom that adjoined the office with its clutter of catalogs, wallpaper samples and designs in progress, she splashed cold water on her face. Then she spent several minutes at the mirror, combing her casual-style, jaw-length auburn hair and repairing her makeup.

Her wide hazel eyes stared back at her, a troubled expression in them. Well, why shouldn't they look haunted? Dissolving a marriage was a painful prospect. Not that she expected Michael to object to her request for a divorce. He no longer seemed to care about anything.

What happened? Karen wondered. In the beginning Michael Ramey had been a loving husband and the perfect father for Livie. But in these last months he had turned into a glacial stranger.

Michael had refused to discuss their problem, wouldn't agree to counseling. He just kept pulling away from her, becoming someone so remote she was no longer able to reach him. She had wondered at first if he was having an affair, but somehow that didn't seem to be the explanation.

Maybe it was all her fault. Maybe she had deceived herself that she'd loved him because she had wanted so much to have a father for Livie. She had tried to be a good wife, needing perhaps to compensate for the passion that was never fully there in their marriage. And if Michael ultimately resented that…

She just didn't know, but she refused to remain in an empty marriage.

Leaving the bathroom, Karen resolutely seated herself at the desk. She eyed the telephone while she waited for the computer to bring up the program she needed. Should she call Michael at his office, tell him she was no longer in Atlanta? No, bad idea. He would want to know why she was home ahead of schedule, and she didn't want to risk getting into anything over the phone. They needed to be face-to-face for this.

She spent another moment struggling with the urge to call Livie's sitter, longing for the reassurance that her three-year-old daughter was thriving but eager to see her mother. But that also wasn't a good idea, not when she had called so often from Atlanta that first day and a half to check on Livie that Mrs. Gustafsson must have considered her a nuisance. Livie was in safe, capable hands, and she would be with her in another few hours. Karen could wait.

She began to enter her trade show data into the computer. When she found herself making repeated errors, her fingers drifted from the keys. It was no use. Though she was able to put Michael and Livie on mental hold, there was someone else who refused to go away.

Devlin Hawke. Why was he here, when in all this time he had never tried to contact her? Why now?

She tried to persuade herself she had nothing to worry about. Since Devlin was probably in Minneapolis in a professional capacity, he'd decided to look her up. Just wanted to say hello.

Yes, maybe. But then why had he visited Dream Makers twice in the same day? As if it was imperative that he see her. She didn't like it. She kept remembering he was a private investigator, that collecting information was his business, and if he had somehow—

As if on cue, the office door opened. Robyn slipped into the room, a look of warning in her eyes. ''The persistent P.I. is back.''

Karen's heart sank. Devlin Hawke was about to intrude on more than just her thoughts.

"Do you want me to stall him?"

She knows I don't want to see him, Karen thought, aware that her face must be guilty of its usual treachery. She had to be careful. She didn't want either Robyn or Maud to start wondering why she was so reluctant.

"No, send him back."

Robyn left. She got to her feet, willing herself not to be nervous. As she faced the door, she folded her hands beneath her breasts, fingers laced together. It was a familiar, unconscious pose meant to convey serenity. Only those who knew her intimately understood how deceptive it was, masking an inner turmoil.

Devlin found her like this when he entered the office seconds later. The first thing she noticed was that he wasn't wearing the warm smile of an old friend paying a casual visit. His lean, good-looking face with its wide mouth and strong nose was as sober as a condolence. Not a good sign.

After that, she was aware of how his rangy, six foot body overwhelmed the small room. There had always been a latent power in him that she had found a little daunting. And that hadn't changed.

She could see that those riveting blue eyes of his were busy reacquainting themselves with her in turn. He nodded slowly, as if satisfied by her slender figure and a face she had always considered as rather ordinary but which, to her secret pleasure, he had once insisted was eye-filling. His husky voice said as much.

"Looking good, Karen. I guess I forgot how good."

She might have returned the compliment. His jaw was as square as ever, his thick hair as black. Only the grooves on either side of his mouth seemed more pronounced than she remembered. Not surprising that they should have deepened. He must be—what? Somewhere in his mid-thirties by now.

But she didn't compliment him. It wasn't safe. All she gave him was a pleasant, innocuous, "It's nice to see you again, Devlin. Uh, sit down, please."

She looked around for a chair for him. All of them were too dainty. She chose what was most likely to accommodate him, a gilded French *fauteuil,* and he settled on it. His hard, long-limbed body was too big for it, but he didn't complain. She seated herself at the side of the desk facing him.

There was a moment of strained silence while those disturbing blue eyes of his captured her gaze and held it. She caught her breath and fought the memory of the incredible six weeks they had once shared.

He leaned toward her suddenly, his expression rigid. "I'm not going to waste words, Karen. This isn't a social call. I'm here on business. *Serious* business."

Here it comes, she thought, tensing to face the blow he was about to deliver.

He surprised her when he reached inside the breast pocket of his suit jacket and withdrew a photograph, which he placed on the corner of the desk with a brusque, "Will you identify this man for me, please?"

She stared at Devlin. This wasn't the accusation she'd been expecting. What on earth—

"The photograph," he reminded her.

She turned her head and lowered her gaze, her bewilderment deepening as she looked at the photograph. It was an informal shot of her husband, Michael Ramey. Not a very good one because the camera must have caught him when he was unaware of it. Like many people, Michael objected to having his picture taken, though he had no reason to mind. His features were good ones, if unremarkable, and he kept his body in trim condition.

"It's your husband, Michael Ramey, isn't it?" Devlin prompted her.

Then he already knew about her marriage to Michael. How had he learned of it? More importantly, why? "I think so," she said cautiously.

"You're not certain?"

Actually she was, though afraid to admit it. There was something wrong here, something she sensed she didn't want to hear. "I've never seen this photograph before. If it is Michael, it was taken several years ago before I met him. He's different here, a little more weight maybe and wearing the mustache. Where did you get this picture?"

"From my client, a woman back in Denver who hired me to find the guy you're looking at. The man who calls himself your husband."

She lifted startled eyes to Devlin's face. "He *is* my husband."

"Yeah, I know. I wasn't idle while I waited for you to get back from wherever it is you went. I checked the records here in the city and learned Karen Howard married Michael Ramey two and a half years ago. It wasn't what I wanted to discover."

"I have to tell you," she said slowly, "that you are beginning to scare me."

"I wish I didn't have to do this to you, Karen, believe me. But there's no way around it. Michael Ramey, who was known as Kenneth Daniels back in Denver, was married to my client. Trouble is, he never bothered to divorce her when he walked out on her and disappeared three years ago."

Jolted, Karen resisted his shocking allegation. "This is preposterous! You've got the wrong man! A—a look-alike!"

"Do you have a recent photo of Michael Ramey in your wallet, Karen? We could compare pictures."

She shook her head. No, she had no pictures of Michael. The several that had existed, mostly from their wedding, had been destroyed. It happened when Michael cleaned out the closet in his study. By mistake, along with the other rubbish, he had carted the box of their photos stored there out to the trash. Karen had the uneasy feeling now that this accident, about which Michael had been so contrite at the time, might not have been an accident at all.

"But we really don't need to compare photographs, do we, Karen?" Devlin pressed her solemnly. "Because there is no mistake. Kenneth Daniels and Michael Ramey are the same man."

"Do you know what you're telling me?" she whispered.

"Yeah, I know, and I'm sorry about it. But there's no avoiding it. The man you thought you were legally married to is guilty of bigamy."

Karen felt as if the floor under her chair was no longer solid, as if it had been rocked off its foundations. Bigamy was the kind of thing you saw in tabloid headlines. It always involved strangers in other places, never anyone you knew. So how could it be happening to her?

"Why?" she appealed to Devlin. "Why would Michael do such a thing?"

He shook his head. "I have no idea."

She hadn't really expected him to know, any more than she understood it herself. Michael Ramey, the man to whom she had been a loyal wife for two and a half years, was suddenly a complete stranger.

But she needed to understand what was happening to her. Questions swarmed into her mind. "This woman back in Denver, this—this other wife, has she been looking for him all this time?"

"No, it was only last week that she hired me to find him. Actually, she'd been granted a divorce from him almost two years ago on the grounds of desertion. But it still makes him a bigamist, since he married you before that divorce."

"Then why is she trying to—"

"She has a successful fitness center in Denver, and she's in the process of selling it. It's her business, but Daniels, Ramey—whoever he is—was somehow involved in it. Her lawyer has advised her that, to avoid possible litigation, she needs him to sign away any claim."

"Only last week," Karen murmured, struggling to sort it out, "and already you've located him."

"Sometimes you get lucky, and sometimes you have the right mother. She's wicked when it comes to computers. Handles a lot of that end of the business for all of us. I sent her a copy of this photograph, and she did the rest."

Karen remembered Devlin once telling her how his parents, who had founded the Hawke Detective Agency, managed the home office in Chicago, networking with all of the other nationwide branches of the firm operated by Devlin's brothers and sisters.

"Ma posted the photograph, along with an inquiry, on the Internet," he went on to explain. "We didn't have to wait long for results."

"Another agency responded?"

"Uh-uh. It was a teenager, one of your neighbors down the block. Kids like him live on the Internet. He recognized our man and contacted us. I flew into Minneapolis and spoke with the kid and his parents first thing this morning. I didn't know then you were involved, Karen. I didn't guess until the kid mentioned Michael Ramey had a wife of almost three years named Karen and that she was an interior designer. And after he'd described you...well, there didn't seem to be much doubt, though I had to make sure of your marriage in the records.''

"So you came to Dream Makers. Why here, Devlin? It's Michael you want. Why didn't you go straight to Michael?''

"I tried. He wasn't at your house or his office.''

"He's away from the office a lot. He handles commercial real estate, which you probably learned, and that means showing properties to clients. His assistant, Bonnie, should have told you as much.''

"She wasn't there either. Place was locked up.''

"Then she's probably with Michael. Sometimes, when the deal is a complicated one, she goes with him. Why, Devlin?'' she persisted. "Why come to me at all, when there's the risk I'll let him know you're looking for him? When you could lose him before you're able to reach him?''

Their eyes locked while she waited for his answer. For a breathless moment Karen felt the memories she had tried to resist flow between them like warm honey. Far too many of those memories were sensual ones. They might not have been a problem, had they remained just memories. Instead, they triggered an awareness of his potent presence. She could almost feel the heat of his solid body as he leaned toward her earnestly, could detect his clean masculine scent.

That she was capable of acknowledging an attraction that still existed, that she could recognize its potential sizzle, shocked her. How could she be experiencing such wildly dangerous emotions at this, of all times?

His voice was deep, almost gruff, when he finally answered her. "Learning it was you and not some stranger…well, it would have been pretty rotten of me not to warn you. I owed you that much.''

"Thank you."

She watched him as he reclaimed the photograph and returned it to his inside breast pocket. His business suit was trim and dark blue. It gave him a dynamic image, but it seemed strange to see him clad so formally. The Devlin she had known had never dressed in anything but jeans and ski outfits. When he had worn anything at all, that is, but that was another memory she had to bury.

Perhaps Devlin, too, had memories he needed to tame, because he was all business again as he got to his feet. "I don't have the right to ask you not to confront Ramey with everything I've just told you before I get the chance to see him," he said, his voice almost curt, as if he didn't trust himself to be sympathetic again. "I hope you won't, but if you feel you don't have a choice, then please make sure he understands I'm not a cop. I'm not here to arrest him, and I'm not interested in making any charges. All my client cares about is having him sign her papers I've brought with me."

"And if he decides instead to disappear?"

"Then I'll find him again," he promised, and she knew he meant it.

Karen stood, and there was another precarious moment when the forceful blue eyes under the heavy black eyebrows sought hers. All out of nowhere the thought struck her that she need no longer consider herself a married woman. It was a treacherous idea. It even felt like an immoral one, and she quickly smothered it. She was suddenly anxious for Devlin to leave. But, maddeningly, he lingered.

"Did your assistant give you my business card?"

"Yes."

"My cell phone number is listed on it. Use it if you need me."

"Yes." Why didn't he just go? She wanted to be alone so she could try to deal with this monstrous thing.

"It may be necessary for you to sign a deposition. You'll have to consult your lawyer about just what your situation is legally."

"Yes."

There was another uncomfortable pause. What was he waiting for now?

"If we had to go and meet again, Karen," he finally said, his voice raspy with emotion, "I would have wished for it to be anything but this."

HE WAS FINALLY GONE. She was mercifully alone again. Too dazed to go on standing, she sank back into her desk chair. She sat there, struggling to accept what she had just learned. Devlin was too careful an investigator to have brought her anything but the truth. She could no longer question it.

Bigamy! Michael was guilty of bigamy, and she was his victim!

Whatever had vanished from their relationship, it was a cruel blow to learn that her marriage to him had been nothing but a lie. Which meant everything he had shared with her about his past—and she realized now it wasn't all that much—must also be a lie. Then exactly who was Michael Ramey, and what other secrets might he be guarding?

Whatever the explanation, she would no longer need to seek a divorce since it seemed she had never been legally married to him in the first place. It occurred to her there was a terrible irony in that.

All of this was too agonizing. She didn't want to think about it anymore. Livie. She wanted to be with Livie, to hold her securely in her arms. She longed for someone she could trust and who trusted her, someone who belonged to her without question in a world that suddenly seemed shadowed with uncertainties. Only her daughter could satisfy her need.

Maud and Robyn must have thought her a little crazed when she rushed away from Dream Makers a few minutes later after the most inadequate of explanations. But they didn't try to delay her with questions she was in no mood to answer. Claiming her blue Camry from the parking garage across the street, Karen drove across the Mississippi River into St. Paul.

The tree-shaded house was located near one of the colleges and not far from a park. It had a soothing quality about it. There was an old-fashioned glider on the front porch and a fenced yard in the back with a sandbox and a playhouse.

Parents were grateful for Mildred Gustafsson. A retired kindergarten teacher, she provided their children with superior care. One of her toddlers, an inquisitive boy named Joey, peered around her leg when she answered Karen's ring.

"Mrs. Ramey!" The lanky woman, who seemed far younger than her mature years, was a little startled to find Karen standing on her porch.

"I know this is way ahead of the usual hour we pick Livie up. But I got back from Atlanta earlier than scheduled, so I thought I'd collect her now. She's not still napping, is she?"

Mildred Gustafsson looked bewildered. "But Livie isn't here."

Karen felt her stomach lurch sickeningly. "What do you mean she's not here? She *has* to be here."

"I thought you knew. I thought he must have told you. Mrs. Ramey, your husband came for Livie yesterday morning. She's with her father."

Chapter Two

Devlin had been far too busy to think of food. It wasn't until he came away from Dream Makers that he realized he hadn't eaten anything since the plane that had brought him from Denver. Locating a fast-food joint, he ordered a burger and fries and carried them out to his rental car.

It was midafternoon by the time he polished off his belated lunch, and the sun was hot. Even though he had removed his suit coat and tie and rolled up his sleeves, it was much too warm to go on sitting here in an unshaded parking lot. But that's exactly what he did.

He had an unconscious habit of whistling a slow tune whenever he was considering all the angles of a difficult case. Or when he was dealing with an emotional situation he didn't like. And since that was exactly what he was experiencing now, he began to whistle so softly that the result was almost inaudible. But the action enabled him to concentrate.

He'd made a mistake, a *serious* one, in going to see Karen. Even though it would have been an insensitive way to give her the brutal truth about the man she'd married, he should have handled it by phone or even left a letter for her with her assistant. But he hadn't expected after almost four years to find himself aching in the gut at the sight of the woman. Never mind how that sweet mouth and lithe body affected another area of his anatomy, stirring unwanted memories of the fantastic nights they had shared in that Colorado chalet. He could still see the snow drifting through the evergreens on the mountain outside the window while a fire blazed on the bedroom's stone hearth. Not that they had needed its warmth. They had created their own heat.

What was he doing? This was stupid. Getting all nostalgic about something that had ended badly. Because if he was going to start examining memories, then he'd better focus on the only one that had any reality. She'd abruptly left him and flown back to Minneapolis, making it clear that her goodbye was a permanent one. No real explanation, just as though she'd offered him some blithe: *Been fun, babe, but gotta go.*

Funny. Devlin would have sworn that, unlike the women who usually appealed to him, Karen Howard's values were traditional ones. That, because of the intenseness of their relationship, she might have been interested in exploring a more lasting connection. But, as intimate as the two of them had been, he hadn't really known her, even though they had been together for many weeks.

He'd told himself he was lucky, that a commitment was the last thing he wanted, anyway. The truth was, she had hurt him when she walked away without a backward glance. Hurt him for a long time, though eventually he'd managed to forget all about her. Or so he had believed. But now...

Damn, this was no good. Even if, technically, she wasn't a married woman, he needed to stay away from her. He'd learned this afternoon that he couldn't trust himself anywhere near her, and he sure as hell didn't want to be wounded again. For all he knew, she was madly in love with the bastard who had deceived her, would forgive him and go on loving him.

Checking his watch, Devlin decided it was time to head back to Michael Ramey's office, which was located near the Metrodome. If Ramey still wasn't there, he was prepared to wait for him. This was the part of his work that he hated, spending long hours in a parked car watching a building and hoping your objective turned up before your backside went totally numb.

He'd hoped surveillance wouldn't be necessary, that Karen could have told him exactly where to find Ramey. Actually, it had been his major reason for seeing her. Yeah, sure it was.

Starting the car, he left the parking lot and edged out into the traffic. He knew that, if Ramey didn't show by closing time, he had no other choice. Despite his promise to avoid Karen, he would need to go to their home.

He was still whistling softly as he neared the Metrodome. Still trying to understand why she had turned her back on him four years ago.

KAREN FOUGHT for self-control as she faced Mildred Gustafsson on her front porch. She tried to quiet the panic that gripped her.

"What you're telling me—I don't understand it. Why did he take Livie?"

The woman was concerned, but she also looked uncomfortable with a situation that had suddenly become awkward. "There's nothing to be worried about, is there, Mrs. Ramey? I mean, he is Livie's father. He had every right to—"

"What did he tell you?"

"That, since you were going to be gone for a few days, he'd decided to spend some quality time with his daughter.

I understood that he was going to forget work and that they were going to enjoy a little holiday together until your return. Livie was all excited about it when he told her, though I'm not sure she actually understood—''

"Where? *Where* were they going?"

"Now that he didn't say. I suppose he could have meant just a holiday at home with outings around the city, like the zoo and that new kiddie park. But, of course, if you've been to your house already—''

"I haven't—not yet."

"Well, there you go. When you get home you'll either find them there or an explanation of where they've gone."

Karen shook her head. "He should have told me what he was planning. I should have known about it before-hand."

The apprehension must have been all too evident on her face. The woman placed a reassuring hand on her arm. "I had the impression it was a spur-of-the-moment kind of thing but that he would let you know. There's probably been a mix-up. He could very well have left a message at your hotel in Atlanta, and they neglected to get it to you."

Karen knew that Mildred Gustafsson didn't share her fear. Why should she when Michael Ramey had always been a responsible, devoted father? The woman was convinced it was nothing but a misunderstanding.

The little boy, Joey, had followed Mildred out to the porch and was now pulling at her slacks, demanding attention. Karen had no further reason to keep her, and she didn't think anything could be gained by telling her about Michael's bigamy. In any case, she was anxious to get home.

Back in her Camry, making every effort to hurry through the frustrating traffic, she tried to tell herself that her alarm was needless. That her recent discovery about

Michael could in no way be connected with this, that he wouldn't have taken Livie and just disappeared. Nothing to be scared about. Michael would never hurt Livie. Just as Mildred Gustafsson insisted, it was all a mix-up. An *innocent* mix-up.

But why hadn't Michael made certain she knew about this holiday of his? Knew about it and approved of it. She had a bad feeling driven by a powerful maternal instinct, and she couldn't shake it. She wanted Livie with her, and she wanted her now.

Her heart was racing with anticipation, and a prayer for delivery from her growing anguish, as she came in sight of their home on Summit Avenue. The house behind a cast-iron fence was a shingled Victorian with a mansard roof and dormers. It was in no way as large and imposing as its red sandstone neighbors along St. Anthony's Hill, but it had always given Karen pleasure. Now it was nothing more to her than a property that was too expensive because Michael wanted luxuries and could afford them.

One of those luxuries was the tan BMW that he drove, which she hoped to find parked in the drive. It wasn't there. When she let herself into the house, there was no familiar squeal of her daughter galloping to meet her at the door on a pair of chubby legs. There was no sound at all. The place wore the silence of desertion.

Karen went from room to room searching for a note that Michael might have left for her, checking the answering machine for a possible message from him. Nothing. She was trembling with terror when she went upstairs to look into his closet. Suppose it was empty, all of his things gone? She kept thinking about that other wife in Denver and how Michael had left her without an explanation and how she had never heard from him again. But this was different. This time he had Livie with him.

Her relief, when she went into his closet and found his suits still hanging there, lasted only a moment. Looking further, she discovered that some of his more casual clothing was missing, along with a pair of their suitcases. And several items of Livie's clothes had been taken from her bedroom as well.

They weren't spending a holiday at home. They had left the city, and she had no knowledge of their destination.

Trying to remain calm, Karen went to the phone. She rang Michael's office. No one picked up. Then she tried to reach his assistant, Bonnie, at her apartment. Again no answer. She began to phone friends and neighbors. But Michael had confided in none of them. No one had seen him leave. No one knew where he had gone.

She was frantic by now, unable to convince herself he had merely taken Livie on a short vacation somewhere. Something was wrong. Very wrong. She *knew* it.

No longer hesitating, she called the police. While she waited for a patrol car to arrive, she made an effort to contact her lawyer. Aggravating. With the long Fourth of July weekend coming up, people were already out of town. He was among them.

Minutes later, she was seated in her kitchen with a uniformed officer who listened to her politely. Even before she finished expressing her deepening anxiety, she knew he wasn't going to help her. She could see it in his narrow face. And she could hear it in the way he cleared his voice when he finally responded.

"Ma'am, I don't see that we can do anything for you. This doesn't qualify as a child abduction or a denial of custodial rights. If your husband legally adopted the little girl, he's entitled to have her with him."

"But they're gone!"

"On vacation for a few days while you were supposed

to be out of town. That's what you say your sitter told you, and there's no reason to think otherwise, even if he did neglect to inform you of his intention. Ma'am, he hasn't broken any law.''

She wanted to shout that Michael Ramey *had* violated the law, that he was guilty of bigamy. That he might not even *be* Michael Ramey. But she didn't think it was wise to bring a charge like this before she talked to her lawyer.

Instead, Karen made the mistake of pleading, ''But you don't understand! Livie is vulnerable!''

He frowned. ''How do you mean, ma'am?''

''She suffers from asthma! She hasn't had a severe attack in some time, but that's because I'm careful! Now she's out there somewhere with him, and anything could happen!''

She couldn't manage to keep the note of hysteria out of her voice, couldn't stop herself from sounding like an overprotective mother whose imagination had run away with her. And, infuriatingly, that's just how he judged her. He offered soothing reassurances, telling her that her husband would surely keep Livie safe, telling her that she had nothing to worry about. Like Mildred Gustafsson, he recognized no threat.

I *should* have told him about the bigamy, Karen thought after the officer left. It might have made all the difference. But somehow, at this point, she didn't really think so. He would have regarded it as a separate issue. And although he would have promised her a police investigation around the accusation, it would have meant a delay. No immediate action where Livie was concerned, which was all that she cared about at this point.

Then who could she turn to, if not the police? There had to be someone prepared to believe this awful fear coiling through her insides was not just the behavior of a paranoid mother. Someone who would help her to recover Livie.

But, of course, there *was* someone qualified to do just that. Nor was this the first time she had thought about him in connection with her missing daughter. Even before she had called the police, he had crossed her mind. Then she had immediately dismissed him as a possibility. The risk in involving him was too obvious.

And there may be an even greater risk to Livie if you don't.

Oh, this was absurd! Why was she hesitating when she ought to be thinking of nothing but Livie's welfare? Devlin Hawke was a solid investigator with a family network behind him. It was all she needed to care about. That and convincing him to help her.

Silencing any lingering resistance, Karen got to her feet and went over to the counter where she had tossed her purse. She found the business card with his cell phone number on it. Lifting the receiver off the wall, she dialed the number. He answered almost immediately, his voice brisk.

"Devlin Hawke."

She wanted to sound calm and composed when she spoke to him and regretted that, instead, her voice was breathless with emotion. "It's Karen. You said if I needed you I should call. I need you, Devlin."

There was a moment of strained silence from him. He had to be in his car somewhere. She could hear the muffled sounds of traffic, and she could sense his reluctance before he responded with a husky, "Where are you?"

"At home."

"I'll be there as soon as I can."

And that was all. There was a click. He had hung up without asking for an explanation. It didn't matter. He was coming, and for the first time since learning Livie was gone, she dared to feel hope.

Far too anxious to just sit and wait, Karen wandered restlessly through the rooms she had planned so carefully with their antiques, comfortable chairs and deep sofas. Rooms she had been proud of, but which suddenly meant nothing.

Livie had left one of her toy animals on a chair in the hall. She leaned over and picked it up, holding it close. It was a kind of connection. When she straightened, she found herself gazing without interest at her collection of Victorian fans mounted on the wall.

She had other collections throughout the house. Far too many of them. Things that had accumulated over the years, many of which were not particularly valuable, or even had sentimental associations, but which she couldn't bear to let go.

She supposed any amateur psychologist could have told her they were substitutes for what she had lacked growing up. She would have agreed with him, but not because she'd had few possessions in her childhood. It was family she had missed and longed for. There had been none.

Her single mother had died when she was an infant. No father, no relatives. None that anyone had been aware of, anyway. Karen had been raised in a series of foster homes, all of them kind and protective but ultimately leaving her disconnected. It was why she'd always been so determined that Livie should never experience that kind of insecurity.

Did it also partly explain her powerful attraction to Devlin Hawke almost four years ago? It probably did, because she had never stopped envying him his big family. Of course, she hadn't known about that family when she'd first met him in a Colorado ditch.

One of Dream Makers's wealthy Minneapolis clients

had hired Karen to supervise a redecoration of his vacation home outside of Aspen. Being a native of the Twin Cities, Karen knew all about driving in snowy conditions. But, as she discovered to her dismay, flat terrain in heavy snow is not the same as a mountain road in heavy snow. She'd been on her way to town to meet with a cabinetmaker when she landed her rental car in that ditch.

Devlin, returning from a day of skiing to the little chalet a Denver friend had loaned him for several weeks, had arrived on the scene in his sports utility vehicle to rescue her. Actually, all he had provided was a lift to the nearest garage, but she had been too dazzled by the cleft in his chin and a pair of intriguing blue eyes to define his action as anything but heroic.

Everything after that had been an intoxicating blur. She did remember learning the essentials about him. That he was a private investigator. That he lived in Denver where he had opened the first branch of the Hawke Detective Agency. That he was the eldest son in a family of three boys and two girls.

It was the last that had impressed her. She recalled wondering how he could bear to be so far away from his family back in Chicago. She wouldn't have been separated from them for anything. But it was understandable. Devlin loved skiing. That would make him want to be near the slopes.

Beyond that, she hadn't bothered with the details of his life. They had been much too busy exploring other interests in each other. It still staggered her to remember how immediate and all-consuming their passion had been. Being largely inexperienced in that area, she had no yardstick to measure what they shared. But surely it was special, a rapture that was more than just temporary. Almost six weeks later reality took an enormous bite out of Karen's naive bliss.

They had been on their way to visit a popular coffee bar in Aspen. Passing a flustered young mother on the sidewalk dealing with a pair of howling twins no more than six months old, Devlin had shuddered.

"Look at that," he muttered. "She's practically a kid herself, and she's trapped. Bad enough to deal with one of them in diapers. But two of them at the same time? Never!"

It was in the coffee bar afterwards that she heard everything she wished she'd dragged out of him before his strong arms had raised her out of that snow-filled ditch, and certainly before those blue eyes had impacted hers. But she was hearing it all now. How the ski slopes of Colorado had been an excuse to put distance between himself and his family. How he'd broken up with a woman back in Denver because she'd suddenly started talking about her biological clock ticking.

"But don't you expect to ever have children of your own one day?" she had asked him, and was stung by his reaction.

"Hell, no. I'm not father material."

"Even though you come from a big family? Don't they matter?"

Yeah, sure, he guessed he loved his family, but not when they were always in his face. Not when they were smothering him, thank you.

He had sounded so resentful, almost bitter, that he had shocked her. And he had opened her eyes. Opened them wide and clear. Whatever the magic of their togetherness, whatever compelling emotion she had convinced herself they had invested in each other, Karen had badly misjudged him. Because other than incredible sex, she and Devlin Hawke had absolutely nothing in common. Why, he had thrown away the very thing she longed for!

Get out now, her head warned her, before it's too late. But her heart feared it might already be too late. She was halfway in love with him by then. Probably even more than halfway. Yet, feeling as he did, there could be no hope of their relationship going anywhere—at least not in any direction she wanted.

It cost her a great deal of pain and effort to part from him, but Karen knew if she lingered in Aspen she would eventually pay an even greater price. She didn't try to explain her departure to him. What was the point? Determined to avoid an agonizing scene, she left him as pleasantly as possible and flew back to Minneapolis where she grieved for weeks.

And in the end she met and married the man who seemed to want everything Devlin Hawke hadn't. Now, ironically, she was turning to Devlin to help her find that man. She was a desperate mother. There was no one else.

"LET ME GET THIS CLEAR," Devlin said. "You have a daughter, and you're convinced her father has taken off with her somewhere, and you want to hire me to find them."

"Yes."

Karen, tense with expectation, waited for him to ask her Livie's age. He didn't, at least not then. He was silent for a moment, absorbing her information. She watched his face in the glow of the late afternoon sun that poured through the window of the plant-filled kitchen where they sat. His good-looking features registered no expression. She couldn't tell what he was thinking. She could only pray that he wouldn't react like Mildred Gustafsson and the police officer, that he would determine her concern was a legitimate one. She trusted him to believe her. It was why she had called him.

"All right," he finally said, "let's start with some possibilities."

"Like what?"

"Like supposing this *is* an innocent holiday."

"But it's not."

"But if it were," he persisted, "where would he have gone with her? Is there some favorite vacation spot, family or friends out of town they could be visiting?"

She shook her head emphatically. "No, nothing like that. Don't you think I would have made every effort to contact them if there were? Devlin," she pleaded with him, "there's something very wrong. I just know there is."

"Convince me," he challenged her.

"Michael has…well, he's been a stranger lately." She went on to tell him how her husband had become remote and indifferent to her and how, after repeated efforts to reach him, she had concluded that a divorce was unavoidable.

One of Devlin's eyebrows lifted when she mentioned her decision to part from Michael, but his only reference to it was an indirect, "Did the two of you have any major quarrel before you left for Atlanta? Couples sometimes punish each other by using the kids as weapons."

"No, he wasn't angry. He was just distant. Except, underneath that detachment…"

"What?" Devlin encouraged her.

"I'm not sure. He was hard to read, but there could have been—oh, a kind of intenseness is the word for it, I guess. Like something was happening with him, or about to happen."

"Could be there's an explanation for that. Could be that—" He broke off, tugging at his collar and glancing around the kitchen. "Do you think we could have a window open? It's warm in here."

"I'm sorry. The air-conditioning doesn't seem to be working." Getting to her feet, she crossed to the nearest window. It resisted her effort when she tried to raise it. "It's stuck, I'm afraid."

"Here, let me." Leaving the table where they had been seated, he joined her at the window.

She moved aside so that he could get at the sash. "It's probably swollen shut from disuse. We never open any of the windows. It's because of Livie," she explained. "She has asthma. The doctor recommended filtered air in the house and no pets. Even her toys are allergen-free."

"Is it serious?"

"She has had some bad attacks. None lately, thank heaven."

"Maybe she's growing out of it. Kids do."

"How would you know that?"

"Because I suffered from asthma myself as a kid, and I grew out of it."

"Oh."

"There." With one sharp tug, he lifted the sash. When he turned away from the window and faced her, his expression was sober. "What I was about to say around this business of your husband's remoteness...."

"Yes?"

"It doesn't surprise me. Karen, I've heard this before. I heard it from his other wife. She described the same behavior occurring just before he walked out on her. And if it is a pattern, I think you have to face the fact that he may have been getting ready to leave you like he left my client in Denver."

"But if that's true, why would he want Livie with him? He's her father, yes, and he cares about her, but she's never been vital to him."

"I don't know. People living secret lives aren't predictable. And if your husband committed bigamy, and we know he did, then he is living a secret life.''

Karen's shoulders sagged under the intolerable weight of a situation that was no longer just a strong possibility to her but an absolute conviction. ''Dear God, he means to disappear, as he did before, and if Livie vanishes with him—Devlin, what if I never see her again? You have to find her for me!'' she appealed to him urgently. ''You have to promise—''

''Easy,'' he said, placing a steadying hand on her arm.

She could feel the tears of desperation welling in her eyes, could feel herself coming apart. ''I can't bear this!''

It was an understandable reaction when he took her in his arms and rocked her slowly in an effort to soothe her. It felt familiar, and it felt right being held against the solid, secure wall of his chest. As though she belonged there. And even when his arms tightened around her, she didn't resist. There was nothing wrong in accepting comfort that was offered in a moment of despair. Even if there had been, how could she be unfaithful when she no longer had a husband to be faithful to?

''You were going to ask him for a divorce,'' Devlin probed, as if reading her. ''That's what you said, isn't it?''

''There was nothing left to save,'' she murmured.

''No doubts about your decision? No guilt?''

''Before you told me I wasn't legally married to Michael? Yes, I suppose then I was feeling some of both. But not now when he's deceived me! Not after he's taken Livie!''

She realized too late that her fierce admission could easily be misunderstood. That Devlin could define it as a kind of invitation. Whatever the impetus, the innocent embrace turned into something intimate and dangerous.

There was a sensual quality now in the way his splayed

hands shifted against her back, his fingers stroking down her spine, then moving around her rib cage and up to the sides of her breasts. Karen felt her flesh sear under his slow caresses. She could hear his breathing quicken with his arousal, could scent his strong, masculine aroma.

A few seconds more and she would be tasting him. His mouth would be on hers, devouring her in one of those deep, prolonged kisses she remembered so vividly from almost four years ago. But it was not his intention that shocked her. It was her longing for it.

The whole thing must have shocked Devlin as well because he suddenly released her, almost shoving her away. They stared at each other, silently sharing the same thought.

This is a mistake. This must not happen again.

"Sorry," he muttered. "I don't know what I was thinking. Your kid is gone, you're sick with worry, and I go and—" He raked a hand through his dark hair. "Look," he said, "this isn't going to work. There are other P.I.s, and they're right here in the Twin Cities. I'll check them out, phone you with a recommendation."

He started to back away toward the side door to the driveway. Karen knew he was probably right, that it would be safer for both her and Devlin if she used another investigator. Safer for them, perhaps, but not safer for Livie. She needed someone absolutely committed to recovering her daughter. And only Devlin Hawke had a reason for moving heaven and earth to find Livie. Maybe.

It was time to find out if he did. Time to give him the truth, whatever the risk. His hand was reaching for the doorknob when she stopped him.

"Devlin, don't go! You *can't* go!"

He gazed at her, impatient to make his escape. "Karen, this is no good. It'll only lead to trouble for us if I stay and work with you. You saw that just now. You know it's true.''

"You have to help me find Livie," she insisted. "It— it's your responsibility."

He frowned at her, his hand now on the knob directly behind him. "And just how do you figure that?"

She didn't answer him. She didn't know how to tell him what he needed to hear. He was still frowning at her.

"You've been holding something back. What is it?"

As usual, the expression on her face must be giving her away, she thought. And he would be shrewd about reading people's expressions. As a P.I., he would have to be. He waited, and still she couldn't bring herself to tell him. She simply didn't know where to begin a revelation that was so potentially explosive. His shoulders lifting in a little shrug, he turned to go. But she couldn't let him walk out that door! Desperation inspired her with the opening she sought.

"Devlin, wait! There's something I have to show you!"

To her relief, his hand fell away from the knob. He even drifted toward her again a few steps. "All right, show me."

She reached for her purse. "I told you at Dream Makers that I don't carry a photograph of Michael," she explained quickly, extracting her wallet and flipping it open. "But I do carry a photo of Livie."

He shifted his weight from one leg to the other, impatient again. "Karen, if you think showing me a picture of your kid is going to move me to—"

"Just look, will you?"

She came forward to where he stood, extending the open wallet. He took it and glanced down at the photograph inside the clear plastic sleeve while she watched his face, waiting for some sign of awareness. There was none. Not yet.

"Her hair wasn't curled for the picture," she said, trying to help him. "It's naturally wavy, and even darker than it looks here. And her eyes—you can't tell in this—but her eyes are a dark blue."

"Uh-huh."

He wasn't interested. He hadn't *seen*.

"Not like Michael's blond hair and gray eyes," she said, striving to encourage his recognition.

This time there was a flicker of suspicion on his face. He looked up, catching her gaze. "How old is your daughter?"

"She's small for her age. I sometimes wonder if the asthma—"

"How old?" he demanded gruffly.

"Livie just turned three."

"Which means she was born before you married Michael Ramey two and a half years ago."

"Michael is her stepfather, Devlin," she told him softly. "Not her natural father. He adopted her after we were married."

Devlin's gaze dropped again to the picture in his hand. He stared at it for a long time, a muscle twitching in his square jaw. And while she waited, she clasped her hands together below her breasts in that familiar pose she unconsciously adopted in moments of intense anxiety.

When she thought she couldn't endure another second of his silent scrutiny, he lifted his gaze. There was disbelief in his eyes. "It isn't possible. We took precautions."

"Yes, and sometimes even the most careful precautions fail."

"Are you sure that she's mi—"

"Don't say it," she cut him off, her anger stirring, "because there was no one else!'' Did he think she was so devious, so unprincipled that she would lie about his being Livie's birth father just to enlist his help in finding her?

Uttering a savage obscenity, he snapped the wallet shut and slapped it down on the counter beside him. An action which could have been rejection or simply rage. Then he looked at her with those stormy blue eyes, his face rigid with accusation while fear swelled inside her.

She could bear his anger. If he never forgave her, she would understand and accept it. What terrified her was the possibility that he would utterly deny his daughter or, just as bad, surprise her by demanding rights she wasn't prepared to surrender.

''And just when,'' he growled, ''were you planning to tell me about her? Or, if I hadn't turned you down just now, would you have ever told me at all?''

''How could I tell you before now? You made it altogether clear back in Aspen that you wanted no part of fatherhood.''

''After knowing me only a month, how the hell could you be so certain exactly what I wanted or didn't want?''

''Six weeks,'' she corrected him. ''We were together for six weeks.''

''Yeah, well, that makes it even worse.''

''It was long enough to realize that the responsibility of parenthood horrified you.''

Like it might have horrified the man who had fathered *her,* Karen thought. The man who had never been there for her. Had he learned of her existence and rejected her, leaving her mother a single parent? The possibility had haunted Karen her entire life. It was why she had turned to Michael Ramey to provide a father for Livie.

''I wasn't the one who ran away from Aspen,'' Devlin

reminded her bitterly. "That was you, Karen. Remember?"

"Yes, I know. And I should have contacted you when I got back here and learned I was pregnant, but..."

"What?"

"Weeks had passed by then. And there'd been nothing but silence. You hadn't made any effort to reach me, so I could only suppose you didn't care."

"And that's reason enough not to inform me I was going to be a father?"

"No, it wasn't. I admit that. And it wasn't morally right to let all this time pass without ever telling you about Livie. But I wanted things to be perfect for her, not her life getting split between Colorado and Minnesota. No complications like that. Just one solid home, one family and *one* father who cared. It was a mistake, and I'm paying for it now."

"I'll tell you another mistake you made," Devlin informed her, his voice hard and unforgiving. "You went and assumed that, if you told me now about my kid, there'd be no way I could refuse to go out there with you looking for her. You were wrong."

Karen's heart dropped like a stone when he abruptly swung around and slammed out of the house.

Chapter Three

Devlin's rental car was parked out at the curb. A sporty white sedan. Karen could see it through the window of the kitchen door. She watched him as his long legs carried him swiftly to the vehicle. He never looked back, never hesitated as he opened the door and swung himself behind the wheel.

Sick with disappointment, she heard the engine turn over with an angry roar. She waited for the car to speed away down the street, taking him out of her life and away from any responsibility connected with her or Livie. To her surprise, this didn't happen. Instead, he went on sitting there behind the wheel.

Puzzled, she went to the door and pressed her face against the glass, straining for a better view. It looked like he was whistling as he sat there staring off into space. Actually *whistling*. What on earth—

A few seconds later, in an attitude of resentment, he slapped the wheel with the palm of his hand, turned off the engine and climbed out of the car. Karen backed away from the door as his tall figure strode toward the house. There was a grim expression in his deep blue eyes when he stormed into the kitchen.

"Will he hurt her?"

Devlin offered no apology, no explanation, just that single gruff demand. But she understood him. He was asking her how serious a threat Michael was to Livie.

"I hope not," she answered him quietly. "I always trusted him with her. But that was before today, before I learned Michael is someone I don't know."

"In other words, you're not sure."

"No. How can I be?"

"Then we have to find them," he said decisively. "We have to get her back."

Her relief must have been evident, and it had to have worried him because he qualified his intention with a swift, "Don't make any mistake about this, Karen. Committing myself to recovering her doesn't mean I plan to get emotionally involved either now or in the future."

It wasn't necessary for him to tell her. She could see it on his face. He didn't want to do this. Didn't want to help her, wanted nothing whatever to do with his daughter, but his conscience wouldn't let him walk away.

He couldn't have been more clear about it, but he must have feared she might not believe him. He was compelled to elaborate on his harsh warning. "I'm not going to turn into a daddy because of this. You understand?"

"Yes."

"I'll break my neck to see that she's safe. And I'll pay child support. No arguments about that. But don't expect anything else from me, because you won't get it."

She was hearing just what she'd wanted to hear. That he would make every effort to recover Livie without any claim on her. Then why did she feel this great sadness? Why did it hurt her that he was so careful to omit any reference to Livie as his daughter, or even call her by name? It was obvious he didn't want Livie to have any real identity for him, that as long as he kept her that way he could preserve his vital detachment. But why should he feel such a fierce need for that detachment?

As usual, her face must have told him what she was thinking because he added an emphatic, "We're not going to talk about this either, Karen."

She had no intention of arguing with him. She didn't want to risk losing him. Whatever his terms, she would accept them.

"There's one more condition," he said.

"Yes?"

"It'll be necessary for us to work together, but as much as it's possible, I want this to remain a business arrangement. A friendly, but impersonal, business arrangement."

What was he afraid of? she wondered. A closeness that might jeopardize some promise he'd made to himself?

"When all this is over," he went on, "we go our separate ways, you here in the Twin Cities and me back in Denver. Understood?"

"I wouldn't have it any other way."

"Good." Wearing a scowl, he glanced around the kitchen while mopping at his brow with the back of his hand. "And if I'm going to spend any time at all in this house, I have another request."

"What is it?"

"Get your damn air-conditioning fixed. And in the meantime, let's get out of here and find someplace reasonably cool while you fill me in on the essentials."

THE SPOT Devlin chose for their conversation was one of the most pleasant in the Twin Cities. Standing side by side at the railing of a paddle wheel boat that cruised up and down a brief stretch of the Mississippi, with Minneapolis on one shore and St. Paul on the other, they watched the scene slide by.

Twilight was stealing over the river, bringing with it a cool breeze. Lights began to wink in the high-rises massed against the pearly sky. The riverbanks were popular in summer, teeming with couples strolling arm in arm, teenagers in-line skating, families dining at outdoor cafes.

It was a serene setting, almost magical in its mood. And Karen found it deeply frustrating, even painful. There were young children among the crowds, safe in the company of their parents. Watching them, she could think of nothing but Livie who might be anything but secure at this moment.

Why were they here on this silly boat? Why weren't they searching for Livie? Karen felt a desperate need for action, and Devlin sensed it.

"Easy," he said in a soothing voice.

And that was another thing. His closeness was disturbing. She was too aware of his warm, intimidating bulk as his shoulder grazed hers. She preferred him as he'd been back at the house, brusque and remote, not trying to comfort her like this.

"I can guess what you're feeling," he said, "but we have to talk. I have to have some answers before I can decide where to begin."

Conceding the necessity for that, Karen relaxed. "What do you need to know?"

"As much as you can tell me about Michael Ramey. Start with how you met him."

"It was nothing out of the ordinary. We were both taking this evening course on financial investments. He asked me out for coffee one night after class."

"And you went."

"Why not? He was very pleasant, attractive. And, like me, he was unattached. He had no family at all, so we had that in common. He said he was just out of a long relationship, but he didn't like to talk about it.''

''So you started to date.''

''That's right. Sometimes Livie would go with us. He was very good with her, and that was important to me. It was all very conventional.''

''Including the marriage that followed, huh?''

''I suppose so.''

''What else? What about his hobbies, his interests?''

''His business seemed to take up a lot of his time. He did play golf sometimes.''

''How about friends?''

''There's no one special.''

''Connections from his past?''

She shook her head.

Devlin pushed away from the rail and turned to gaze at her, his expression accusing. ''You don't know a whole lot about this guy you married and lived with, do you?''

''I knew what counted,'' she said defensively. ''That he loved Livie and me and that he offered us security.''

She turned away from the look in his eyes and stared out at the lighted shore, listening to the sound of the paddle wheel churning the waters, smelling the aromas of the river. After a moment she stirred restlessly.

''All right,'' she admitted, ''I was vulnerable, and I suppose that made me blind. Michael was so pleased about the marriage, about getting a wife and a daughter at the same time. I wanted to believe he was everything he seemed to be, because I needed to be—''

''What?''

''Safe,'' she whispered.

Which, Karen thought unhappily, is exactly what I went and convinced myself Michael was. Safe, dependable. And because I trusted him, I very foolishly didn't ask questions.

What have you been hiding from me, Michael? What awful secret are you protecting?

Devlin, recognizing her fear, offered a comforting, "Being a bigamist doesn't necessarily make him dangerous, Karen. Although…"

"What?"

"Why commit bigamy at all? Doesn't make sense in this situation. I mean, if a guy risks having two wives at once, it's because he manages somehow to shuttle back and forth between them. But in Ramey's case he walks away completely from the first wife before he goes on to acquire the second one. Why didn't he just divorce the first wife and save himself the threat of jail? And if he is going on to a third identity…"

"Why take Livie along? That's what you're thinking, isn't it, Devlin? Why have Livie with him when she'd only complicate his new life?"

"Yeah, it always comes back to that, doesn't it? Which means we have to try to figure out that *why,* because without it we may never learn the *where.*" It was Devlin's turn then to express a sudden restlessness. "Let's get off this boat. I need to stretch my legs."

The vessel made regular stops along the river, discharging passengers and picking up new ones. Several moments later, its whistle tooting, it pulled into another landing. Karen and Devlin went ashore and began to stroll along the broad, tree-lined river walk with its busy bars and boutiques.

Devlin was silent as they walked. She assumed he was busy sifting through what little information she had been able to provide, putting it all in some kind of order. Karen knew he was very good at what he did. He had described some of his cases to her back in Colorado. Like everyone else in the family firm, he had a specialty. The other members of the Hawke Detective Agency consulted him in that area whenever necessary, just as he drew on their particular skills. Devlin excelled in finding missing persons. Karen was counting on that talent.

"There's something here that's giving me a lot of trouble," he finally said. "Assuming Ramey is neither a fool nor a lunatic, he must realize that you'll move heaven and earth to find your kid."

"Which makes it even harder to understand why he'd go off with her."

"Unless we look at it from another angle, one that isn't so straightforward."

"What does that mean?"

"Suppose he has no intention of keeping Livie with him permanently. Suppose he's just—for want of a better word—*borrowed* her for a time. Didn't you tell me he left most of her clothes behind? That could indicate he was planning to return her. Maybe he meant to have her back before you even knew she was gone, before you had any reason to be alarmed."

"But I *have* learned she's missing, and I *am* alarmed."

"Yeah, because you came home ahead of schedule. Just when were you supposed to return from Atlanta?"

"The trade show ends late tomorrow. I was to fly out the next morning, Friday, which was a change from my original plan around Sissy Baldwin and her latest house, but that has no bearing here since—"

"Whoa!" Stopping her, Devlin drew her out of the stream of pedestrian traffic and off to one side of the walk. "Now run that by me again. What original plan?"

She explained it to him. "Dream Makers has this client, Sissy Baldwin. She's a tiresome woman, but she's good for business."

"Rich?"

"So rich that she can afford to indulge her hobby. Sissy collects houses, and she hires us to redesign them. Her newest toy is this historic row house in Savannah. When she learned I was going to be in Atlanta for the trade show this week, she invited me to come down to Savannah on Friday. I was supposed to spend the holiday weekend as her guest discussing possibilities for the house."

"Through the Fourth on Monday?"

"Yes, and then we'd fly back here on Tuesday. But, Devlin, there's no point in my telling you all this, because I canceled that visit my first morning in Atlanta. With what I was going through about ending my marriage, there was no way I could spend a weekend with Sissy Baldwin."

"And what about your husband? Did you inform *him* that you wouldn't be staying on through Monday?"

"Yes, certainly. I phoned him at his office right after I called Maud at Dream Makers. Well, I didn't speak to him directly. He was tied up with a client or something. I told his assistant, Bonnie, and she promised to give him the message."

"What if he somehow didn't get that message? What if he still thinks you'll be in Georgia through the Fourth, and he has all that time to use Livie without you being aware that he's taken her?"

"*Use* her? Dear God, for what?"

"I don't know. It's only a possibility, maybe a wild one. But in my work you examine all the possibilities, because more often than not, one of them turns out to be right."

Karen felt her insides tighten all over again with fear. "I don't know how I'm going to stand this," she said in a small voice. "It just seems to get worse."

"I can't promise you it won't be rough. Just keep hanging on to the thought that she's going to be safe and that we are going to get her back."

Did he earnestly believe that? she wondered. Or was it just his professional way of calming a client?

"Come on," he urged, "let's keep moving. Even a useless action is better than none."

She fell in step beside him again. They continued along the river walk, moving in the direction of the lot where they had left his car. As they walked, he reviewed in a speculative murmur what she had told him on the paddle wheel boat about Michael and her.

"Conventional. That's the word you used about how the two of you got together, isn't it? Including the way you dated, even your marriage. All very conventional."

"You make it sound like it was something deliberate."

"Maybe it was."

"To what purpose?"

"Conventional lifestyles draw no attention. I mean, the guy even looks bland in that picture I showed you. Goodlooking maybe, but bland all the same. Speaking of which, do you have any current photos of him back at the house?"

Karen shook her head, explaining how the few that existed were destroyed. "Yes, I know," she said. "It was no accident, was it?"

"Probably not. But you are carrying that picture of Livie in your wallet. Let me have it, please."

She produced the photograph from her purse and handed it to him. He took it without glancing at it. His gaze was busy in another direction, searching the shops they passed. At this season along the popular river walk nearly all of them were open late.

"What are you looking for, Devlin?"

He didn't answer her until a moment later. "That," he said, pointing to a convenience store featuring a small office service open twenty-four hours a day.

Standing beside him at the counter inside, after supplying him with a description of Michael's car, she watched him as he addressed a fax message to his mother at the home office in Chicago.

"Ma will post the particulars, along with Livie's photo, on the Internet," he explained. "Maybe we'll get lucky."

Though out of necessity he'd been referring to Livie by name since the boat, she noticed that nowhere in his message to his mother did he make any mention of his paternal connection with her. And when the material had been faxed, he returned the photograph to Karen without further comment. And, again, without looking at his daughter's likeness. Well, he'd warned her, hadn't he?

Twilight had faded into a balmy summer evening by the time Devlin delivered her to her front door. He had been silent again on the drive back to Summit Avenue. Deciding their next course of action, she hoped. She meant to know just what that was before they parted for the night.

He didn't reveal it, however, until she faced him on the stoop, asking an anxious, "What now?"

"You get a good night's sleep."

"You don't really suppose that I can possibly—"

"Try," he urged, "because there's nothing more we can do until tomorrow."

"Then what?"

"We go to your bank when it opens in the morning. Providing, that is, you and your husband have any joint accounts that we can examine."

"We share a checking account." She understood Devlin's intention. If Michael had cleaned out that account, it would be a strong indicator that he wasn't coming back. "There's also a safe deposit box. It doesn't contain any valuables like jewelry, just the usual essential documents."

"Good. What's inside a deposit box can sometimes tell you more than any account."

Or what's *not* in it, he might have added. But Karen didn't want to think about that.

"I'll say good night then," he said. But he lingered for another moment on the stoop. There was something obviously nagging at him. He finally made up his mind to address it. "Got something to ask you."

"What is it?"

"Were you in love with him?" he blurted.

The question startled her. Why in the world had he asked it? "I thought so," she said.

"And what about now?"

"No, but does it matter?"

"I guess not." He started to leave and then turned back with a husky, "I'm sorry I wasn't able to offer you that safety you were looking for when you turned to Ramey. I'm just not a safe kind of guy."

Was he warning her about himself? "I'll remember that," she called after him as he started down the walk to his car.

"There's something else I want to ask you to do," he said over his shoulder. "Try again to reach what's-her-name, this assistant of Ramey's. Could be she has the answers."

"Bonnie Wodeski, and I will."

She watched him drive off to his hotel, and then she went into the house and rang Bonnie's apartment. As before, she got nothing but the answering machine. Leaving another message, she went up to her bed.

As she had predicted, sleep was impossible. And not just because she was sick with worry about Livie. The image of Devlin Hawke, with his black hair, blue eyes and killer smile, troubled her thoughts. He was a necessity. She couldn't find Livie without him. But their essential alliance was as uneasy as the atmosphere before a summer storm, charged with issues and past conflicts as volatile as chain lighting. Karen didn't know how she was going to survive him.

HER FIRST CHALLENGE in that area occurred early the next morning. Exhaustion had finally permitted her to drift off, but she couldn't have been asleep more than a few hours when she was roused by the insistent ringing of her door-bell.

Disoriented, it took her several moments to struggle out of bed and into her robe. By the time she groped her way down the stairs, the ringing sounded so urgent that her heart was in her throat. All she could think of was that the police were here to report the worst.

She didn't know whether to be relieved or angry when she arrived in the kitchen and saw Devlin at the door, signaling through the glass to be let in. Still groggy, she fumbled with the lock and opened the door.

"What is it?" she demanded. "Is something wrong?"

"Not unless the coffee gets cold." He held up a bulging paper bag. "I brought breakfast."

"You scared me to death!"

"Sorry." He pushed past her into the kitchen.

When she closed the door and turned to confront him again, he was already busy at the counter unpacking the bag, lifting out juice, two containers of coffee and a selection of Danish. The sight of him fully awake, with a brisk, take-charge attitude and wearing a pair of crisp tan slacks and a fresh oxford shirt that managed to emphasize his rugged good looks, irritated her. She was conscious of looking less than human herself in her wrinkled robe and with her auburn hair uncombed.

"What are you doing here at this ungodly hour?" she accused him. "The bank doesn't open until nine."

"We've got other errands before then. I want to get inside Ramey's office and look at his records. That is, if you know where to lay your hands on a key."

"There's a spare one in his desk here, providing he didn't take it with him."

"Good. And along the way, I'd like to stop off and turn in my car. No point in paying rent on it when we've got yours."

"I see," she said dryly. "Anything else?"

"Yeah, how do you like your Danish? Warm or cold?"

"Neither until I've showered and dressed. And while I'm doing that, you can make yourself useful." She slapped a phone book in front of him. "You'll find the air-conditioning service listed at the back. See what you can do about arranging for a repair. Bonnie Wodeski's number is there, too. Maybe you'll have better luck reaching her. All I get is her answering machine."

Devlin had made himself at home and was removing the Danish from the microwave when she returned to the kitchen fifteen minutes later in a summer top and matching cotton pants.

"Looks like we won't have to break in," he said, eyeing the key to Michael's office that dangled from her hand. "Air-conditioning people will be out this afternoon, and the machine is still answering at Bonnie Wodeski's apartment. Sit down to your breakfast and tell me what she looks like."

Karen seated herself and reached for the juice that was waiting for her. "Bonnie is a bottle-blonde and a bit on the flashy side. Why are you asking?"

"Because that juice you're drinking, along with the coffee and Danish here, came from a cafe near Michael Ramey's office."

"You have been out and busy, haven't you?"

"That's right. I was checking the neighborhood there, asking a few questions. The man behind the counter in this little cafe is the talkative type. He said Ramey came in there all the time for lunch. And guess what? On more than one occasion he was accompanied by a blond woman. The guy said the two of them were very cozy."

Karen stared at him. "If you're saying Michael was having an affair with Bonnie and the two of them have run off together, I don't believe it. She simply isn't his type."

"Look, I'm not saying it's true, but it is another possibility we have to consider."

Devlin offered no further argument, but Karen knew what he must be thinking. Bonnie wasn't answering her phone. Could that mean she, too, was missing? Maybe their visit to Michael's office would provide an explanation.

Anxious now to be underway, she quickly finished her breakfast. After leaving a message on Dream Makers's answering machine, informing her partner she wouldn't be in today and would explain later, she followed Devlin to the agency where he turned in his rental car.

The morning rush hour traffic was beginning to thicken when he joined her in her Camry. He was silent as they headed in the direction of the Metrodome, but Karen was strongly aware of him beside her in the car. He was so close that she could feel the warmth of his hard body, detect the faint, appealing smell of his soap. She found his presence daunting.

An impersonal business arrangement. That's what both of them wanted. What they had promised each other. But how could she maintain that agreement when his nearness was so disturbing, taunting her senses at every turn?

It was unfair and wrong that he should affect her like this when she was so worried about her daughter. Nothing should be on her mind but Livie. Certainly not any treacherous longings involving broad shoulders and a pair of blue eyes that had the power to soften her with a glance.

Steeling herself to resist temptation, Karen concentrated on her driving. A moment later she spoke to him quietly. "I think we're being followed."

Devlin turned his head, staring at her. "There are a million cars back there. How can you say one of them is tailing us?"

"Because I've been aware of it in the rearview mirror ever since the rental agency. A burgundy-colored van that's right behind us every time we make a turn. Doesn't seem to have a front license plate, but it has a chunk out of one corner of its left headlight cover."

"You're serious, aren't you?" He twisted around to look. "It isn't there now."

"It dropped back just a second ago."

"You get a look at the driver?"

"Not really. The van's windows are tinted. Besides, the sunlight keeps glaring off its windshield. You think I'm imagining it, don't you?"

"No, but it's probably just a vehicle going our way. Karen, I'm a P.I. Don't you suppose I'd know if we were being tailed?"

"All right, so everything that's been happening has made me paranoid. But I still say it was following us."

There was no further sign of the van, however, when they reached Michael's commercial real estate agency. His operation was located within a brick, single story building containing other offices. It was still too early for any of those offices to be open yet. Karen and Devlin were alone in the corridor that brought them to the rear of the structure where the Ramey suite was situated.

The reception area was unlighted and unoccupied when

they let themselves in with the key. Mail that had been slid through the slot in the door was piled on the floor.

"Looks like it's been accumulating for a couple of days," Devlin said, gathering up the stack.

"Which means Bonnie hasn't been here to deal with it."

Devlin flipped rapidly through the contents. "Nothing very interesting. Bills and circulars. But we'll take them with us, examine them later, because right now..." He gazed around the dim reception area.

"What are we looking for," Karen asked, "and where do we start?"

"I'd like to get into the files on his clients, see what they can tell us." He eyed the computer on Bonnie's desk. "Any idea how we can access them?"

Karen shook her head. "But we don't have to go that route. Michael kept hard copies of all his records. They're in the file cabinets in his office."

"Wait," he said as she started toward the inner office. "We'd better relock the outer door. We don't want to chance someone wandering in here and asking us a lot of awkward questions."

Seconds later, with the outer door secured and Michael's office door screening them so that they could risk his lights without arousing curiosity, they tackled the pair of oak file cabinets.

Less than twenty minutes later they stood there gazing at each other in perplexity.

"This just doesn't add up," Devlin said. "It's all penny-ante stuff, every bit of it. There aren't enough worthwhile clients or listings here to sustain an operation like this."

Karen was equally bewildered. "Then where did all the money come from, because it was Michael who bought the house and his luxury car and designer clothes, even our trip to Europe.''

''Investments?''

She shook her head. ''Nothing to support the way we lived. At least nothing I was made aware of.''

Devlin eyed the massive desk and the other handsome furnishings of the office. ''It's like all this was a sideline. Or maybe a cover-up of some kind.''

''I don't understand it. If this is part of that secret life he's been living, then—''

Devlin interrupted her, holding up his hand for silence. Karen listened, and then she heard it, too. They had left the inner office door slightly ajar. Through the crack came the scraping sound of a key as it was fitted into the lock of the outer door.

''Bonnie?'' she whispered.

He shook his head.

No, Karen thought, he's right. It couldn't be Bonnie. Whoever was out there was rattling the key impatiently, as if he was unfamiliar with the lock and was having difficulty opening it.

There was a sudden snap. The lock had yielded. A second later came the soft sounds of the door opening and someone slipping furtively into the outer office.

Chapter Four

The intruder must have reached Bonnie's desk. They heard the sound of a drawer being yanked open. And that was when Devlin went into action. Motioning Karen to remain where she was at the file cabinets, he slipped silently across the office.

When she realized that he intended to take their visitor by surprise, and that this was a reckless thing to do, she started forward. Before she could stop him, he was through the door.

What followed happened so swiftly that she froze in alarm. There was a startled curse, the clatter of a chair overturning, then the sickening sounds of two bodies locked in savage combat.

Overcoming her fear, Karen rushed toward the door. By the time she arrived in the reception area, the nasty, but brief, struggle was over.

She found Devlin dragging a thin figure up from the floor. He looked fresh out of his teens, a scruffy young man with a goatee, a gold ring in one ear and a surly expression on his narrow face.

"All right," Devlin demanded, "let's have some answers. What are you doing here?"

He shook off Devlin's grasp. "I wasn't breaking in. I got a key, don't I?"

"And how did that happen?"

"It's Bonnie's key. I'm her brother, Scott Wodeski."

Devlin glanced at Karen for confirmation. She shook her head and shrugged, indicating to him she had no idea if the young man's claim was true or not.

"And does that give you the right to enter this office?" Devlin challenged him.

"Does if she sent me." Scott rubbed his arm where Devlin had gripped it and glared at him. "And who the hell are you to attack me like that?"

"You tried to run for it. I'd call that suspicious."

"Yeah, well, you scared me." His eyes narrowed. "You ain't Bonnie's boss. Maybe you don't belong here yourself."

"I'm Michael Ramey's wife," Karen informed him.

"And I'm a licensed P.I. hired by Mrs. Ramey," Devlin added, "which is all you need to know. Now let's have some more answers. Why did your sister send you here? Why didn't she come herself?"

"Because she ain't in Minneapolis, that's why. She called me from the road. Her boss told her he was shutting down the office for a few days, and she could take a vacation. And that's what she's doing until after the Fourth."

"Where?"

"I dunno. Somewheres up north in the lake country. Said she'd phone me again at the apartment when I got what she left behind in her desk."

"And what would that be? Show us."

Scott turned to the desk, seizing a colorful brochure from one of the drawers he'd been searching. He waved it at them defiantly. "See, this is all it is. A travel folder on one of them resorts up there. Bonnie figures she might like to try the place, providing she can afford it. She wants me to read her the prices, and all this other junk on it, before she tries for any reservation.''

"Who's with her on this vacation?'' Karen anxiously asked him.

"Nobody.''

"You're sure of that?''

"Yeah. Why all these questions, anyway?''

"We need to talk to her,'' Devlin said. "We've left messages on the answering machine at her apartment, asking her to return—'' He broke off, looking at Scott as another thought occurred to him. "And just where do *you* live?''

"With Bonnie.''

"Then you must have heard all those messages on her machine. Didn't you realize how important they were?''

"Man, I don't pay no attention to her machine. I got my own phone line in the apartment. Look, if you're through grilling me, can I go? I gotta get back to the apartment. Bonnie's paying me to build her some shelves while she's away.''

"All right, but when your sister calls you again, you tell her we need to speak to her. Have her phone Mrs. Ramey at her house, and ask her to leave a number if we're not there.''

"Fine.''

Obviously relieved, Scott started to leave. Devlin stopped him with one last question. "You wouldn't happen to drive a burgundy-colored van, would you?''

"No way. I got a wagon.''

When the young man had fled from the office, Karen turned to Devlin. "What do you think? Was he lying?''

"I don't know, but seems like a funny reason for him to come here. I mean, why did his sister need that brochure when she could have phoned the resort itself and asked for the information in it?''

''Maybe she forgot both the name of the place and its number.''

''Could be. Damn, why didn't we think to take that key away from him?'' He was thoughtful for a second. ''Do you know who manages this building?''

''Yes.''

''Let's call them and recommend that the lock be changed, just in case it was something else Scott Wodeski came here for and he tries to get back in.'' He glanced at his watch. ''Then we'd better see what your bank has to tell us.''

KAREN STARED down at the meager contents of the safe deposit box that had been placed on the small table of the cubicle they occupied. She had been shaken by what they discovered in the file cabinets back at Michael's office. This was far more disturbing.

''Go through it again,'' Devlin urged. ''This time tell me exactly what's missing.''

She obeyed him. ''Our marriage certificate, his birth certificate, his passport...''

All of them, and more, were gone, she realized. And even though she had prepared herself for the worst, the reality was a cruel blow. This, along with the disclosure from a bank officer minutes ago that Michael had emptied their checking account, made it a certainty. He was not merely off on some innocent holiday with Livie. She could no longer live with the hope of that possibility.

''In other words,'' Devlin concluded grimly, ''he took every document that could legally prove someone named Michael Ramey actually existed.''

"It must be his real identity," she argued. "I saw his birth certificate."

"Doesn't prove anything, Karen. My client back in Denver could have seen another birth certificate that said he was Kenneth Daniels."

She shook her head. "But I remember he was annoyed when I saw the certificate and asked him about his birth-place listed on it. As if he didn't want me to know. He said he had unpleasant memories of the town. Couldn't that mean it *was* his home once?"

"And that he actually is Michael Ramey this time around? It's possible. You happen to remember the name of this town?"

"Rocklyn. It's in Iowa, just off the interstate about one hundred and fifty miles south from here. I looked it up on the map once, thinking maybe we could visit. The suggestion seemed to upset Michael. He said there were no family connections there anymore, so I forgot about it."

"Then," Devlin said decisively, "I think we'd better go to Rocklyn."

"Do you believe that's where Michael went?"

"I don't know, but what I've learned from years of P.I. work is that when people go missing, they rarely give up established habits and they often go back to old haunts. So, if the Michael Ramey identity is a genuine one, then maybe he did return to Rocklyn. If not, there could be people there with vital information. With nothing else to go on right now, it's our one hope."

Karen nodded. "We ought to stop off first at your hotel and my house to grab a few essentials. Just in case we have to stay overnight down there. And I'll need to leave a key with my neighbor so the air-conditioning people can get in."

They were practical decisions, but all the while her mind

was seething with the prayer that Rocklyn, Iowa would provide them with answers.

THE LONG HIGHWAY was flat and straight, a monotonous ribbon of concrete bordered by endless cornfields. Driving it demanded the minimum of concentration. Devlin, at the wheel of the blue car, found his thoughts drifting in unwanted directions. Most of them were connected with the woman beside him.

Karen, fast asleep, hadn't stirred in over an hour. The exhaustion resulting from her bad night had finally caught up with her. She had drifted off to the sounds of a tape she had popped into the player. Country and western. He wouldn't have figured her for that type of music. Just showed how much he didn't know about her.

Devlin glanced down at her from time to time. Her hands were linked at her waist in a pose that made him think of a demure little girl. It aroused something protective in him, and that was dangerous. As dangerous as his awareness that there was nothing girlish about the swell of her breasts, because that aroused another need he had promised himself to resist.

Damn it, he didn't want to be interested. He didn't want to care. All he longed for were his Colorado mountains, a pitcher of ice-cold beer, and maybe a willing blonde snuggled against him. No demands, no commitments he couldn't handle.

Instead, here he was involved in something that with each passing mile was dragging him into emotions that threatened to tear him up. Why couldn't he just get back to his life? Why did he have to keep remembering a three-year-old child who was at risk?

Asthma. The child he had fathered suffered from asthma. Had she inherited it from him? Was that possible?

Even though it had been decades ago, Devlin could remember what those attacks were like. The tightness in his chest, that panicked feeling of not being able to draw a decent breath. The wheezing that accompanied a fear of suffocation.

No, he hadn't forgotten. Of course there was a far more painful memory from his youth that had nothing to do with asthma, but he never permitted himself to think about that. It was enough to deal with the knowledge that his daughter was vulnerable. Devlin was still brooding about it when Karen awakened several minutes later.

"Got something to ask you," he said.

He could feel her gazing at him in surprise. She was probably startled by the gruffness in his voice that he couldn't seem to help.

"Yes?" she said hesitantly.

"Uh, about the kid and her asthma..."

"Her name is *Livie,* Devlin, and what is it you want to know?"

"Does she take any medicine for her condition?"

"When she needs it. A bronchodilator. We always kept a supply on hand. And if you're asking whether Michael took it with them, I can only assume that he did since it was missing. Believe me, it was one of the first things I checked on at the house. At least that much I can be thankful for."

"But can you count on him to give it to her?"

"I'd go crazy if I let myself believe that he wouldn't."

Yeah, she was probably right, Devlin thought. If Ramey did have some need for the child, then he would make sure he took good care of her, kept her healthy. And if not, if he neglected her in any way...

Enough, he ordered himself fiercely. *You swore you*

weren't going to concern yourself on that level, remember?

He could tell Karen was still looking at him. He was afraid she would start asking him questions he didn't want to answer. Instead, to his relief, she turned to something else.

"You didn't happen to spot any burgundy-colored van with a broken headlight behind us while I was napping, did you?"

"Karen, it's an interstate. There are all kinds of vans out here, burgundy ones included. It's a popular vehicle, but I didn't spot any particular one following us."

As though not trusting his vigilance, she twisted her head to look behind them. He didn't object, and he tried to be patient with her on the subject. But Devlin still believed she was wrong about any certain van having tailed them this morning.

IF CIRCUMSTANCES were different, Karen thought, she would be delighted by Rocklyn. It was the embodiment of everyone's ideal rural community, with mature trees shading its peaceful residential streets and a town square that boasted a bandstand from another era.

As it was, all she could do was to try to picture the man she had married growing up in this place. Somehow, though, Rocklyn didn't fit his image. Not the Michael she knew, anyway.

All that interested Devlin was the county courthouse situated on one end of the square. "If there's any record of Michael Ramey, we'll find it in there," he said, parking the car at the curb.

The tall brick structure, with a clock tower rising from its steep roof, had a sleepy look about it. Karen realized that wasn't just imagination either, because when they climbed the steps they found the doors locked.

"Closed already," Devlin said in disgust. "They must keep banker's hours here." He turned to survey the square. "But *that* wouldn't."

Karen saw him pointing to a newspaper office facing them across the square, its name prominently displayed on the window.

"A local paper like that is as good as a courthouse," he explained. "Maybe even better. If they haven't printed it, it isn't worth knowing. Come on, let's go visit the *Rocklyn Examiner*."

The hot afternoon sun beat down on them as they crossed the square. But Karen noticed that the sky on the eastern horizon was as purple as a bruise. There was a storm on the way.

An old-fashioned bell tinkled above the door as they entered the *Examiner*. It looked as though time had stopped in this place somewhere around World War I. Karen was certain that the tin ceiling was original, as was the scarred oak counter that stretched across the front of the newspaper's office. The only modern touch was a computer at which an elderly man was working.

There was an impassive expression on his seamed face when he rose from his desk and approached the counter where they stood.

"Help you?" he asked.

"I hope so," Devlin said. "We'd like to find out about a local family named Ramey."

The old man wasn't impressed by Devlin's friendly smile. His face remained wooden when he answered them. "Sure, there used to be a Ramey family in Rocklyn. Moved away years ago, though."

"Actually," Karen appealed to him, "it's Michael Ramey we're interested in. Is there anything you can tell us about him?''

He was silent for a few seconds, studying their faces while Karen waited tensely for his response. ''You looking for him?''

''That's exactly what we're doing,'' Devlin said.

''Well, he's right here in Rocklyn.''

Devlin leaned toward him, his tone matching Karen's own excitement. ''Are you sure about that?''

''You'll find him at 459 Pine Street. That way.'' He pointed casually to the eastern end of the square.

Armed with the address, Karen and Devlin thanked him and hurried out to her car.

''Just like that,'' she said as they drove away from the square.

''We don't have him yet. Let's just hope he's still at this address.''

They didn't speak after that. Both of them were busy concentrating on the house numbers as they crawled along Pine Street. The sky had darkened, and the rumble of distant thunder heralded the approaching storm.

They passed a thick wall of lilacs, and Karen announced triumphantly, ''There it is on that brick pillar, 459!''

Devlin parked the car at the curb, and they sat there and stared at the address to which they had been directed.

''But this can't be right,'' Karen whispered in dismay. ''It's got to be a mistake.''

''It isn't any mistake. We've just been had, that's all.'' Opening his door, he started to slide out of the car. ''Come on.''

''What's the point?''

''We're going to do what we came for. We're going in there to locate Michael Ramey.''

''Devlin, it's a cemetery.''

He didn't answer her. He was already out of the car and on his way through the gate between the brick pillars. By the time she followed him he was off among the graves, searching the headstones as the clouds gathered overhead. It would rain soon.

"Here it is," he called to her.

Understanding now, she joined him. They stood there gazing down at the small headstone. It read:

Michael Ramey
Born October, 1965
Died June, 1966

"Well, the sly old coot wasn't lying," Devlin said dryly, "but I can't say I appreciate his wit."

Karen was too disappointed to answer him.

"You know what the explanation is here, don't you?"

"I think so," she murmured sadly. "The man I married took this poor child's identity."

"It's an old trick, and I fell for it. Your Michael Ramey—and for want of his real name I suppose we have to go on calling him that—helped himself to the ID of a deceased infant who would have been his age now if he'd lived. This is why he discouraged your interest in Rocklyn. He didn't want to chance your discovering what he'd done."

"But the birth certificate… How could he obtain the birth certificate?"

"By simply requesting a copy of it, something anyone can do with no questions asked. And once he had it, he could use it to acquire other documents in the name of Michael Ramey."

Thunder rumbled again.

Devlin turned to her, his voice solemn. "Karen, we have

to face it. We're dealing with more than just a bigamist here. This guy's masquerade has all the signs of a professional. But a professional *what?*''

He lowered his gaze to the headstone again, frowning at it as though he expected it to provide him with answers. Karen couldn't bear to stare any longer at the stone. She looked away, and that was when she saw it. A movement at the back of the cemetery. She peered in that direction.

The light was bad now, the shadows even murkier under the thickness of those trees. But she was almost certain she wasn't imagining it. A figure stood there.

The possibility that someone was concealed under the trees and spying on them struck her as so sinister, so chilling that, even though the air was heavy and sultry, she shivered.

''Devlin!'' She grabbed his arm. ''Someone is watching us!''

He glanced in the direction she indicated. ''There isn't anyone.''

''There was,'' she insisted.

''Man or woman?''

''I couldn't tell. It was too dark.''

''Karen, are you sure it isn't just the setting? A storm, a graveyard?''

He thought she was seeing ghosts that were no more real than the burgundy-colored van.

''Let's go,'' he said. ''There isn't anything more for us here.''

He started toward the car. Before she could turn and follow him there was a flash of lightning. In its brilliant glow she caught the gleam of metal through the shrubbery off the back side of the cemetery. *Burgundy-colored* metal.

Without pausing to think about it, Karen raced in the direction of the street at that end of the cemetery. The thunder rolled again, but she swore that under its growl she caught the sound of a door slamming and then an engine roaring to life. She rushed on, ignoring Devlin's shout behind her.

He caught up with her outside the rear gate where she stood gazing frantically up the empty street. "It's gone!" she cried.

"What is?"

"The van! It must have been parked right here, and then—"

"Karen, no."

"Don't you understand? It could have been Michael! Livie could be in that van!" She knew this was wildly improbable even as she said it, but she had reached a stage of desperation where she was prepared to snatch at any possibility.

"Karen, Ramey and Livie aren't here in Rocklyn. There's no reason for them to be anywhere near this place."

He was being reasonable in an effort to calm her. She found his patience infuriating. "You don't know that!"

"Karen, listen to me—"

"No! You think I'm hysterical, that I imagined both the figure and the van!"

"What I think," he said as the first raindrops pelted them, "is that you've had enough. Let's get you to a motel where we can both try to get a good night's sleep before we head back to the Twin Cities, because there's nothing more to be learned in Rocklyn."

She didn't argue with him this time. The rain was beginning to fall in earnest, making it necessary for them to run for the car.

THE MOTEL was out on the edge of town, a plain but comfortable facility that provided them with connecting rooms.

Karen, not bothering with the lights, stood in the gloom and stared at the rain slashing at the window.

Devlin appeared from his own room, bringing her her bag that he'd carried in from the car. "You going to be all right?"

She appreciated his concern, but it didn't relieve her. She turned to face him, struggling with her despair. "It's looking worse, isn't it? The more we dig into this thing, the more alarming it gets. If Michael went to so much trouble to create a false identity for himself, and then risked stealing Livie, he must be up to something very serious. Devlin, I'm frightened."

He placed her bag on the floor and came to her, standing so close that she could see the raindrops glistening in his dark hair. Both of them were wet, but that didn't seem very important right now.

"We're going to get her back," he promised her in a low, solemn voice. "Whatever it takes, we're going to get Livie back."

"How?" she whispered.

"I don't know. But I'm a good P.I. I never give up, and this is one battle we're both going to fight until we win."

She searched his face, wanting to believe him, wanting to trust him. Time seemed suspended as they stood there in the snugness of the room, gazing at each other while the rain went on beating at the window.

Maybe it was just to comfort her in her anguish when his arms went around her, drawing her against his solid length. Or maybe he was surrendering to a temptation he could no longer resist. Either way it didn't matter because, whatever the danger of their intimacy, she found herself longing for him.

There was a slumberous quality now in his dark blue

eyes that seemed to slowly caress her face. Karen trembled at the sensual invitation in their depths, at the allure of his wide, bold mouth.

"Devlin," she whispered.

"What?" he demanded, his voice raw, husky with need.

"Should we—"

He didn't permit her to finish. That strong mouth of his angled across hers, claiming her in a deep, prolonged kiss. Memories of all the feverish kisses they had shared almost four years ago in Colorado assaulted her. She had never forgotten them.

This kiss was no less intense, no less wonderfully compelling as he plundered her mouth. Their breaths mingled, his tongue stroked hers, teasing her, challenging her, and the rain lashed at the windows in a frenzy. Was it the sound of the rain pounding in her ears that she heard, or was it the roar of her own blood?

He felt so good, tasted so familiar, smelled so clean and masculine to her. Her breasts pressed against him were swollen and tender with wanting him.

It was not until she felt Devlin's arousal straining against her with yearning that sanity surfaced through her blind desire. What was she doing? Was she falling in love all over again with the man who had been one of her most serious mistakes? Worse, how could she even think about giving herself to him when she lived with the nightmare of her missing daughter?

His mouth lifted from hers when she squirmed in his arms, signaling with a panicked whimper her wish to be released. He let her go. Maybe he, too, realized that they had been about to repeat the error of Colorado. That neither one of them wanted to deal with that hurt again.

He backed away from her, plowing a hand through his thick black hair. "Sorry," he muttered.

"I know," she murmured. "Me, too."

"I, uh, guess I'd better get into some dry things. Then maybe we'd better see about getting something to eat. Rain's beginning to let up."

He moved toward his own room next door. She didn't try to stop him. They weren't going to discuss what had just happened. Nor was there any point in talking further about the burgundy-colored van or the figure she had spotted in the cemetery.

It was late when Karen finally got to sleep that night. It must have been somewhere in the small hours of the morning when she was startled awake. At first she thought it was the sound of the rain that had disturbed her. It was coming in sheets against the window.

Then she realized it wasn't the rain. It was something else. She lay there in the darkness without moving, straining to identify it. That was when she caught the sound of a stealthy movement just a few yards away. Her heart kicked with fear. Someone was in her room!

Chapter Five

Karen was so paralyzed that she couldn't find the breath to cry out. As the intruder moved furtively from the direction of the bureau, pausing at the desk to check its surface, she realized he must be searching for something.

When he crept toward the bed, she tensed, prepared to defend herself any way she could. But that proved unnecessary. The connecting door was slightly ajar, admitting a thin bar of light from Devlin's room. She almost gasped aloud when the shadowy figure slid through its feeble glow. She recognized him now. It was Devlin himself!

Why had he stolen into her room like this? What was he looking for? She was about to angrily challenge him when he reached the table beside her bed, his hands groping along its top. She decided then that she would have a better chance of learning what he was after if she kept silent and let him think she was still asleep.

She heard him whisper a curse under his breath as his fumbling fingers almost upset the lamp. A second later his hands closed around the article he was seeking. Seizing it, he retreated, slipping quietly back into his own room.

The only thing she had placed on the table beside the bed was her purse. What did Devlin want with her purse, and why didn't he want her to know he had taken it?

Taking care not to make a sound, Karen left her bed and padded softly on bare feet to the connecting door. He had left it ajar again, presumably to avoid the sound of the latch awakening her. She pressed her face against the lighted crack, peering into his room.

She could see Devlin seated on the edge of his bed, half turned away from her. He wore nothing but his briefs, which made him powerfully appealing even in this suspicious circumstance. She tried not to think about all those expanses of hard flesh and exposed muscle as she concentrated on his activity.

He had lifted the wallet from her purse and was now flipping through its contents. When he located what he wanted, he removed it from its clear plastic sleeve and held it in his hand. He didn't move, didn't make a sound. He simply gazed at the face in the photograph.

It was Livie's picture that he'd taken from the wallet, Livie's face that he was hunched over and studying so intently. She watched him, and even though he was nearly in profile she could see his expression. It was one of the most haunted looks she had ever seen on a man.

Why? she wondered. Why, if he didn't care about her, should the image of his daughter cause such blatant suffering in him? And why, if he didn't care, should he go to the trouble of sneaking the photograph out of her purse so that he could gaze at it in secret?

Or maybe he did care, more than he wanted to admit even to himself. She remembered how he had asked her on the way to Rocklyn about Livie's asthma, as though it mattered to him. So why did he go on resisting the reality of his daughter? Why did he deny his fatherhood?

Would he discuss it if she asked him? She didn't think so. Otherwise, he wouldn't be prowling around like this in the middle of the night just to steal a glimpse of his daughter's likeness.

Devlin was punishing himself in private, and she longed to understand it. But she wasn't entitled to know. Hadn't he made that clear when he agreed to recover Livie? No emotional attachments.

Except there was emotion involved. She could feel it in him, see it now when he suddenly shuddered, as if in the grip of both pain and longing. She found it bewildering, heartbreaking when seconds later, plainly renewing his resolve not to acknowledge his child, he fiercely shoved her photograph back into Karen's wallet.

Not wanting him to know she had witnessed his vulnerable moment, she retreated from the door. She was in bed again and feigning sleep when Devlin returned her purse to the table beside her bed. This time, when he went back into his room, he closed the connecting door all the way, leaving her in total darkness and feeling unutterably sad.

THE RAIN had stopped and the sky was clearing when Devlin tapped on the connecting door early the next morning. Already up and dressed, she opened it to find him looking far too inviting in a bath towel snugged around his waist.

"I haven't shaved or showered yet," he apologized. "Give me fifteen minutes, and I'll be ready."

He turned away without another word, leaving the connecting door open. She knew that neither one of them was going to mention his visit to her room in the night.

Karen was gathering the last of her things when his cell phone on the table next to his bed started to trill. Devlin was in his bathroom, the door shut and the shower running. She knew he couldn't possibly hear the phone.

Should she answer it? It might be urgent, something

connected with Livie. Hurrying into the adjoining room, she scooped up the phone.

"Devlin Hawke's number," she greeted the caller.

There was a brief pause. Karen could sense surprise on the other end. Then a woman's low voice, the throaty kind that men appreciated, asked, "Is Dev available?"

A girlfriend? Karen wondered, knowing she had no right to be curious. "I'm sorry, he isn't at the moment," she said politely. "Can I take a message?"

"There's something he needs to know. Ask him to call me back as soon as he can." She paused again. Karen waited for her to leave her name and number and was a little startled when, instead, the woman said impulsively, "Is this his client, Karen Ramey?"

"Uh, yes," Karen answered cautiously.

The woman's voice changed then, suddenly becoming very warm and friendly. "Karen, I'm Devlin's sister, Eden Hawke."

She remembered Devlin having mentioned back in Colorado that this particular sister operated a branch of the Hawke Detective Agency in Charleston. But how had Eden learned about her? "You're calling from South Carolina then?"

"No, from my parents' in Chicago. I flew home to visit over the Fourth. Ma asked me to call Dev for her with an update. Listen, I hope you don't mind my knowing about you and your situation, but the family often shares cases. Trust me, it can help. Karen, I can't tell you how sorry I am about your little girl. I know how awful it must be for you. Do you mind my talking about her? If you do, just say so, and I'll shut up."

She was chatty, and she was also understanding and sympathetic. Karen immediately liked her. "No, I don't mind."

"Because it can help sometimes to talk about it," Eden said. "Her name is Livie, isn't it?"

"Yes, Livie."

"We have her picture that Dev faxed the other night, and everyone here is ready to do whatever we can to get her back to you. Karen, she's beautiful."

Genuinely interested, Eden went on to ask her other particulars about Livie. Small things that probably only mattered to a mother, but Karen valued the opportunity to share them.

Eden Hawke was the kind of warm woman who invited confidences. It was so easy to talk to her. So easy to surrender to temptation.

"Thanks for caring, Eden." She hesitated and then found the courage to go on. "Uh, there's something else I'd like to tell you about Livie. Something you and your family have a right to know…"

In a breathless rush Karen confessed her secret. Then, as she listened to Eden being thrilled by her news, she realized too late what a terrible mistake she had made. Why hadn't she stopped to think before she so recklessly opened her mouth? Devlin was going to— Well, she didn't want to think about what Devlin was going to do.

She had her hands tightly and nervously folded together under her breasts when he finally emerged from the bathroom, buttoning his shirt.

"Your sister, Eden, called while you were in the shower," she informed him. "She's with your parents in Chicago. I told her you'd call her back. She has information for you."

He nodded and started toward the phone she had returned to the bedside table. "Ma must have results from the material I faxed her the other night."

"Wait a second before you call her."

He came to a stop and gazed at her. She knew that guilt must be written on her face like a colossal headline. "What's wrong?" he demanded. "What did she tell you?"

There was no avoiding it. "It isn't what she told me. It's what I told *her*. Devlin, I... Well, I let Eden know that you're Livie's father."

His reaction was immediate and explosive. "I don't believe this! You actually went and—"

"Before you say anything more," she swiftly interrupted him, "let me apologize. It was wrong of me. It was your place to tell your family, not mine."

"If you knew it was wrong," he thundered, "then why did you do it?"

She had been wondering that herself. Maybe it was just because Eden had been so irresistibly compassionate about Livie, interested in her in the enthusiastic way Devlin should have been and wasn't. Or maybe it was because Karen had no longer been able to bear the gnawing guilt of concealing Livie's existence from the Hawkes, who were entitled to know about her. Or was it simply because she had needed this family connection for her daughter? Any one, or all of them, could have been her reason. And what did it matter now? It was done.

Obviously, however, it mattered a great deal to Devlin. He was still furious. "All these years you keep her a secret from me, and now over the phone to a stranger you go and—"

"She's not a stranger. She's Livie's aunt. And is it so terrible that she knows?"

"Yes, because it won't stop with Eden. It'll go through the whole family like wildfire. They'll be smothering me with their damn joy."

He actually groaned over the prospect. What was wrong

with him? How could he mind something that she would give anything to experience?

She tried to reason with him, tried to turn her mistake into an advantage. "Devlin, their knowledge that you're Livie's father could benefit us. This way they'll be all the more committed to helping us recover her."

"You don't know what you're saying. When the Hawke hotline kicks in on this, and believe me it will, they'll be coming at me from every direction with advice and questions. How come I never told them about Livie? Why did I go and let you get away? How could I be apart from my own kid all these years? It'll never let up."

She envied him his wonderful family, and all he wanted was to maintain both a physical and emotional distance from them. Why couldn't he see how lucky he was to have them?

"You're not being fair to them, Devlin. You're not giving them a chance to understand and accept."

"And how would you suggest I accomplish that? 'Sorry, Ma. Sorry, Pop. Gee, the truth is I never even knew I had a kid until just the other day.'"

Karen was hurt by his sarcasm. "And that's what your anger with me is really all about, isn't it? You still haven't forgiven me for Livie. Oh, not for hiding her existence from you like you claim, but for having her at all. I actually think you would have preferred to never know about her."

She must have struck a raw nerve, because when he answered her his voice was raspy with pain. "Which would make me a real bastard, wouldn't it?"

"Devlin, I'm sorry," she whispered swiftly, "I shouldn't have—"

"Forget it. I've got to call Eden and find out what's up."

He turned away to the phone, dismissing their argument as though it had never occurred. But Karen wasn't able to forget their quarrel.

This just isn't working, she thought, too despondent to pay attention to the conversation that followed as Devlin talked to his sister. We promised each other it would be nothing but a dispassionate business arrangement. Only we weren't being realistic, because there are just too many issues involved.

But what choice did she have? She had to go on working with Devlin. They had to find some way of supporting each other. Without him, she couldn't hope to find Livie.

Maybe Devlin realized this, too, because his mood was altered when he got off the phone. He was sober but gentle with her when he told her the news.

"Ramey's car was found abandoned in Milwaukee, which means two things. He's already far away from the Twin Cities, and he's probably switched vehicles."

"They're certain it was his car?"

"The Hawke connections are reliable ones, Karen. It's definite."

"What if it's a van he's driving now? What if he doubled back to this area and is in that van?"

"Karen, don't go there again. It's a dead end. This guy is not hanging around chasing us. He has his own agenda elsewhere. What bothers me is we don't have a clue what it is, where it is, and what he's using now to reach it. So all we can do is get back to the Twin Cities and start digging again."

THEY WERE headed north on the interstate when Devlin, who had been quiet since they'd left Rocklyn, cleared his throat and spoke to her in gruff-voiced remorse.

"Listen, I'm sorry about that scene back at the motel. I shouldn't have lost my temper like that."

"I guess you were entitled to be mad at me." He had given her an opening, and she took advantage of it. "Devlin, I don't know what the problem is with you and your family, and of course it's none of my business, but if you'd like to talk about it...."

She saw him tense behind the wheel, and she knew she had trespassed.

"There's nothing to talk about. I get along with them just fine."

He wasn't going to explain. It was something he intended to keep sealed up inside himself, along with his resistance to fatherhood. Something as private and personal as that moment she had witnessed last night when he had sneaked Livie's photo out of her wallet. He wouldn't thank her for knowing about that.

"So are we okay?" he asked her.

"We're okay," she assured him, knowing it wasn't true. There was a strain in their relationship that no simple apology could eliminate. And it was made all the more complicated by an unrelieved sexual energy that continued to strum between them, like a taut wire waiting to snap.

THEY WERE CROSSING the bridge to St. Paul when Karen reminded Devlin of his decision.

"You said we'd have to start digging again. But where? What's left to us?"

"We'll begin by checking the answering machine at your house. And if Bonnie Wodeski hasn't left any message yet, then we're going to pay a visit to that brother of hers. My instinct tells me there's something happening there."

"You think he's holding back?"

''Oh, yeah,'' he said grimly, ''and this time I mean to persuade him to share it.''

The Twin Cities were still in the grip of a heat wave, but a welcome coolness waited for them inside the house on Summit Avenue. The air-conditioning service had obviously been here in her absence and taken care of the problem.

After dropping her things, Karen went straight to the answering machine. ''No messages,'' she reported in disappointment to Devlin, who had trailed her into the kitchen.

She was about to ask him if he was interested in having her fix them lunch before they headed to the Wodeski apartment when the phone rang.

Devlin was instantly alert. ''That could be her now. Wait,'' he said as she started to answer it. ''Put it on the speakerphone so I can hear.''

Stabbing the speaker button, Karen picked up. ''Ramey residence.''

''Oh, good, you're back!''

The exuberant voice belonged to a woman, but she wasn't Bonnie. Karen didn't recognize the caller, but Devlin did.

''Ma, what are you doing calling this number?''

''I don't like that cell phone of yours. It's not clear. You should get a new one.''

''Ma, my cell phone is just fine. You need to have your hearing tested. We've been telling you that for—''

''Nonsense. I'm hearing both of you perfectly on this instrument, aren't I? Except it does sound a little hollow.''

''That's because we're on the speakerphone so we can both listen.''

''Good. Hello, Karen.''

''Hi, Mrs. Hawke.''

"I don't answer to that name, Karen, except when Devlin's father thinks he's being cute with me, which thankfully doesn't happen too often. It's Moura, please."

Karen found herself already liking her, just as she had immediately liked Eden. Mother and daughter had the same friendly warmth in their voices.

"You still there, Dev?"

"Right here, Ma. I, uh, suppose Eden filled you in on what's been happening at this end after I talked to her earlier."

"Yes, I've been brought up to date."

Devlin captured Karen's gaze, mouthing a silent: *Here it comes.*

But, to their surprise, it wasn't the subject of Livie that Moura Hawke addressed when her cheerful voice suddenly became earnest.

"Now it's my turn to give you the latest. Karen, I hate to add to your distress, but you need to know this. There's been another response from our original inquiry on the Internet. Make that *two* responses. It's a shocker, I'm afraid." She paused, and they could hear her draw a quick breath before she went on. "We've turned up two more wives that Michael Ramey married and then abandoned without bothering to divorce them."

Karen, feeling weak, leaned against the kitchen counter to steady herself. Devlin eyed her in concern. She shook her head, indicating to him that she would be all right.

"Ma, are you sure it was the same man in both cases?"

"It seems pretty certain. He used other identities of course, but both women recognized his photo and the description that I posted with it. My darlings, this has been one very busy man."

"And a devious one," Devlin added angrily. "Ma, this

will need positive verification and some further investigation.''

''Already in progress,'' she assured him. ''The first wife lives in Sacramento. Mitch is on his way from our branch in San Francisco to interview her. The other woman is in Mobile, which makes her accessible to Christy, who's also on her way from the New Orleans office.''

Karen remembered that Mitch was one of Devlin's two brothers and Christy another sister. The impressive teamwork of the Hawke Detective Agency was again in motion.

''When do you think you'll have results on those interviews, Ma?''

''Call me later this afternoon, and we'll see what Mitch and Christy have turned up. I'll let you go now. You two take care of each other. And, Devlin?''

''Yes, Ma?''

''Find my granddaughter.''

And that was Moura Hawke's one and only reference to Livie before she rang off. She'd managed, however, to make it a plea from the heart, simple and brief though it was. Which meant Devlin was wrong about his family, Karen thought. Because Moura, somehow sensitive to her son's reluctance on the subject of his fatherhood, had neither asked questions nor offered opinions, though she must have wanted to express both.

There was silence in the kitchen after the phone call. Devlin looked worried about her. ''Can I get you anything? A glass of water, a chair?''

''No.''

''This is tough, huh?''

''Two more wives,'' she whispered, stunned and bewildered by his mother's revelation. ''Devlin, what's it all about? Why is he marrying all these women and then deserting them?''

He shook his head.

Karen thought about her daughter. "I miss Livie. The house feels so empty without her. *I'm* empty without her."

For a moment she thought he was going to hold her, comfort her again. But this time he must have considered the risk, and he resisted. Karen recognized the wisdom in his decision, but it didn't stop her from yearning for the shelter of his arms.

"Let's forget lunch," he said. "We can grab something later. Right now I'm interested in Scott Wodeski."

He's right, she thought. We can't rest. We have to keep digging, no matter what the result. Because without action, and the hope that drove it, she would lose her sanity.

"You know the address?" he asked.

She did, and twenty minutes later they emerged from the elevator on the fifth floor of the Columbia Heights building that contained the Wodeski apartment.

The place wasn't in the best condition. Karen noticed that the carpet in the corridor was worn and stained, and the walls would have benefitted from a fresh paint job. Potted plants stood in the corners. Plastic ones that had a layer of dust on their leaves.

"This is it," she said, arriving at the door of 510.

There was the sound of hammering inside, but when Devlin rang the bell it produced a silence. Long seconds passed before the door was cautiously pulled back on a chain. Scott Wodeski, with his goatee and narrow face, peered out at them. He didn't look happy to find them standing there.

"Whatcha want? I'm busy."

"We need to talk to you again," Devlin told him. "It'll only take a few minutes."

"Please," Karen added earnestly.

The young man considered their request, then nodded reluctantly. "Okay, hang on."

He closed the door, but another few seconds passed before he released the chain and admitted them into the apartment. Tools and raw wood were strewn around the small living room. Karen remembered that Scott had told them yesterday he was building shelves for his sister. He didn't invite them to sit down, which was just as well. Every chair was littered with junk.

"Make it fast, huh? And if this is about Bonnie again, I haven't heard from her yet."

"A little odd, isn't it," Devlin challenged him, "considering she was so anxious to have that information she sent you to get from her desk at the office?"

The young man shrugged. "I guess she just got too busy to call."

"Busy doing what, Scott?"

"How should I know. Probably just having fun. She's on vacation, ain't she?"

Karen noticed that he was nervous as he stood there twisting the hammer in his hand. He obviously didn't appreciate their visit. He might not have answered their ring at all, except he'd probably figured they had heard the hammering and knew he was in here. Devlin is right, she thought. He's hiding something. Something that has him worried.

"Know what I think, Scotty?" Devlin said, his smile friendly but steel in his voice. "I think maybe Bonnie isn't on vacation at all. I think maybe she's with her missing boss, Michael Ramey."

"That's nuts."

"Oh, I don't know. Your sister is young and attractive, isn't she? She and Ramey worked together, right? So why couldn't the two of them be having a hot affair? In fact,

Scotty, I talked to someone in this cafe near their office. Know what he told me? That Ramey and a blond woman were in there a lot and that the two of them were always cozy with each other. Bonnie's a blonde, isn't she?''

Scott stared at them, and then to Karen's surprise he laughed, revealing a couple of missing teeth. "That's a good one."

"Why?" Karen demanded.

"Because if you think your husband has a blond girl-friend, then you're looking in the wrong place. If I were you, I'd start with that partner of yours."

"Maud? Are you talking about Maud Dietrich?"

"That's the one. Bonnie caught them together over lunch and recognized her. She said they looked interested in each other. *Real* interested."

Karen was incredulous. Her friend, Maud, involved with Michael? "That just isn't possible!"

"Yeah? Then why don't you go and ask her?"

"We'll do that," Devlin promised him, a severe tone in his voice. "And if we don't like what she has to tell us, Scotty, you could be hearing from us again. And in the meantime, when your sister contacts you—"

"I know, I know. She should call you."

Karen was in such a state of shock that she didn't remember Devlin leading her out of the apartment. The next thing she knew they were in the elevator and descending to the street.

"We shouldn't have left," she objected. "We should have stayed until he gave us the truth. Devlin, Maud is a trusted friend. She wouldn't have cheated on me with Michael. It's all wrong."

"Then let's hope she gives us a solid explanation."

"You don't really think—"

"I'm not jumping to any conclusions, Karen. I'm just

saying we need to find Maud Dietrich, because it's possible she has some answers. And right now we need them.''

SCOTT STUCK the hammer in his belt, opened the door of one of the apartment's two bedrooms, and spoke to its occupant. "It's all clear."

Bonnie Wodeski, flipping her long blond hair back from a face heavy with makeup, strolled past him and out into the living room. Her brother followed her, wearing a rebellious expression.

"You hear what they had to say?"

"Yeah, I heard," Bonnie said, gazing critically at the bookshelves he was building. "So what?"

"Easy for you to say. I'm the one who's got to come up with all the lies while that P.I. looks at me like he's ready to take a piece out of me. If you hadn't screwed up getting the message to Ramey that his wife was comin' home early from Atlanta, maybe he wouldn't have taken the kid and they wouldn't be on our backs."

"Yeah, well, it went clean out of my head when he told me all out of the blue that he was shutting down the office. Time I remembered about the message it was too late, he was gone."

"Why do you have to keep hiding out in here, anyway? Why don't you just face those two?"

Bonnie rounded on her brother. "Let's not start that again. You want the cops here asking questions, maybe learning about me? This way I'm safe."

"Not if those two keep nosing around. They're bound to find out sooner or later that you never left town. Why don't you just phone 'em and get them off our backs?"

Bonnie shook her head stubbornly, her long hair swinging from side to side. "Not until I get this all put together and decide exactly what it might be worth."

"And when will that be?"

Bonnie didn't answer him. She moved restlessly to the window and stood playing with the drape cord while she stared down into the street.

This was getting tricky, she thought. With her history, she couldn't afford to get involved in something illegal. Not that she wouldn't risk it if it meant a nice profit for her. And after what she'd read in the Green Bay newspaper that had come in the mail less than an hour ago, she was beginning to think what she had was worthwhile.

Bonnie chuckled to herself. Worthwhile? Hell, it was better than gold. Besides, it would earn her personal satisfaction to outwit a man who'd regarded himself as superior to her.

For a long time Bonnie had wondered why Michael Ramey hired her. She'd always known she wasn't exactly brilliant. Then, when she'd begun to suspect his classy business wasn't all it claimed to be, she had finally figured it out. Michael had wanted someone just dumb enough not to ask the wrong questions.

Well, he had made a mistake. Because, while she might not be a brain, she had the shrewdness of a survivor. And that shrewdness had led her to a certain file he'd kept locked away in his office. She had caught him intently studying it once. He had been angry about that.

Bonnie had decided that, if the file was a secret, then it must be valuable. Maybe something that would benefit her. Stealing his key, she had removed and photocopied the contents while Michael was out on a call. Then, after returning both the original file and the key, she had examined the photocopied material at leisure. And been disappointed. It had looked to her like nothing more than a profile he was building on a potential real estate client. She had buried her copy in the bottom of her desk and forgotten about it.

That was before a couple of very private phone calls Michael had taken in his office just the day before he abruptly told her to take a vacation. Calls that had seemed vital to Bonnie, even though she hadn't managed to overhear them. Those calls, along with his furtive behavior, which had included his destruction of the original file, had convinced Bonnie something funny was going on. Something that warned her to lie low until she saw what developed.

And now, with her employer missing and after what she'd read in the newspaper, together with her memory of the file, Bonnie was fairly certain she had the pieces all in place. Yeah, had to be the explanation. But to be positive she needed the file.

Suddenly impatient for results, she swung away from the window. Scott was on the floor measuring a board. "Forget that," she told him. "I want you to go back to the office, and this time don't come away until you get me the photocopy of that file."

"I *was* back, and the lock's been changed, remember?"

"So break in. It won't be the first time you've done something like that."

He scowled at her. "Why don't you do your own dirty work?"

She exhaled in exasperation. "Because Hawke and Karen Ramey could be watching this building. It won't matter if they should see you leaving, but I don't want them to know I'm here. Not yet. Not until I have what I'm planning to sell them."

"It ain't worth it if I'm caught."

"Don't be a fool. You aren't working, and it's pretty clear now I'm out of a job, too. We need the money, and that file is going to earn it for us."

Chapter Six

After leaving the Wodeski apartment, Karen borrowed Devlin's cell phone and made a quick call to Dream Makers. Robyn answered. No, Karen was informed, Maud wasn't there. She was working at the diner their interior design firm had been hired to renovate.

Karen knew the place, and this time she took the wheel of the car. Her familiarity with the city left Devlin free to observe the passing scenery.

The noonday sun was blistering, but as far as he could tell it had no affect on the energy that seemed to charge Minneapolis at all hours. Sidewalks were crowded, and the River City trolley buses, replicas from another era, scooted in and out of the traffic like busy red beetles. Homes and storefronts wore an abundance of Fourth of July decorations. Flags and bunting were everywhere, and a marching band on a school playground practiced its drills for an Independence Day parade.

It was all normal, Devlin thought, watching the crowds. All bright and cheerful. He wished he could say the same for the woman beside him. The taut expression on her face told him what she was suffering. She had been dealt one cruel blow after another since her return to the Twin Cities, and now she had to contend with the possible treachery of her friend and partner.

He wouldn't have blamed her if she had collapsed long ago. But she hadn't. With each of those blows she had faltered and then picked herself up and gone on. He admired her courage. But how much more could she take? He was worried about her. Hell, he was worried about himself.

Devlin didn't know how long he could endure this thing that seethed between them, as sizzling as the summer heat. He was aware of her every minute. Little things like the way her auburn hair brushed her cheeks when she leaned forward. The soft love in her hazel eyes whenever her daughter was mentioned. The desirable curves of her slender body. And at this particular moment he found himself aroused by her subtle flowery scent that emphasized their closeness in the car.

Devlin squirmed in his seat with the temptation of that fragrance. He wanted her. Wanted her even more fervently than he had back in Colorado when they'd first met. But Karen came attached to something he couldn't handle.

There were moments, *dangerous* moments like now, when Devlin wished he could be like other men. That he could devote himself to a wife and kids. But he was unable to risk the responsibilities of a family. Not when that thing in his past continued to haunt him.

His promise to recover the child he had so recklessly fathered was tough enough as it was. It nagged at him all the time, tearing him up inside. But he was committed. He couldn't escape his obligation. Whatever his resistance, Livie was his daughter, and he had to find her.

"It's there again," Karen said in a low voice.

Jolted out of his thoughts, Devlin glanced at her sharply. She was gazing into the rearview mirror while they waited for a traffic light to change. He knew immediately that she referred to the burgundy-colored van.

Twisting around, he searched the street. A compact car directly behind them separated them from the van. He was unable to make out its driver.

"You're sure it's the same van?"

Karen nodded without hesitation. "I saw the broken headlight before that other car got between us."

The light turned to green. The traffic moved again. This time, as the compact began to edge over into the other lane, Devlin caught a glimpse of the van with its damaged headlight. It couldn't possibly be a coincidence, which meant Karen hadn't been imagining it. Her van was no phantom. It was a reality, and it was tailing them.

"Pull over," he directed her.

"What are you going to do?"

"Challenge this guy, if I can."

But he never got that opportunity. When Karen started to draw to the edge of the street, the van flashed around a corner and disappeared into the traffic. The tinted glass had kept its driver a mystery.

"Damn," Devlin muttered in disappointment. "How long was it back there before you noticed it, I wonder?"

Karen shook her head. "I have no idea."

"Which means it could have been following us ever since we left the Wodeski apartment, maybe even before then."

Karen didn't say anything as they sat parked there at the side of the street. She merely looked at him, her expression plain to read.

"Yeah, I know," he said. "I should have believed you from the start."

"What do we do now?"

"Go on to the diner. There's nothing we can do about

the van unless it turns up again, and then we'll worry about it.''

But Devlin couldn't help thinking about that van as Karen pulled away from the curb. Why was it following them? Who was driving it, and what did they want? Frustrating. He didn't know what the hell was going on here, but he meant to find out. Starting with Maud Dietrich.

IF THE SITUATION had been otherwise, Karen would have taken the time to leisurely examine her partner's latest project. Even so, being a professional, she couldn't help but briefly admire the results as she and Devlin arrived on the scene.

The diner, located near Loring Park, had been remodeled in the retro style of the 1950s. There was a great deal of polished chrome and red vinyl, a garish jukebox and walls plastered with framed posters of such icons of the era as Marilyn Monroe and James Dean.

The smell of fresh paint assaulted their nostrils as they came through the door. Karen remembered that her friend was making an effort to ready the diner for a Fourth of July opening.

Maud was consulting with the contractor behind the counter when they appeared. Excusing herself, she hurried to join them. There was a look of concern on her square, attractive face.

''At last! Karen, I've been fretting with worry! Where on earth have you been? And just *what* is going on?''

''Too much, I'm afraid,'' Karen answered her solemnly. ''Maud, we need to talk to you. It—well, it's pretty serious.''

A moment later the blond woman sat across from them in one of the booths, her pale blue eyes registering her shock as she heard Karen's story and their efforts to locate the missing Livie.

"You know I'll do whatever I can to help you find her," the sympathetic Maud assured them.

"If you mean that," Devlin said, "then you can start by telling us what's been going on between you and Michael Ramey."

Maud stared at them. "You can't be serious. You don't really believe that—" She broke off, aware of their grim expressions. "You *do* mean it. You think that Michael and I were *actually* involved."

"I'm sorry, Maud," Karen said, "but I don't know what to believe anymore. We were told that Bonnie Wodeski saw you and Michael having lunch together."

"That doesn't mean I was having an affair with him."

"Then it's true. You and Michael did meet each other in that cafe near his office."

"Yes," Maud admitted, "on one occasion about a week ago."

"There was another source," Devlin said, leaning toward her intently, "that informed me Ramey had lunch on a regular basis in that cafe with a blond woman."

Maud shook her head. "I don't know anything about that. Michael and I met just the once, and that's all."

"And you kept it from me," Karen said, accusation in her tone. "Why?"

"Because he made me promise to keep our meeting confidential. I thought I was helping both of you."

"How?"

"Karen, the reason he asked me out to lunch was to discuss your troubled marriage."

"Which means you already knew that my marriage was coming apart."

"No, just that you were having difficulties."

"But you never said a word."

"I was waiting for you to tell me in your own time. Look, I realized after the lunch that I'd made a mistake in accepting his invitation, so I figured it was time to just keep my mouth shut."

"I don't understand why he should have wanted to talk to you about our marriage. That wasn't like him."

"I didn't think so either. But he seemed so anxious to make things right that I thought he had your best interests at heart and actually wanted to save your marriage. I can see now, after everything you've just shared with me, that what he really wanted was to get me alone so he could convince me he had nothing to hide."

"Why should he think you might suspect him of hiding anything?" Devlin demanded.

Maud was thoughtful for a second. "Maybe," she said slowly, "because I caught him at something I wasn't meant to see."

Karen knew it was her partner's words, and not the powerful air-conditioning in the diner, that made her suddenly feel chilled.

"And what was that?" Devlin urged her.

"Probably nothing. At least it didn't seem important at the time. Now I don't know."

Maud's faint German accent became more pronounced as she went on to describe the situation. Karen knew this was a sign of the tension her friend was experiencing.

"It happened the morning of that lunch. I went to check out this new draper's near the Convention Center. There was a fabric I was interested in for that condo model we're doing. I had a bolt of it at the front window of the store where the light was bright enough to show me the quality of the stuff. And that's when I saw him."

"Ramey?"

Maud nodded. "He came out of a health club across the street, and then he went into the place next door. It was one of those mail drops. He wasn't in there more than a few seconds, and when he came away he had a letter in his hand. That's when he looked up and saw me in the window."

"How did he react?" Devlin asked her.

"At the time I thought he was just surprised. But after everything you've told me, I guess it was more than that."

"You're telling us he was worried because you'd spotted him? That he *was* hiding something?"

"That's the impression I have now, yes. But I'm not sure why. They were just a health club and a mail drop, except it did cross my mind that the mail drop itself was a little unusual. I mean, people use them when they have very private correspondence to protect, don't they?"

Devlin nodded. "That's the general idea. What happened next?"

"He came into the draper's and invited me to join him for lunch. I tried to turn him down, but, Karen, you know how persuasive he can be."

"All right," Devlin said, "you've told us why you went. Now tell us what he had to say for himself over lunch."

"He wondered if I'd seen him leaving the health club. I told him I had. Then he asked me not to mention it, because he was a little embarrassed about his visits there. He'd been regularly working out in secret, trying to make himself more attractive to Karen. He was afraid of losing her."

"And you bought that?"

"I know, it sounds pretty weak now, but he was so sincere about it. And he admitted I was right when I told him that building muscles wasn't going to impress Karen, that he'd have to do better than that if he was going to save his marriage.''

"Did the mail drop get discussed?"

"He mentioned in passing that a few of his clients preferred this method for sending him their more sensitive documents. I said I could understand that, and the subject was forgotten.''

"And that was all you talked about?"

"That's it. I've told you everything." She leaned toward Karen, her expression contrite. "Karen, I'm so sorry. I had no business discussing your marriage with him, but at the time I didn't see it as interfering. I saw it as—"

"Maud, it's all right. It's not important. All that matters now is learning where he went with Livie.''

"And I haven't told you anything that will help you to do that, have I?''

"Could be that you have," Devlin said mysteriously.

Before Karen could ask him to elaborate, he put his hand on her arm, silently telling her it was time to leave. She understood him. He wanted to wait until they were outside before he explained.

Sliding out of the booth, they got to their feet. Maud came and hugged her. "I know you'll find her, Karen, and until you do, don't waste a thought on Dream Makers. Robyn and I can manage everything between us, and if there's anything else I can do...."

"There is one more little thing," Devlin said.

"Name it.''

"Would you happen to know anything about a burgundy-colored van with a broken headlight cover?"

Maud gazed at him, puzzled. "I can't think of anyone I know who has a van like that. Is it very important?"

"Maybe.''

Before Maud could ask them any further questions, the

manager of the diner came out of the kitchen and began to tell her about the pedal pushers and ponytails the waitresses were going to wear. He wanted to know if Maud thought they would complement the diner's decor.

Karen and Devlin used the opportunity to slip away. Once back inside the car, she turned to him expectantly.

"That comment you made to Maud that maybe she did provide us with something useful…you were referring to the mail drop, weren't you? You think if we go there we stand a chance of learning just what it is that Michael's involved in."

"Forget it."

She stared at him in disbelief. "How can you say that when the mail drop could tell us what secret he's protecting, because it must be connected with something he's been receiving there?"

"It won't. Karen, believe me when I tell you that no P.I. can crack a mail drop, and the best of them have tried. Mail drops preserve an absolute confidentiality. It's why people with something to hide use them."

"Then, if not the mail drop, what did you mean?"

"The health club."

"If that makes sense, I don't see it."

"Think about it. You don't for a minute believe his explanation to Maud about why he was there was an honest one, do you?"

"Not to save our marriage, no."

"And if he was there on a regular basis simply to exercise for himself, then why keep it from you? Wait a minute. Where's that mail we carried away from his office yesterday morning?"

"I stuffed it into the glove compartment. Why?"

"Because I seem to remember when we glanced through it…" Opening the glove compartment, he pulled out the stack of mail and flipped rapidly through its contents. "I was right. Here it is." He waved the envelope in front of her.

"It looks like a bill from the health club."

"That's just what it has to be. Maybe this time Ramey slipped up by giving the club his office address. Let's see what it says."

Devlin tore the envelope open and unfolded the statement that was inside.

"It isn't a bill," Karen observed. "It's a receipt for several months of service."

"Yeah, paid in full and the account closed by customer request."

"And nothing secretive about it," she said, scanning the items in disappointment. "Just a record of the exercise equipment he used. He was telling the truth, after all."

"Not so fast. Look at these last ones." His finger indicated a series of identical listings at the bottom of the statement. "They're more than all of the other charges put together."

Karen frowned over it. "But there's no explanation. Just the initials F.R. beside each of the charges. What do they stand for?"

"Don't know, but whatever it is he used it almost daily for a considerable length of time." Devlin looked at her with determination. "I may not be able to crack a mail drop, but a health club is something else. Let's go."

KAREN THOUGHT that the attendant behind the counter was a poor advertisement for a health club. He was overweight, and his clothing smelled of cigarette smoke. The man wasn't impressed by Devlin's P.I. credentials or her own identity.

"Being his wife," he said stubbornly, glancing from her

to the itemized statement she had placed on the counter
for his inspection, "doesn't entitle you to privileged information about Mr. Ramey's membership here."

"Maybe you need something more convincing," Devlin
said, slapping a twenty dollar bill on the counter. "Will
this do it?"

The man didn't hesitate. Looking quickly over his
shoulder to make sure they were alone, he whisked the bill
into his pocket. Karen didn't care for either the greedy
attendant or Devlin's action, but this was no time to get
moral about a bribe.

"So, what is it you want to know?"

"The F.R.," Devlin said, tapping the initials on the
statement with his forefinger. "What does it stand for?"

"Firing range."

Karen noticed Devlin's face suddenly tighten, and she
realized her own face must be wearing a startled expression.

"You're telling us this club has a practice range for
handguns?"

"Sure, out back. It's one of our most popular services."

"And Ramey used it?"

"Yeah, all the time when he wasn't keeping in shape
on the other equipment. Nothing illegal about that."

"He ever mention why he was practicing on that
range?" Devlin pressed him.

The attendant shrugged. "I don't ask questions like that.
It's none of my business. All I know is he was a damn
good shot when he started and a perfect one before he quit.
Hey, it's a dangerous world. People like to know how to
defend themselves."

The man had nothing else of any consequence to tell
them. Devlin was silent when they left the club and returned to the car. There was a hard look in his blue eyes

that worried her. She was afraid to ask him what he was thinking. Afraid of her own growing suspicions, but she needed the truth, no matter how terrible it might be.

"What does it mean?" she asked him.

He shook his head. "Not sure."

"But you think you know, don't you? Why won't you tell me?"

"Not yet." He glanced at his watch. "Let's go back to your house and the speakerphone. Ma should have some results for us by now."

Devlin sat beside her as though she had ceased to exist, staring off into space as she drove them back to Summit Avenue. His silence was infuriating. Except he wasn't silent. She could hear him whistling softly under his breath. He had done that before, and she thought she understood the habit now.

His whistling meant he was sorting through the pieces, shifting them around, fitting them together until they were assembled into a picture that satisfied him. This explained his refusal to form any conclusion for her. Nor would he be ready to share his result until he had the final, few missing pieces within his reach. Pieces that he must be expecting his mother to supply him.

It was how Devlin's mind worked. And it was understandable to Karen now, but it was no less frustrating. By the time they reached the house, she could hardly bear the suspense, or her own mounting apprehension.

All she could see was Livie's small, bewildered face, an image that made her sick with dread as Devlin dialed his mother. To her relief, Moura answered immediately, the briskness of her voice offering a measure of reassurance.

"Hello, my darlings. Are you making any progress?"

"I think so, Ma, but I'll save it until you tell me what

Christy and Mitch have come up with. You hear from them yet?''

''I have. Both of them phoned from the road on the way back from their interviews. You're going to find this interesting, because the two wives—''

''Hold it, Ma,'' Devlin interrupted her. ''I want to get paper and pencil in case I need to jot down the essentials.'' He scanned the kitchen counter in the area around the phone.

''In the drawer in front of you,'' Karen informed him.

She'd forgotten the contents of that drawer until he opened it, discovered the evidence of her addiction, and then looked at her, one of his thick eyebrows arched quizzically.

Worried by the silence, Moura demanded, ''What's going on there?''

''Nothing, Ma. I've just discovered she's a pack rat, that's all. Twist ties?'' he said to Karen. ''Nobody hoards twist ties. Must be a million of them in here.''

''Don't you let him make you feel guilty, Karen,'' Moura sided with her. ''I save rubber bands myself.''

The extent of Karen's various collections in the house might have daunted even the robust Moura Hawke, but Karen didn't think this was exactly the moment to mention them. Burrowing under the twist ties, she located a pad and pencil and placed them in front of Devlin.

Levity forgotten, he was all business again. ''All right, Ma, you were saying....''

''About the two wives,'' she continued. ''They had almost identical stories to tell about him. Only the names and occupations were different. In Sacramento, Michael Ramey was Oliver Jordan, an investment counselor. In Mobile, he was David Adams and operated a travel agency.''

"Meaning," Devlin said, "he always used something low-key and respectable. Careers that wouldn't draw attention to himself."

"Exactly," Moura agreed. "His behavior was just as conservative, and the marriages were always traditional ones. And get this. Money never mattered in his choice of a wife, because neither woman had any real money to speak of."

"Yeah, we've already established he wasn't motivated by profit when he married them."

"Then you've probably also figured out what did count with him."

"I think I know the pattern now," Devlin said, gazing apologetically at Karen. "He wanted wives who were attractive and accomplished, but there was something more essential. They had to be women without families who might ask a lot of questions about his past."

Karen, listening to their exchange with a heavy heart, could relate to those other wives and the ultimate despair they must have experienced. "You're leaving something out," she said quietly, finding the courage to add what had to have been Michael's most important requirement. "Because I'm sure there was something else we all had in common. Every one of us must have been vulnerable, and that made us gullible. I know I was."

"I'm afraid that's true, Karen," Moura said sympathetically.

"What else, Ma?"

"This is the part that counts," Moura went on. "Christy and Mitch said the women reported the same scenario about the failure of their marriages. It matches Karen's and your client's back in Denver. Almost overnight their devoted husband emotionally detached himself from them. Then, before they had opportunities to understand why he'd suddenly turned into a stranger, he was gone. Vanished, just as though he'd never existed.''

"Either wife have any clue he was a polygamist?''

"None at all. Both women were shocked when Christy and Mitch explained the situation to them. This is not a nice man we're talking about, my darlings.''

"That the extent of it, Ma?''

"Pretty much, except to add that in both cases he cleaned out the bank accounts before he disappeared, but that's all. He left them with everything else. Unlike Karen,'' she added gently in reference to Livie.

"All right, Ma. There's one more thing I'd like you to do.''

Karen caught Devlin eyeing her with concern as he spoke. He's worried about how I'm going to handle what he needs to ask his mother, she thought. She knew it had to be something alarming. Steeling herself, she nodded slowly, indicating to him that she was prepared for whatever it was.

"What is it, Dev?'' Moura asked him, her grave tone telling Karen that she, too, sensed his request would be a disturbing one.

"This won't be easy, but maybe the rest of the family can help us out.'' He paused to cast another worried glance at Karen. "See if the dates Ramey left his wives are closely followed by unsolved murders of people who were either important or wealthy, and where individuals had something major to gain by their deaths.''

If Moura was shocked, she was careful not to show it. "That's a tall order.''

"I know, because they could have occurred just about anywhere. But we can narrow this down. Look for killings where any suspects with strong motives had solid alibis. If I'm right, if we can establish a time line here that fits…''

He left the rest unsaid. A further explanation wasn't necessary. Karen understood now what he was thinking, and she guessed that Moura understood it, too.

She stood there and numbly watched Devlin scribble doodles on the pad as he and his mother went on to make sure of the dates that were to be investigated.

It's bad, Karen thought. Even worse than I imagined. Because if what Devlin believed was true, and logic convinced her it must be true, then she had married Michael Ramey, lived with him in contented ignorance, and all the while he had been carefully guarding an appalling secret.

Feeling as though her legs would no longer support her, she sank down on one of the chairs at the kitchen table. Her mind was so dazed that she was only half aware of Devlin now describing to his mother their efforts on this end. It was Moura who brought Karen back to a hard reality when she directed her closing comment to her over the speakerphone.

"Karen, trust Dev to bring you and Livie through this safely. He will, you know."

There was a brief silence after Moura made her goodbye. Then Devlin came to her where she sat. Hunkering down on the floor in front of her, he gazed perceptively into her haunted face.

"Do you understand it now?" he asked, a strong compassion in his deep voice.

She shook her head. "All I'm certain of is that terrible possibilities are going through my mind. Which is the right one?"

"That the man who calls himself Michael Ramey is a professional killer for hire."

The shock of his conclusion was even worse than she had anticipated. "How could I?" she whispered. "How could I have been married to him and never guessed?"

"Don't be so rough on yourself. He played his role very well."

"Are you sure that's the explanation?"

"I think so. I think that's what everything points to."

"Yes," she said, seeing it all now and unable to keep the edge from her voice, "that's just what it points to. The firing range where he perfected his skill, the mail drop where he must have had contact with whoever wanted his vile service, the unexplained luxuries. He probably commands huge fees, which means there's got to be another account somewhere with big money in it. Something only he knows about. That's right, too, isn't it, Devlin?"

"It's more than likely."

"The wives," she remembered, fighting hysteria. "We were all a part of it, weren't we?"

"Looks like it."

"We *were*," she insisted. "We had to be, because what could be more safe than a respectable marriage? Cunning, so cunning. Disappear after each hit and find yourself a new identity in another part of the country and a new wife to hide behind. And he probably enjoyed it. We were no more than a game to him. He used us, and none of us ever knew who he really was, and we don't now."

"Karen—"

"And then he would get a new contract, so it was time to pull out again. Time to move on, because—" She broke off, staring at Devlin in horror as the full realization kicked in. "Dear God, do you know what this means? If it's come *my* turn to be abandoned, and we know it has, then he has a new assignment! He's out there somewhere ready to strike again! He's going to kill someone, and we don't know who or where!"

"It's very possible, yes."

"And Livie is with him! Why Livie, when he never took

anything before but the contents of bank accounts? Why does he need Livie?''

''I don't know.'' Devlin reached for her hands, clasping them tightly in his own.

''Devlin, we have to tell the police! We have to bring the police in on this now!''

''Not yet. What we've got amounts almost entirely to speculation, and we can't afford to have them refuse to believe you again when we go to them. We need real evidence, and I'm praying Ma and the family come up with—''

''That's no good! It could be too late by then!''

''Karen, a few hours. That's all I'm asking for. A few more hours for the Hawke network to produce something.''

''A few hours with Livie at risk! Because now that we know just how dangerous he is, she *is* at serious risk!''

''I realize that, but putting our faith in the family agency is the best we have.''

''It doesn't matter to you, does it?'' she said angrily. ''Why should it when you barely acknowledge her as your daughter?''

''I do care,'' he insisted. ''More than you know.''

She didn't listen to him. She tried to drag her hands away, but he held onto them. After a brief, breathless struggle, she realized she was being unreasonable. Losing her self-control and firing wild accusations at him wasn't going to help Livie.

Karen gave up the battle and outwardly calmed herself, but inside she couldn't prevent the anguish of the silent plea she sent to Livie: *Wherever you are, be safe for me, sweetheart. I need you to be safe for Mama.*

Did Devlin somehow feel her cry to their daughter? Was

that why he suddenly surged to his feet, hauling her with him? Why he growled a savage, "The hell with this!"

It was his own restraint he was talking about. The promise he had made both to her and himself that he would avoid any intimate contact with her. She understood that, just as she understood in this agonizing moment that her need for his comfort was so desperate he was prepared to abandon all caution.

She didn't resist him when his arms went around her, when he drew her tightly against his solid length. This wasn't just Devlin, the man she'd been fighting not to love. This was Livie's father, and on that level there was a bond between them too strong to deny.

It was a connection she welcomed when he rocked her tenderly, crooning reassurances in his mellow voice. She gazed up into his riveting blue eyes that looked back at her from a face that was all angles and planes. Compelling eyes that willed her to trust him. And she did, even when he began to kiss her between his soothing murmurs.

They were harmless kisses lightly planted on her forehead, her cheeks, her throat. It was when his parted mouth settled possessively on hers that those kisses, now involving his sensual lips and searing tongue, became serious. That they threatened to escalate into something deep and intoxicating.

It would have been so easy to surrender to passion, to lose herself in the mindless haze of his sweet lovemaking. But she couldn't. There was Livie. Her fear for Livie that made such an indulgence unthinkable.

She could already feel her defenses weakening dangerously under the assault of his shameless kisses. Aware of his arousal, of how much he wanted her, Karen forced her mouth away from his.

"We can't," she pleaded with him. "Not now. Not when Livie needs us."

She watched the heat in his eyes cool. He nodded slowly. His arms dropped, releasing her. She felt empty without his protective embrace, vulnerable. As though she had sacrificed an essential security.

"Yeah, there's Livie," he said.

Did she detect resentment in his tone? "Why, Devlin?" she asked him solemnly.

"What?"

"Why are you so resistant to fatherhood and family? Just what is that all about?"

Tugging restlessly at the lobe of one ear, he turned away from her. "Forget it," he said abruptly.

He wasn't going to tell her. It was something private and perhaps very painful, something he didn't want to share. His refusal saddened her. She watched him as he plunged his hands into his pockets and prowled around the kitchen. It was time for her to change the subject, get back to what was immediate and vital.

"What if the Hawke agency comes up empty this time?"

"Then we go straight to the police, just like you wanted."

"And what if, as you said, they don't believe us?"

"I don't know, but we won't give up. We'll find them. Whatever it takes."

Karen clung to that renewed promise. It was all she had.

The afternoon dragged on while they waited for Moura to get back to them. Karen knew it could be hours before they heard from her.

They hadn't eaten anything since breakfast in Rocklyn early this morning. Karen fixed them a belated lunch. Though neither one of them had much of an appetite, they dutifully ate the sandwiches and drank the iced tea. It was a way of passing the time, of trying to fill the awful hollowness inside them.

The phone remained frustratingly silent. She and Devlin were equally quiet. It was late afternoon when Karen, unable to bear the tension any longer, was ready to ask him if there wasn't something more they could do. Something they might have overlooked in their efforts to prove to the police that Michael was lethal and that they had to conduct an organized hunt for him. Anything but this empty waiting. And that was when the phone rang.

Moura, Karen thought, hurrying to answer it, praying that Devlin's mother had useful results for them. But it wasn't Moura Hawke on the speakerphone. It was another voice that spoke to them, edgy and cautious. Karen and Devlin exchanged excited glances as the caller identified herself.

Chapter Seven

"This is Bonnie Wodeski."

"We've been trying to reach you," Karen said.

"Yeah, Scott told me."

"Where are you?" Devlin demanded. "If it's at all possible, we need to meet with you."

Bonnie was immediately suspicious. "Who's that talking?"

"It's all right," Karen assured her. "His name is Devlin Hawke, and he's a friend. We're both here on the speakerphone."

"Yeah, I heard about him, too. And he's more than just a friend. Scott said he's a P.I. Why do you need a P.I.?"

"Michael is missing," Karen explained, "and Livie is with him. Do you know where they might—"

"Hold it," Bonnie interrupted her. "Have you got anyone else there listening in?"

She's nervous, Karen thought. Worried about this conversation. Why?

"There are only the two of us here," Devlin promised her. "And you haven't told us where you are."

"I'm in town," Bonnie admitted, and Karen could tell she was not willing to be more definite than that.

"What about Michael?" Karen pressed her. "Do you have any idea where he went?"

"Maybe."

"I think you do," Devlin insisted. "I think you know exactly where he is and what he's up to."

"I didn't say that," Bonnie countered swiftly.

"And what's more," Devlin went on, "you knew when you called here that Karen hired me to help her find Ramey and her daughter. Yeah, I think you already had that all figured out."

"Smart guy, aren't you?"

"It's what I get paid for. So why the act, Bonnie? What is it you want?"

Don't, Karen pleaded with him silently, afraid that he was alienating Bonnie and that she would hang up on them.

There was a long pause while Karen prayed not to hear the sharp click that would indicate Bonnie had abruptly ended the call. But Devlin knew what he was doing.

"I just need to be careful, that's all," Bonnie grumbled, to Karen's relief. "So, okay, there is something I want."

"Let's hear," Devlin said.

"I've got this item to offer you, and it's dynamite. Interested?"

Karen caught her breath in taut anticipation, but Devlin remained cool. "If it leads us to Ramey, we are."

"It will," Bonnie promised them, "and for the right price it's yours."

"I figured that was coming," Devlin said. "All right, what is it?"

Bonnie hesitated. She's afraid, Karen thought. Wondering if she can trust us not to turn her in for extortion. Bonnie must have decided the risk was worth it, because she went on.

"Michael Ramey isn't what he pretended to be," she said, her words rushed now, as if she feared any further reluctance might change her mind. "He's into murder for hire, and if you think that's impossible, I've got the proof right here in my hands."

"We've already figured out exactly what Michael Ramey is," Devlin assured her. "And you still haven't told us what this item is."

"It's a file. Everything he researched to prepare him for his next victim, and never mind how I got my hands on it. All you need to know is that it's genuine, and it contains all the details. It tells who and where and when."

"Then it's not too late?" Karen asked her anxiously. "We need to be certain of that."

"You've got time, but if I were you I wouldn't waste it."

"I don't suppose we can persuade you," Karen appealed, "to take this file and go with us to the police."

"And what would I get out of that?" Bonnie sneered. "Now are you buying or not?"

"How much?" Devlin asked.

"Three thousand in cash, and don't ask me for any samples of the merchandise."

Karen and Devlin's gazes silently questioned each other. But they both understood they had no choice. Without the precious information in Bonnie's possession, there would be little hope of recovering Livie and preventing a murder.

"This had better be legitimate material," Devlin warned Bonnie. "All right, where do we meet you?"

"I've got to think about protecting myself, so let's make it a neutral place. I figure one of the skywalks is good."

Devlin lifted an eyebrow in puzzlement. Karen nodded, assuring him that she knew exactly what Bonnie was talking about.

"Which one?" she asked.

"Let's say the one on Sixth closest to Marquette. Make it just after sundown. Should be real quiet by then. No one to disturb us. And, listen."

"Yes?"

"Don't even think about involving the cops, because if the two of you aren't there on your own I disappear along with this file."

"I understand," Karen said.

"Good. Nice doing business with you, folks."

A silence told them she had hung up.

"I'd guess she was never away on vacation at all," Devlin said. "Looks like the little witch has been busy right here in the Twin Cities the whole time. Skywalk?"

"Enclosed pedestrian bridges," Karen explained. "There's a regular maze of them in downtown Minneapolis. People can move from building to building over the streets without ever having to go outside. In a climate like ours they're very appreciated."

"And useful to Bonnie Wodeski. Probably no way to be cornered and the opportunity to watch who's coming and going."

"Devlin, are we doing the right thing?"

"You heard her. If we don't meet her, we don't get the evidence to convince the police, or the FBI if it comes to that, to stop Ramey before it's too late."

"But the information you've asked your mother and the family to come up with—"

"Too much of a long shot. It was a possibility when it was all we had, but this sounds like a certainty. We need that file, which if it's all she claims—" He broke off as a realization occurred to him. "The three thousand dollars in cash! We've got to come up with that money, and we only have a few hours to do it!"

Karen glanced at the antique school clock on the wall. "If we hurry, there's just time to make the bank before it closes."

"Unless that clock is wrong, it's already too late. Karen, it's almost five-thirty."

"This is Friday," she reminded him, "and some of the banks stay open until six or later on Fridays. Thank heaven, mine is one of them."

"I'm assuming," he said, grabbing her hand and hurrying them toward the door, "that you've got something there besides the joint checking account Ramey cleaned out."

"My own money market account," she assured him, "and he wouldn't have been able to touch that."

"Bless you and your bank, because I've gotta tell you, on my own I'm not sure I could come up with three thousand in cash on short notice like this."

They were outside and on their way to the car in the driveway when Karen remembered something. "The call we've been waiting for from your mother. Shouldn't we phone her and—"

"No time. Let the answering machine take her call. She'll realize we got busy on this end. Anyway, it could be hours before the family has any results, and maybe not even then."

THE CENTER OF Minneapolis had all the bleakness of a ghost town, Karen thought as they left the Camry in a parking facility and made their way toward the rendezvous with Bonnie Wodeski. It was Friday evening at the start of a long holiday weekend, which meant there had been an exodus from the stores and offices hours ago. Most of the businesses were closed by now, the downtown streets nearly deserted.

The sun was setting, casting long, lonely shadows. Many of the streets were already gloomy canyons. And without the hum of traffic in them, the quiet seemed unnatural to Karen, contributing to her sense of uneasiness.

I'm just tense because of this meeting, she told herself. That's all it is.

But she was thankful for Devlin at her side. Even in her distracted mood, she was conscious of his reassuring closeness, of his long stride as he hurried them along the sidewalk. There was something distinctly sexy about his unhesitating gait, maybe because it marked him as a man of confidence, and she needed that.

"This way," she said, leading him into one of the highrises.

They took the escalator to the second floor, followed a broad corridor, and emerged onto the glass-enclosed skywalk that overhung the thoroughfare below. They had met no one on the escalator or in the corridor. The skywalk connecting the two buildings was equally empty.

"I guess we wait," Devlin said.

They strolled out past the center of the skywalk and stopped. Neither of them spoke. Devlin stood close to the windows, watching the thin traffic passing below them. Karen, trying not to be restless, clutched her purse and was aware of the three thousand dollars stuffed down inside it. They remained the only two people on the skywalk as the minutes crawled by.

The sun had gone, leaving a flaming sky in the northwest, when Devlin expressed his growing impatience. "Where the hell is she? She should have been here by now."

He swung his head, searching both ends of the skywalk, but there was no one else in sight. Then he turned his attention back to the scene from the eastern windows.

Karen saw him frown as he gazed at another enclosed bridge almost a half block away along the street.

"What if we're on the wrong skywalk?" he wondered. "What if she's waiting over there on that one?"

Karen shook her head. "I'm sure this is the one she specified. It's closest to the intersection."

But Karen, too, was beginning to think something was wrong. What if Bonnie never appeared at all? It was a depressing possibility. She kept thinking of Livie, worrying about her as they waited.

Devlin wasn't satisfied by Karen's answer. Another long moment passed, and then he shook his head. "I don't know. You said yourself this skywalk system is a complicated one, with bridges everywhere over the downtown streets. Maybe there *was* a misunderstanding."

Shoving away from the eastern side of the bridge, he crossed to the western windows behind them. "There's another of them out there," he said, indicating a skywalk that was much nearer to them than the one to the east. It was probably less than a hundred yards away.

The glow in the sky behind the structure made it not much more than a silhouette. It was difficult to distinguish any details, but as Karen joined Devlin at the glass she caught a rapid movement out in the center of that other skywalk. There was someone standing over there. Someone with a mane of long blond hair. And then the figure was gone, ducking back behind a window divider.

"Yeah, I saw it, too," Devlin said as Karen clutched at his arm. "It's Bonnie, isn't it?"

"She knows we're here. I could swear she knows we're here."

"She's been watching us," he said grimly. "Probably been there the whole time."

"Then we are on the wrong skywalk, after all."

''No, you were right. This is the one she intended.''

''Then why—''

''She's making sure we're alone before she joins us, that we didn't bring the cops with us. That's why she's over there.''

They waited anxiously, and a few seconds later the figure they were convinced was Bonnie edged out cautiously from behind the divider. At the same time another shape detached itself from the shadows along the left side of that skywalk. Karen was aware of the second figure in her peripheral vision, but she was too busy trying to wave a reassurance to Bonnie to pay the new arrival any attention.

That all changed within seconds. A startled Bonnie was suddenly confronted by the newcomer. They couldn't tell whether it was a man or a woman. Not only was the distance too great, but the individual stayed away from the windows, remaining just a dark form against the frustrating backlight from the sky. They knew only that this was not simply some innocent pedestrian on his way across the skywalk.

Karen's grip tightened on Devlin's arm, her fingers digging into his hard flesh as what appeared to be a heated exchange followed. Then, as they watched in horror, unable to prevent it, a gun barked. Muffled, but they heard it. Bonnie crumpled to the floor. Her attacker bent over, snatched something from her grasp and fled from the skywalk.

''Dear God!'' Karen cried. ''She's been shot!''

''How do I get over there?'' Devlin demanded. ''Which way?''

Karen tried to think. ''That way,'' she said, pointing in the direction opposite the one from which they had arrived. ''Just follow the markers. But I'm coming with you.''

''You have something else to do,'' he insisted. Reaching

into his back pocket, he withdrew his compact cell phone, grabbed her hand and slapped the instrument into it. "Call 911 and get an ambulance and the cops over here!"

"Devlin, don't go!" she pleaded with him as he started to move away. "That lunatic could still be on the loose over there, and he's armed!"

"I have to go," he said urgently.

She knew he was right. If Bonnie was still alive, she might need attention that couldn't wait for the paramedics.

"Make that call," he said, "and then get out of here. I want you off this skywalk system and safe down on the street by the time the cops arrive."

"Be careful!" she shouted after him as he rushed away.

She was suddenly alone on the skywalk. With fingers that trembled, she flipped open the cell phone and punched in the numbers. When she held the instrument to her ear, she heard nothing but a crackling. Muttering in exasperation, she tried again and had the same result.

Was the skywalk the problem? Something about this enclosed space that caused an interference? Whatever the explanation, Karen knew there was no time to waste. She had to get out into the open, reach help.

Devlin, she thought, worried about him as she raced toward the exit. Where was Devlin now?

The blinding glow that had been in the sky on the heels of the sunset had faded into a gray dusk. There were only the lights of the city now, including overheads here and in the skywalk where Bonnie lay. They must have come on automatically with twilight. But they revealed no sign yet of Devlin over there.

And then the skywalk was no longer in Karen's view. She was back in the corridor, headed toward the escalators. The broad passage came to a fork. She took the left branch,

and when it turned she came up against the solid barrier
of a metal screen that hadn't been there before.

She stared at the locked gate in dismay, and then she
remembered. Certain sections of the skyway system had
more limited hours than others. This route must have been
blocked off by security since their arrival earlier. She
couldn't reach the escalator.

Pressing against the steel mesh, she called a frantic,
"Can anyone hear me?"

Silence. She was alone in the corridor. Maybe the phone
would work this time. She tried it, but again there was
nothing but static.

Panic is not an option, she told herself sharply. Just go
back to that other branch. They wouldn't shut down a skywalk without some way out.

Swinging around, she rapidly retraced her steps. She
came to the fork and, without pausing, plunged into the
other passageway. There were office doors along this
route, but they were all locked and dark. No windows either, and though the hall was adequately lighted, it felt like
a tunnel stretching into the heart of a mountain. She met
no one, heard no sound but her own footsteps echoing
hollowly on the hard tiles.

Her growing apprehension added to the eerie quality of
her aloneness. Where was Devlin? Comforting a wounded
Bonnie, or was it too late for Bonnie? Karen shuddered
over that possibility and their powerlessness to stop her
murder.

Devlin must be wondering why he wasn't hearing the
sirens announcing the police and an ambulance were on
their way. Frustrated by her inability to contact help, by
the maddening delay, Karen increased her pace, trotting
along the corridor.

This was ridiculous! There should have been another

escalator by now or a stairway to the street level. Someway out of here. The corridor seemed endless, twisting and turning. She crossed on another skywalk, a short one linking the two high-rises over a narrow alley.

By now, even with the markers, she had completely lost her bearings. She wasn't familiar with this section of the skyway system. What's more, she was winded. It was when she paused briefly to catch her breath that she heard it. The soft sound of approaching footsteps. She wasn't certain whether they were behind her or in front of her, or even whether she might be imagining them in her desperation.

"Devlin!" she called out. "Is that you?"

The footsteps were silent now.

"Who is it?" she shouted. "Please, I need help!"

No answer. And then, her throat tightening with alarm, it occurred to her that a killer could be stalking her. Bonnie's killer!

Hands shaking, she fumbled for the cell phone that she had shoved into her purse. She prayed that this time it would work. She never got the chance to find out. In her nervousness, the instrument slipped from her hand, shattering on the tiles.

Sick with terror, she abandoned the useless phone, fleeing up the corridor. If she was running toward her pursuer instead of away from him…well, she had no choice. She had to find an exit, and none had been available on the route behind her.

The corridor turned again, emerging into a lobby. Weak with relief, she reached a bank of elevators. But there was no open car sitting on this level. She stabbed a down button and waited, on fire with tension.

There were no more echoing footsteps. She must have imagined them, after all. But she didn't like standing here.

She had the feeling of being cornered in this place where the corridor ended.

Although there was another, narrower passage that joined the lobby, it was unlighted. A well of sinister darkness. Karen tried not to think about it. She faced the elevators, controlling an urge to pace.

What was taking so long? Why wasn't one of the cars arriving?

"I have a message for you, Karen Ramey."

The footsteps might not have existed except in her mind, but the voice, chilling in its suddenness, was very real. It came out of the blackness behind her. Spinning around, Karen flattened herself against the elevator doors, staring into the unlighted corridor. Whoever it was knew her name, which made this encounter all the more frightening.

"Who's there?" she called, challenging a figure she couldn't see. "What do you want?"

The low voice, disembodied, androgynous, warned her in a gruff monotone, "For you and your P.I. to do the smart thing. Stop investigating. Stop interfering, the both of you, or I promise you'll regret it. Just remember Bonnie Wodeski."

Karen wished she had the courage to go into that tunnel and confront the nameless danger watching her from the darkness, but whoever it was must be armed with the weapon that had shot Bonnie. She was trapped here against the elevators.

"My daughter," she pleaded. "You know where she is, don't you? What have you done with Livie?"

The voice, still unrecognizable, replied with rancor, "Why did you come back from Georgia? Why couldn't you have just stayed down there? If you'd waited until next week to return, like you were scheduled, there would have been no problem. Everything would have been taken care of by then. Nothing for you to worry about, but now—''

"Livie!" Karen cried. "Why does Michael need Livie? I want her back!"

"If you ever expect to see her again, safe and unharmed, then call off your P.I. Otherwise…"

The rest was left unsaid, but the speaker's meaning was altogether clear. Until this instant, Karen had been able to do nothing except cower there in terror. But the threat to Livie so infuriated her that she no longer cared about the risk to herself.

"You can threaten me all you like!" she raged. "But I won't stand for you threatening Livie! If she's hurt in any way, if either you or Michael so much as touch her, I swear you'll suffer for it! Do you understand? *Do you?*"

There was no response from the dark corridor, no sound at all. Karen suddenly realized she was alone again. The menace had silently retreated, melting away into the blackness.

She was so shaken by her experience that she didn't hear the elevator until the door slid back, startling her. When she turned to board the car, she gasped aloud at the sight of the figure inside. Then she flung herself into Devlin's arms.

He held her, crooning soothing words. She had never been so grateful for his solid, protective embrace.

"It looks like you've had a bad time of it," he murmured. "What happened? I've been looking everywhere for you and imagining the worst."

Karen realized for the first time that her face was wet with tears. She brushed them away and rapidly described the episode to Devlin. She hung onto him when he looked like he was ready to thrust her aside and race up the unlighted corridor in pursuit of the enemy.

"Devlin, no. Whoever it was is long gone by now."

"Was it a man or a woman?"

She shook her head. "I don't know. The voice was flat and low-pitched. It could have been a woman disguising herself. I am almost positive it wasn't Michael himself. Whoever it was, though, had to be Bonnie's attacker." She searched his face questioningly. "Is Bonnie—"

"There was nothing I could do for her. She was dead by the time I reached her."

Karen made a sound of despair, and then she remembered something. "Devlin, I never got the chance to contact the police."

"It's been taken care of," he assured her. "I ran into a security guard when I went looking for you. He's alerted them. Look, if you're up to it, we'd better get downstairs. The cops are probably here by now. I think we're going to have one hell of a bunch of questions to answer."

"I know."

"The worst of it is," he warned her, pressing the button for the street level, "we don't have the file Bonnie was going to sell us. Her murderer has it. And without that proof, I think we have some tough explaining ahead of us."

HE HADN'T BEEN exaggerating. Karen felt drained when she and Devlin emerged from the old stone building that housed the downtown police department at the corner of Third and Fourth. They had undergone a grueling two-hour session with the team of investigators, recounting in detail their every action since Michael had disappeared with Livie.

They stood there for a moment in weary silence on the sidewalk, gazing at the lights of the city, listening to the sounds of the passing traffic in the warm summer night.

Karen finally framed the question that had been on her mind since they had been told they were free to go. "Do you think they believed us?"

Devlin's voice was husky when he answered her, as though strained by too many lengthy arguments and appeals. "That we weren't responsible for Bonnie Wodeski's death? Yeah, I think in the end they were convinced of that much."

That hadn't been easy, either, Karen thought. Not when she and Devlin had been unable to provide a worthwhile description of the killer. Nor had the police, after searching the vast skywalk system, found any sign of the murderer. Whoever it was had managed to get away.

"As for all the rest—" He shook his head. "I don't know. My gut feeling is that they think it's a pretty fantastic story."

"But they did promise us that they would put out the net for Michael."

"Yeah, but there wasn't a lot of enthusiasm in that promise. They still want evidence, and we don't have it to give them."

The car was parked a couple of blocks away. They were turning in that direction when a police cruiser pulled up to the curb. Two uniformed officers emerged from the vehicle, escorting a young man in torn jeans and a stained T-shirt.

"But maybe *he* does," Devlin said.

Not pausing to think about it in his urgency to find answers, Devlin strode toward the thin figure between the two officers. Karen, recognizing Scott Wodeski with his gold earring glinting in the streetlight, hurried after him.

One of the officers raised his arm protectively in front of Scott as Devlin approached, barring his way.

"I just have a couple of quick questions to ask him, Officer," Devlin requested.

"Not now, sir," he was politely refused.

"But they're important."

"They'll have to wait."

Scott's gaze met Karen's as she joined the group. There was a haunted look in his eyes. He's been told about his sister, she thought, and was deeply sorry for him. The young man also looked scared and worried, the goatee on his chin wobbling with emotion. Did the police think he had something to do with Bonnie's death? Is that why they had brought him here?

"It will only take a minute," Devlin persisted.

Karen tugged at his arm. "This isn't a good time," she told him softly.

The officers moved on with their charge, disappearing into police headquarters.

"Damn it, Karen, why did you stop me? There's a chance Scott Wodeski knows what's in that stolen file."

"If he does, then the police will learn about it and hopefully share it with us. Devlin, he's her brother, and he must be suffering. They're probably going to have him identify her body."

Devlin heaved a sigh. "You're right. I wasn't thinking. Come on, let's get out of here."

Karen's mind was busy as they walked to the car. At one point in their long session with the police, they had been questioned separately. She felt the need to examine that with Devlin.

"They asked me who I thought the figure was on the skywalk," she said.

"What did you tell them?"

"That I was sure it couldn't be Michael. Not tall enough."

"Yeah, I got the same question."

"And what was your answer?"

"That Ramey, himself, is probably nowhere in the area, but that he must have an accomplice still here. Someone he left behind to make sure his latest assignment isn't discovered before he executes it. And that someone killed Bonnie to prevent her from revealing the contents of the file."

"Yes," Karen agreed, heartsick over their series of failures, "which is why I told them about the burgundy van that's been following us. It's how Bonnie's killer learned what we were doing and that we were getting too close to the truth. That's right, isn't it, Devlin?"

"It makes sense, even though we don't have the full explanation yet."

"The blond woman Michael was seen meeting on several occasions in that cafe…is she his accomplice? There's a good chance she is, isn't there? And they counted on everything being over and done with before I got back from Georgia and found Livie missing. Why do they need her, Devlin? Why is Livie so important to them?"

He shook his head, unable to relieve her torment. It was in this bleak mood that they drove back to the house on Summit Avenue.

What could they possibly do now in their effort to find Livie? Karen wondered dismally as she threaded her way through the late-hour traffic. Devlin's silence beside her told her that he, too, had run out of ideas. It looked like they had reached a dead end, but she refused to accept that. Refused to give up hope.

Nor was she ready to uselessly wait for the police to produce results. Devlin is right about that, she thought. We can't count on them to locate Michael when they're still suspicious of our claims, reluctant at this point to perform more than a local investigation of Bonnie's death. And certainly not willing yet to involve the FBI. But if we don't convince them to use all of their resources, and to do it soon, it will be too late to stop an assassination. And maybe, unthinkable though it was, too late to recover her daughter.

Where are you, Livie? Tell Mama where you are.

There was no answer to her silent plea. No solution to her misery.

The house was dark when Karen turned into her driveway on Summit Avenue. But not deserted. The headlights of the car picked out a figure casually perched on the back steps. The lanky figure of a man in Stetson and boots who rose to his feet with their arrival.

Karen had no idea who their visitor was. But Devlin must have immediately recognized him. To her surprise, he muttered a curse of pure exasperation.

Chapter Eight

"What's wrong?" Karen demanded, faintly alarmed by the appearance of this strange cowboy ambling toward the car. "Who is it?"

"Someone I don't need right now," Devlin growled.

Concerned by his resentful reaction to their visitor, as well as his failure to identify him, Karen followed Devlin out of the car.

"What in hell are *you* doing in St. Paul?" Devlin asked, confronting the tall stranger as he reached them.

The inadequate glow from a streetlamp didn't permit Karen to make out the man's features, but there was no mistaking the crooked grin on his face.

"That's what I love about you, Dev. Your sweet greetings always make a man feel real welcome." And to Karen's astonishment, he grabbed Devlin in a rough embrace. What was even more surprising, Devlin suffered the bear hug without objection.

"Yeah, I missed you, too," Devlin said when he was released, his sarcasm evident and his suspicion even plainer. "Now would you like to explain how and why you turned up here?"

"Just a stopover between flights. Taxi dropped me from

the airport. I'm on my way to San Francisco. Mitch needs my help with a tricky case.''

"By way of the Twin Cities?" Devlin said dryly. "A little indirect, isn't it?''

"Well, you know the airlines. Never a straight route between destinations.''

"Uh-huh. That route wouldn't have also involved another stopover in Chicago, would it?''

"As a matter of fact, it did. Got to spend a few hours this morning visiting with the folks.''

Karen, impatient for an explanation, interrupted their exchange. "I don't suppose that either of you would care to, uh—''

"Sorry," Devlin mumbled, offering a hasty introduction. "My brother, Roark Hawke. Rory, Karen Ramey.''

Karen, who had already guessed by now that the cowboy was his brother, offered her hand. It was met with a firm, genuinely warm clasp. "My pleasure, Karen.''

"All right, Rory, you've shaken her hand. You can let it go now.''

Karen glared at Devlin. What was the matter with him? Why was he being so rude to his brother? Not that Roark seemed to mind. He still wore his infectious grin.

"Do I get invited inside?" he wondered, releasing Karen's hand with a lingering reluctance that seemed to irritate Devlin. "Or are we going to stand out here in the drive slapping at the bugs?''

Karen, fishing for her key, led the way to the back door. "How long is your stopover, Roark?''

"A couple of hours.''

"Long enough to have a late supper with us? Devlin and I haven't eaten anything since this afternoon.''

"I wouldn't say no to a pizza. My treat.''

"A couple of delivered pizzas isn't a bad idea," Karen

agreed, unlocking the door and switching on lights as she led the way into the kitchen, "but you're my guest, so keep your wallet in your pocket."

Roark didn't argue with her. Now that they had the benefit of the lights, Karen took a moment to satisfy her curiosity about Devlin's younger brother.

The physical resemblance was a strong one. Though Devlin's shoulders were broader and his face more mature, they were both tall and with powerful builds. They shared the same square-jawed good looks and compelling blue eyes.

But in other respects they were very different. It had been immediately apparent to her that Roark Hawke had a good-natured attitude that contrasted sharply with Devlin's often cynical, and sometimes explosive, temperament.

Karen found Roark easy to like, maybe because of the wicked grin he perpetually wore and the witty way he addressed himself. She even found his outfit amusing, but the cowboy boots and Stetson seemed to annoy Devlin.

"Still dressing like Roy Rogers, I see."

"I'm a Texan now, remember."

"For pete's sake, Rory, you're a P.I. in San Antonio, not a ranch hand riding the range."

Devlin was being positively nasty, and Karen didn't understand why. She could have smacked him, but Roark merely laughed.

"Hey," he said, exaggerating a lazy drawl, "if you can be a ski bum in Colorado, I can be an urban cowboy in Texas. Karen, how about those pizzas?"

His reminder was a timely one. Calculated, she suspected, to ease the tension. Obliging him, she asked their preferences and went to the phone. The pizza parlor she called promised to deliver their order in forty minutes. Hanging up, she suddenly remembered the answering machine. She checked it quickly and was disappointed. There were no messages.

Devlin, sensing her anxiety, joined her at the phone. "Nothing from Ma? There should be something by now."

Karen shook her head. They both glanced at Roark. He was leaning against one of the counters, looking casual and innocent. Devlin went to his brother, challenging him.

"All right, Rory, let's have it. What's the real reason you're here?"

"Told you. I'm on my way to help out Mitch," he said, referring again to the youngest Hawke brother, who operated the San Francisco branch of the agency.

"That might be true, but you came by way of Chicago and you knew just where to find us here in St. Paul. Which means the family told you everything. Ma sent you, didn't she?"

"Hell, Dev, they're worried about you and Karen and this whole mess. And you weren't around to answer the phone since this afternoon, and since I was heading west again anyway..."

"Yeah, I get it. Rory gets sent to check it out and report back. How is ol' Devlin bearing up? Could he use some on-the-spot assistance?"

Karen was frustrated and angered by Devlin's resentment. Roark's presence here was more evidence of the Hawkes closing ranks in a crisis, a demonstration of family support that deeply moved her. His family cared. He mattered to them, and so, too, did the daughter he'd never wanted. Why couldn't Devlin appreciate that? Why did he have to see it as the family ganging up on him? It was maddening.

Devlin considered his brother for a moment, and to her relief his attitude softened. "So, now that you're here, what can you tell us? Any progress yet on the family's search to match up the dates Ramey left his wives with unsolved assassinations?''

Roark shook his head. ''It's a slow, tedious business. All we've got so far came from Mitch's office—the murder of a wealthy industrialist in San Francisco that occurred shortly after your man deserted the wife in Sacramento. The killer was never found.''

Devlin nodded. ''Which means Ramey was probably responsible, but it isn't conclusive. And by itself it's not enough to convince the police and the FBI to commit themselves to a nationwide manhunt for this guy. And that's what we need right now because we keep running into brick walls.'' He went on to tell his brother about Bonnie Wodeski.

Roark's grin had vanished. He listened with sympathy, understanding their urgent need to find Michael before he struck again. ''Well, look,'' he said, offering them encouragement, ''you know how respected Pop is. He's trying to use his influence to get his FBI connections to act on this.''

But it's a big country, Karen thought, and Michael could be anywhere in it. Without some direction, how could even the FBI locate him before it was too late? And, meanwhile, he had Livie. It always came back to that.

Struggling against that anguish, Karen occupied herself making a simple salad to go with the pizza and plugging in the coffee. She only half listened as the brothers talked, speculating on the methods Michael might have employed to make his services available to anyone without a conscience and the right price. Roark had a theory that professional assassins made use of both the Internet and certain underground paramilitary magazines to offer themselves for hire.

But what difference did it make, Karen thought desperately, how Michael Ramey got his vile contracts? All that mattered was stopping him before he destroyed his latest victim, and before he used Livie to do it.

She wondered if Roark sensed the direction of her thoughts. Was that why he got up from the table where the two brothers had settled, crossed the kitchen to the bulletin board on the wall, and gazed with a smile at the bright crayon drawing Karen had proudly mounted on it a little over a week ago?

"Did your little girl do this?"

"Yes."

She watched him slide a glance in Devlin's direction and then nod thoughtfully. Before she could explain that the picture was meant to be a pair of clowns Livie had seen on a visit to Mall of America, the phone rang.

"It was the pizza parlor," she explained when she hung up. "The pizzas are ready, but the delivery boy's car won't start. They're asking us to pick them up ourselves." She reached for her purse and the car keys. "I'll go."

It would give the brothers a little private time together, she thought. But to her surprise Devlin surged to his feet. "No," he insisted, "you stay here and visit with Rory. I'll collect them."

He asked for directions, and before she could argue about it he had taken the car keys and was gone. She could have sworn that leaving her alone with his handsome brother was something he would have avoided. She didn't understand it until after the door had closed behind him.

Livie, she thought, remembering that the subject of his daughter had been introduced just before the phone rang. He was afraid that if he stayed behind, Roark would ask him questions about Livie. Questions he didn't want to answer. Once again Devlin was running away from any emotional connection with Livie.

"You're worried about him, aren't you?" Roark said, looking up at her perceptively from where he sat at the table, long legs stretched out in front of him.

"What I'm worried about," she said with a sharp edge to her voice as she went back to preparing the salad, "is how unpleasant he's being with you."

"Oh, that," he said casually. "Don't let it bother you."

"But it does bother me," she said, assembling ingredients for the dressing. "I know I don't have the right to apologize for him, but he shouldn't treat you that way. You're his brother."

Roark didn't respond to that, at least not immediately. Unfolding his length from the chair, he tossed the Stetson on the kitchen counter. "If you'll point me in the direction of your dishes," he said, "I'll set the table while you finish that salad."

She indicated the cupboard that held the tableware and napkins. He was silently busy for a moment transferring plates and cups to the table. Then he began to talk.

"Look," he said with that attractive drawl he had acquired in Texas, "I don't mind Dev's abruptness with me because I know that underneath, where it counts, he does care and that he'd be there for me if I needed him."

It didn't seem a very adequate explanation to Karen. "Is that how it's supposed to work with siblings? Being an only child, I wouldn't know, but it just seems wrong to me."

"Well, sometimes," he admitted, "there's this rivalry between brothers, and I guess that's true where Dev and I are concerned. Doesn't mean we don't love each other."

He wasn't giving her the truth, at least not the truth she needed. She stopped working on the salad and faced him. "But it's not just you he's resisting. It's all of you in the family. And Livie...when all of this is over, he doesn't want anything to do with Livie.''

Roark stared at her and then nodded soberly. ''Yeah, I guess that doesn't surprise me.''

''Why, Roark?'' Karen pleaded with him. ''What's it all about?''

''Have you asked him?''

''He won't discuss it. I was hoping that you...''

He considered her appeal and then shook his head. ''No, that would be a mistake. If he wants you to know, he'll tell you himself. Just give him some time.''

''You're as mysterious as he is,'' she complained.

He grinned at her outrageously. ''It's part of the Hawke charm. I do have a solid piece of advice for you, though.''

''What's that?''

''Don't fall for him, Karen.''

She had no answer to that. But a reply wasn't necessary. Her face, that perpetual curse, gave her away.

''Uh-oh,'' he murmured. ''Too late, huh? You're already in love with him. Yeah, I should have known that.''

''You mean because we once had an affair that resulted in Livie?''

''No. It's the way you look at him.''

''I thought I've been looking at him like I could kill him.''

Roark laughed. ''Yeah, that's what I mean.''

Karen could feel her face go hot. Was she so apparent? Did Devlin, himself, know how hard she had fought not to love him and that somewhere along the way, without realizing just when or how, she had lost the battle? It could be very painful for both of them if he did know.

Roark must have thought the same thing because he cautioned her gently, ''Just be careful. He could end up hurting you badly.''

Devlin, himself, had warned her of the same thing, and she understood it no better now than she had all along.

"Do you think I should just give up on him then?" she asked. "Is that what you and your family have done?"

"No," Roark admitted, "we haven't. It's been tough where Dev is concerned. There are some real issues there, but we're not about to let him divorce us. We just keep hanging in there, loving him, trying to be patient with him, and hoping that one day he'll come back to us."

If she applied that same love, Karen wondered, exercised that same patience with Devlin, would he ever love her and Livie? Want both of them in his life? Or would she just be letting herself in for a lot of heartache?

"Yeah," Roark said, reading her, "it's a risk. I guess you just have to ask yourself whether he's worth it."

Karen feared she already knew the answer to that question. If she didn't fight for Devlin, she would lose him. And that prospect was suddenly unbearable.

DEVLIN STRUGGLED with his guilt all the way to the pizza parlor and back. His brother never failed to have this effect on him. Whenever they were together, Devlin found himself snapping at him. He didn't really understand it. Maybe it was because he resented Rory's easy self-confidence, that carefree, rascal-like quality that seemed to endear him to people. He had none of Devlin's own intense nature.

The worst of it was, Rory never seemed to mind his rudeness. He would just laugh it off. And then, afterwards, Devlin would be left dealing with his guilt. Because in spite of everything, he did love his brother, as he loved every member of his family. He just couldn't bear to be close to them anymore. Not with his bitter memories.

It was worse this time, though. He wasn't quite sure why. Maybe it was because Rory's appearance tonight somehow reminded him that he was no longer young. That it was growing increasingly difficult for him to resist the responsibilities of fatherhood that had been thrust on him out of nowhere. An emotional commitment he didn't want and couldn't handle.

"What about your little girl, Dev? What are you going to do about her and her mother?" That's what Rory seemed to be asking him on behalf of the whole family. It was a question he wasn't able to answer.

He was quiet when he got back to the house. The three of them seated themselves around the table and ate the savory pizza, munched on salad and drank coffee that was too hot. And all the while Karen and Rory, damn them, ignored his silence. They were too busy enjoying themselves.

Rory asked her all about Livie. Was she shy and introspective, or open and full of energy? What were her interests? Who did she favor in looks, Karen or the Hawkes? They were questions that Devlin should have asked for himself and hadn't. Now he had to listen to his brother framing those questions, and he minded that more than he was ready to admit.

He sat watching them, a brooding expression on his face. They were entirely comfortable with each other, like they'd been friends for years. Devlin's gaze narrowed suspiciously. He could swear that Rory was flirting with her. What's more, Karen was enjoying his attentions. Rory's charisma seemed to make her momentarily forget her frantic tension of the past three days.

Devlin decided that he could cheerfully break his brother's neck. Make that both their necks. The worst of it was, even after all she had been through today, he had never seen Karen look so sexy. Devlin felt himself aroused at the sight of her, with her auburn hair gleaming in the lamplight and her hazel eyes shining. That Rory might be responsible for these, as well as the attractive flush on her cheeks, infuriated him.

Devlin refused to acknowledge that he was jealous. But he was deeply relieved when Rory, realizing he would miss his flight if he lingered, called for a taxi.

It was late when they said their goodbyes. Devlin stood at the door and watched the taxi bearing his brother to the airport disappear down the street. Rory was gone, and Devlin had a smile on his face. That was before he turned around and faced a woman who looked ready to annihilate him.

"YOUR OWN BROTHER!" she reproached him. "And you were positively rude to him!"

"What?" Devlin said, all innocence as he moved across the kitchen to where she stood, hands tightly locked together under her heaving breasts. "I never said a word to him. Not after I came back with the pizza."

"No, you just sat there scowling at him like a spoiled brat. Do you know what I'd give to have a brother of my own? Or a sister? How much I'd value them? And stop that when I'm being angry with you!"

Devlin was staring at her breasts with an expression on his face that threatened her concentration.

"Can't help it," he muttered. "They're damn alluring with you blazing away like that."

"I'm in no mood for this, Devlin. Not after the way you treated Rory."

"I'll call him and Mitch after he gets to San Francisco. I'll apologize."

He started to touch her, and she slapped his hand away. "Why can't you appreciate the family you have?"

''Tomorrow,'' he promised. ''I'll phone him tomorrow.''

Refusing to be discouraged, he slid his arms around her, pulled her close. She squirmed in objection, but he went on holding her.

''This isn't going to work,'' she warned him.

''Sure it will,'' he murmured, his voice thick and husky. ''You just have to relax, that's all.''

His hands, those skillful, wonderful hands, began to stroke the length of her, sliding with slow, exquisite seduction down her back and over her hips. She was squeezed against him so snugly that she felt his powerful arousal. This had to stop! She struggled against his embrace. But perhaps her effort wasn't convincing enough, because he failed to release her.

She tried to maintain her self-control. ''I'm still mad at you,'' she said with what she hoped was a cool detachment.

''We'll fight later.''

His hands crept around to the sides of her breasts, his fingers caressing their silken fullness.

''Don't do that,'' Karen ordered him, feeling her insides turn to jelly.

''I have to,'' he said, his voice drowsy as his hands continued their enticing exploration.

''This is a mistake.''

''Probably,'' he agreed.

What was the matter with her? She wasn't helpless. All she had to do was insist that he let her go, and mean it. He wouldn't force himself on her. Instead, she submitted to the torment of his hands teasing her willing flesh.

''Devlin?''

''What?''

''That's enough.''

"You're right. I won't touch your breasts anymore."

And he didn't. His hands left that area and reached up to frame her face, creating a target for his mouth which angled across hers. His kiss was deep, searing and utterly disarming, robbing her of all reason. She was dazed when his mouth finally lifted from hers.

"What was I mad about?" she whispered.

"I wasn't very nice to Rory," he reminded her softly.

"Oh, yes." She attempted again to lecture him. "You sulked the whole time he was here. There's no other word for it. You *sulked.*"

"Uh-huh," he said, and he kissed her again, his tongue warm and wet in her mouth, wantonly sensual.

When she could breathe again, she managed to croak a feeble, "Didn't we promise ourselves and each other that this wasn't going to happen again?"

"I think so."

"That we weren't going to repeat Colorado?"

"You're right." His hands shifted, scooping her up into his arms. "Upstairs?"

"What?"

"Your bedroom, sweetheart. Is it upstairs?"

"Yes."

He carried her out of the kitchen and along the hall, pausing just long enough at a wall switch to flip on a light. "This the way?"

"Yes."

She no longer had a will of her own. No longer cared about the consequences. Nor, she assumed, did he. Maybe it had to do with this desperate situation concerning Livie. A need to find a measure of comfort in each other. A release from an intolerable tension. Whatever it was, she wanted him. Wanted to feel him deep inside her, a part of her. Because, for better or worse, she belonged to him. At least for this night.

There was a magic in the way he carried her almost effortlessly up the stairs and into the room she indicated. It was the guest room, seldom used but always kept ready. She refused to profane their magic in the master bedroom she'd once shared with Michael.

The wide bed on which Devlin placed her was fresh, untouched. A new beginning, like the lovemaking they were about to experience. Stretching out beside her, he gathered her into his arms and began to kiss her again. Sweet, feverish kisses which she returned with a mounting urgency.

"Are you sure?" he tried to warn her between those kisses, his voice raw. "Remember, I'm not a safe kind of guy."

"I haven't forgotten. And that hasn't changed, has it?"

"No," he admitted, trying to be fair.

"I'll risk it," she whispered.

"Thank God," he said in gratitude, obeying her invitation with a further assault on her mouth.

When did they shed their clothes? Peel the cover away from the bed? Karen had no memory of either action. But they must have happened because she was suddenly aware of their naked bodies clasped together on the cool, scented sheets.

Encouraged by his hoarse pleas, her hands traveled the length and breadth of him, rediscovering the hard body she had once known as intimately as her own. The expanse of dark hair on his deep chest, the thickness of his muscular thighs, the sensitive place in the hollow of his strong back. They all became familiar to her again.

Devlin, breathing hard, dealt with his own renewal of her willing flesh. Branding the taut buds of her breasts with his eager mouth, learning again all the secret places of her body with his gentle hands, cherishing her with whispered endearments.

Unable to endure his prolonged torture, it was with a sob of relief that Karen welcomed his swollen length slowly, tenderly parting the petals of her womanhood. He eased into her, and when they were finally, completely one, she felt as if not only the vessel of her body had accepted him but her soul as well.

He murmured her name, and she answered him, their words blurred, breathless. And when he stirred inside her, her body responded with a rhythm as old as time. Straining against him, consumed by him, she scaled the pinnacle toward which he urged her with his inflamed kisses.

Their release was a blinding victory accompanied by unrestrained, joyous cries.

Afterwards, snug in his arms, Karen gazed at his face beside her on the pillow. His eyes were closed, and there was a mellow little smile on his wide mouth. Looking at him, treasuring the precious thing they had just shared, she felt as if a part of her that had been missing for too long had finally been restored to her. But would she be able to keep it?

DRUGGED BY CONTENTMENT on the heels of a long, exhausting day, they slept deeply and without interruption.

Karen was startled when she opened her eyes and found the room bright with sunlight. Morning. Saturday morning, and Livie had been gone since Wednesday. The burden of her missing daughter settled on her shoulders again. It was Devlin's burden as well. Only after last night it was more complicated, with a need only he could satisfy but which she had to find the courage to win from him.

He was no longer at her side. And though she knew by

the sound of running water in the adjoining bathroom that his absence was only a momentary one, it still gave her a sense of loss. She was relieved when the door opened and he reappeared, a towel snugged around his waist. Fresh from the shower, bearing the tantalizing aromas of soap and shampoo, he was a riveting sight, his virility never more evident.

He greeted her with a drowsy grin that tugged at her insides and a cheerful, "Morning. I found a razor and helped myself to a spare toothbrush. Hope you don't mind."

"We aim to please."

He crossed the room and perched on the edge of the bed. "How far does your hospitality extend?" he wanted to know, a meaningful glint in his blue eyes.

In another second he would reach out for her. He would take her in his arms, capture her with his potent kisses. With the memory of last night roaring in her head, it would be so easy to surrender to him again. But Karen resisted the temptation. She still had that need to be answered.

Sitting up against the headboard, she drew the sheet up high enough to cover her breasts. An action that wasn't lost on him. He gazed at her, his expression sober now.

"What's going on?" he wanted to know.

"Could we talk for a minute?"

He nodded, but there was a wary look in his eyes.

Karen approached the subject indirectly and with care. "I don't think I ever told you, Devlin—there would have been no reason to tell you—but I never knew my father. I mean, I didn't even know who he was. Nothing about him, not even his name. You'd think, wouldn't you, that you couldn't possibly miss what had never existed for you in the first place?"

She paused, eyeing him, knowing by the way his mouth

tightened that he understood where she was headed. But he said nothing.

"Only it doesn't work that way. It didn't for me, anyway. I never stopped feeling the hole in my life that he left behind. In all fairness," she went on hastily, "it mightn't have been his fault. It's very possible he was never even told of my existence, but all the same...."

"We're not talking about you, though, are we, Karen?" he challenged her. "We're talking about Livie."

"It's too late for me," she pleaded, "but it's not too late for Livie."

"What have I missed?" he said, a harsh edge to his voice. "The last I heard, once your daughter was recovered you'd be happy to see the last of me."

"I was wrong." She had known it even before last night, but last night had strengthened her realization.

"What do you want from me, Karen?"

"The father Livie deserves. I want you to love her, be a part of her life." And mine, too, she thought with longing, but she couldn't bring herself to say it. Her courage didn't extend that far.

He got off the bed and began to prowl around the room. There was a panicked, trapped look on his face. "You don't know what you're asking."

"Would fatherhood be so difficult, Devlin?"

He rounded on her. "Some men just aren't meant to be fathers. I'm one of them."

She didn't believe that. She remembered the other night in the motel room in Iowa when she had caught him staring at Livie's photograph. There had been a haunted expression in his eyes, as if he longed for something he could never have. He wore that same look now.

"If you would just talk about it," she tried.

"All the talk in the world isn't going to change my

mind. I'm sorry, Karen, but what you're asking isn't going to happen, so let's just forget about it.'' He snatched up his discarded clothes. "I've got to get dressed."

He left her abruptly, returning to the bathroom and shutting the door behind him. Karen got out of bed, gathered up her own things and crossed the hall to the master bedroom. She went into the bathroom there, brushed her teeth and took her own shower.

And all the while her heart ached with disappointment. She had planned to tell him that she loved him. She couldn't do that now. There could be no hope of any future for them together. His not wanting Livie was the same as not wanting her. Last night had been a mistake, a gamble she had lost.

Her misery and sadness felt like more than she could bear when she emerged from the bathroom. She was pulling on jeans and a fresh top when the phone on the bedside table rang.

The police? They had promised to call if there were any new developments. She hurried to answer it.

"Karen Ramey," she identified herself briskly.

There was a pause. And then a tiny voice, sounding as if it spoke from a million miles away, said breathlessly, "Mama?"

Chapter Nine

She would know that voice anywhere! Livie!

Karen's heart began to pound. She tried to steady herself, to sound calm. "Yes, sweetheart, it's Mama."

"I don't like it here anymore, Mama. I want to come home now, please." The voice was plaintive and small, still sounding far away.

"Where are you, Livie?" she pleaded. "Tell me where you are, so I can come and get you."

"With Poppy."

"Livie, where did Poppy take you? Can you tell me—"

There was a sharp click and then a cruel silence. The connection had been severed.

"Livie!" she shouted uselessly into the phone.

Devlin must have heard her cry. He was suddenly at her side. He took the phone from her trembling hand and held it to his ear.

"There's no one there," he said.

"There was!" she said frantically. "It was Livie! Livie was calling me!"

"Karen, are you sure? At three years old—"

"Of course, I'm sure! She was taught how to use a phone and to memorize her number! We were cut off!

Michael must have caught her calling and cut us off! Dear God, the way she sounded—''

''How?''

''Her voice was faint and—and maybe a little breathless.'' She clutched at him, stricken by a fearful possibility. ''What if it was the asthma? What if she's starting to have one of her attacks, and I'm not there for her?''

''Was she wheezing? Gasping?''

''Not yet, but—''

''Karen, I know you're sick with worry and scared, but don't start imagining the worst. That won't help Livie.'' He laid the phone back in its cradle and took her in his arms, making an effort to soothe her fears. ''Look, there could be any number of explanations for the way she sounded. Maybe the connection wasn't good, or maybe it was the kind of phone she was using. And even if it was her asthma starting to act up, bastard though he is, Ramey knows what to do for her.''

''How can you say that,'' she said, wild with anxiety, ''when there's nothing about him that I trust anymore?''

''Because as long as he needs her, and whatever his reason is we know that he does, he'll keep her safe. We have to believe that, Karen, or we lose all hope.''

She knew he was right. Drawing a deep, shuddering breath, she fought for self-control. She was still in his arms. It was a dangerous place to be. ''I'm all right now,'' she murmured.

He released her. She stared down at the phone with the vain hope that it would ring again, that she would hear her daughter's voice and that this time— And then it struck her!

''Devlin, the phone company! Don't they keep records of all incoming calls to numbers and where those calls originated from? If we contact the phone company—''

"They won't tell you," he said, stemming her excitement. "Believe me, I've had occasion to try it. But that information can be made available to the police."

"Then we have to convince the police to get it. If we can learn where Livie made that call, then we'll know where Michael is holding her."

He stopped her as she started to reach for the phone. "We'll be more convincing if we turn up at the department in person."

KAREN WAS LESS enthusiastic about his suggestion an hour later when, once again, they emerged from the old stone building at Third and Fourth. They had spent another frustrating session with the detective in charge of Bonnie Wodeski's death.

Yes, he would be in touch with the phone company, but they had to understand that results like that weren't as immediate as people expected. It was a holiday weekend. It would take time. He would have to get back to them later with what he learned.

No, Bonnie Wodeski's killer hadn't been caught yet. With the same reluctance, he admitted that the police had no reason to hold her brother. Scott Wodeski had been released after questioning.

Progress on locating Michael Ramey? Nothing so far, but they were working on it.

Delays, Karen thought, feeling angry and helpless. Nothing but delays. And all the while Livie was out there somewhere needing her.

Once they were back inside the car, she gave into her despair. "I went and asked you to be a father for Livie. Why did I do that, Devlin? Was it because I convinced myself that, if I had your promise, fate wouldn't fail to return her to us? Only it was foolish of me, wasn't it, because I realize now I may never see Livie again, and if that happens—'' Her voice broke on a quick sob.

This time Devlin made no effort to comfort her. This time he spoke to her sharply. "Stop it, Karen. No more tears for Livie. She *is* coming home. You and I are going to make certain that she does. Do you understand?''

"How, when it may already be too late?''

"It isn't too late. You're forgetting what Bonnie Wodeski's killer told you on the skywalks. That if you'd returned from Georgia on Tuesday as originally scheduled, you would have had nothing to worry about. Do you see what that means?''

She shook her head, too miserable to comprehend.

"I think it means Livie is needed up to that point, that whatever they've planned is going to happen just before then. On Monday, Karen.''

"The Fourth of July,'' she murmured.

"Yeah, Independence Day.''

"But if it's true, that's only two days away.'' Two days, she thought desperately, to prevent an assassination and save her daughter.

"Right,'' he agreed, "and they could be anywhere, and police manhunts take time. But if we could provide them with what they need to locate them immediately…''

He lapsed into silence, his eyes narrowed in thought, his lips pursed. She expected him to start whistling softly, his familiar habit when he was concentrating on a problem, but he was quiet this time.

"I think,'' he finally decided out loud, "that it's time to pay another visit to Scott Wodeski.''

"Why? What can he possibly tell us that he hasn't already told the police?''

He turned to her. "Haven't you noticed, Karen? Authority makes our Scott very nervous. People like cops and P.I.s worry him.''

''You're saying he has something to hide? Something he withheld from the police?''

''I think so. I think he knows what we need. Or at least he knows how we can get it and he's been too scared to share it. I believe I'll try again to persuade him to part with it. Let's go.''

There was a haze over the city, and heat shimmered up from the pavement as she drove them in the direction of Columbia Heights and the Wodeski apartment. But the sweltering weather that continued to stress the Twin Cities was of little interest to Karen. She could think only of Livie.

Hang on, sweetheart. Mama will find you.

It was early and the Saturday traffic was light. They had no delay in reaching Columbia Heights. Finding a parking spot on the street less than half a block away from the apartment building, they left the car and headed toward the front lobby. They were passing the entrance to the parking lot for the residents at the side of the building when Karen spotted something.

''Look,'' she said, indicating a thin figure emerging into the lot from a back door.

He carried a battered suitcase, and he was in a hurry. It was Scott Wodeski.

''He's running away,'' Devlin said. ''Told you he was hiding something.''

Devlin had also told her Scott was frightened. And that had to be true as well, Karen realized, because the young man was seized with an obvious panic when he glimpsed them out on the sidewalk. Bulky suitcase bumping against his legs, Scott fled in the direction of a rusting vintage station wagon parked on the far side of the lot.

"Not so fast, Wodeski!" Devlin shouted to him. "We need to talk to you!"

But Scott, interested in nothing but escaping the scene, continued to race in the direction of his car. Devlin uttered a curse of pure exasperation and sprinted after him.

Karen watched what happened in the tense seconds that followed with helpless alarm. Reaching the station wagon, Scott jerked open a door, tossed his case inside and dived behind the wheel. The car rumbled to life and, with a clashing of gears, squealed out of its space.

Devlin never hesitated. Gaining the lane, he planted himself directly in front of the oncoming wagon, arms waving. Karen's breath stuck in her throat as she prayed for the station wagon to screech to a stop. But the young man behind the wheel was no longer thinking clearly. The heavy wagon hurtled toward the man in its path.

With the agility of a matador sidestepping a charging bull, Devlin squeezed out of the way. But as the vehicle roared by him, he threw himself with reckless determination across its hood. Desperate to rid himself of the figure spread-eagled so threateningly in front of him, Scott twisted the wheel sharply. The force of his sudden turn flung Devlin from the hood. It also cost the driver the last shreds of his control. With a crunching of metal, the station wagon crashed into a low concrete divider, rocked to a halt and stalled into silence.

Finding her wind at last, Karen issued a cry of fear and sped across the lot to the tall man sprawled on the pavement. By the time she reached Devlin, he had picked himself up from the ground.

"I'm okay," he assured her and started toward the wagon where a stunned Scott continued to sit behind the wheel.

Yanking open the door, Devlin asked a quick, "Are you all right?"

"Yes," Scott whispered, goatee wobbling on his bony chin.

"In that case—" Devlin hauled him out of the car, confronting him with a furious, "What were you trying to do, you idiot? Kill us?"

Karen was angry with both of them. "The two of you are a pair of suicidal fools!"

Trembling in shock, Scott blubbered, "I don't know what to do anymore. Bonnie always told me what to do, and Bonnie's gone."

No longer able to stand, the skinny young man sank down on the concrete divider. He sat huddled there, confused and miserable. Karen perched beside him, prepared to offer him her comfort.

Scott turned and gazed at her, tears welling in his eyes. "I was building bookshelves for Bonnie. Now she'll never see them finished."

"I know," she said gently. "I saw the shelves. She would have loved them."

Devlin hunkered down in front of Scott, his tone still gruff. "What you can do is help us to find her killer."

Scott stared at him, dazed. Karen, impatient with Devlin's lack of compassion, shot him a look of warning.

"Sorry, Scotty," Devlin said, this time with kindness. "But you *were* running away."

"I didn't have anything to do with Bonnie's death, if that's what you think."

"Then why were you cutting out of here in such a hurry?"

"I don't want the cops bringing me in again. I—" He hesitated, then mumbled a worried, "I been in trouble with them before, back in Wisconsin where me and Bonnie lived before we came here. If they find that out, they just might decide I was involved somehow in Bonnie's death.''

''Scott, they would have already checked you out and learned you had a record. I'm surprised they didn't discuss that with you last night. What kind of trouble?''

''Auto theft. But I was just a kid.''

''Then what *did* they talk to you about last night?'' Devlin pressed him.

Scott shrugged. ''Asked me if I had an alibi for the time of Bonnie's murder, which I did. A buddy and I were hanging out at the mall.''

''What else?''

''Nothing.''

''Didn't they ask you about the file your sister was going to sell us?''

''Yeah, I guess it got mentioned. But there was nothing I could tell them. I never knew anything about a file.''

''No?'' Devlin paused and gazed directly into the narrow face before going on in a slow, uncompromising voice. ''Know what I think, Scotty? I think you do know about that file. Yeah, I figure that's why you were in Michael Ramey's office that morning we caught you there. It wasn't any travel folder Bonnie sent you for. It was the file, right?''

''That's bull.''

''Know what else I think? That when you didn't bring Bonnie the file, she sent you back to the office later, and this time you got her what she wanted.''

''That's not true. I would have told the cops.''

''No, you wouldn't, Scotty. Because you would have had to break in that second time after the lock was changed. And with your record, that's the last thing you wanted the police to learn.''

''You've got it wrong.''

"You forget, Scotty. I'm a private investigator. It's my business to take all the pieces and fit them together until they make sense. And this does finally make sense."

Scott stared at him, saying nothing.

Karen put her hand sympathetically on his arm, appealing to him in a low, earnest voice. "Devlin is a P.I., Scott, not a police officer. He isn't going to arrest you, and I promise you that neither one of us will mention that break-in. All we care about is finding the man who has my little girl, and in doing that we find your sister's killer. You can help us by telling us exactly what was in that file."

Scott tugged nervously at his gold earring.

"Please," she begged him.

He shook his head, admitting reluctantly, "I don't know what was in the file, except it was stuff about some bigwig, and that's the truth. Bonnie said it was better if I didn't know. All I know is she wanted the thing, and I got it for her."

"Wait a minute," Devlin said, needing for them to fully understand the situation. "Why did she send *you* for the file? Why didn't she go herself?"

"Couple of reasons. For one, Bonnie said I was better at getting in and out of places. Anyway, she didn't want people knowing she was here in town when she was supposed to be away. See, she was laying low until she could figure out exactly what her boss was up to. I mean, she knew something wasn't right about his operation, especially when he pulled out like that. Also—" The young man squirmed uncomfortably. "Well, Bonnie didn't want to risk anything where the cops might be involved."

"Are you telling us your sister had a record, too?" Devlin asked him.

"No, but she come close to having one back in Green Bay where we came from. This guy she was involved with in the office where they both worked was dipping into funds. He went to jail for it. Her boss suspected Bonnie of helping him. Cops did, too. Only thing that saved her was her boss making a deal with her not to press charges.''

"Why?"

"Guess he was afraid she might tell his wife about the affair they'd had the year before. He said he'd let Bonnie go, even give her a nice reference, if she agreed to leave Green Bay and stay away.''

"Which," Karen said, "is how you came to the Twin Cities where Michael hired her."

"Yeah."

There was a long silence. Karen was only dimly conscious of the sun beating down on them where they sat in the open. She was too discouraged to mind its heat. She knew that Devlin shared her disappointment. They already knew from Bonnie's phone call to them that the stolen file contained Michael's research on his next victim. What they hadn't known, and hoped Scott could provide them, was who, where and exactly when. But now…

"Scotty," Devlin asked him one last time from where he continued to crouch on the pavement, "are you sure you didn't get so much as a peek at that file?"

"Told you I didn't. Hell, I didn't even have a look-see at the newspaper article she clipped out and added to the file just before she called you."

Devlin and Karen's eyes met, their expressions registering a morsel of fresh hope.

"What newspaper, Scotty?"

"Wednesday's *Green Bay Bugle,* which came in our mail Friday morning. Bonnie liked to keep up with what was happening back home."

"This article she stumbled across…did she mention at all what it was about?"

"No, kept it strictly to herself, just like the rest of the file. Except—"

"What?"

"I think she was excited about something in it."

"What happened to the newspaper, Scotty?"

"It ain't gonna do you any good. I told you, the article's gone from it."

Scott didn't have the shrewdness of his sister. He wasn't bright enough to realize the value of that newspaper. They had to make him understand its importance to them.

"Is the newspaper still up in the apartment?" Karen asked him. "We need to see it."

"No, I pitched it with the rest of the trash on my way out."

"Where?"

"In the bin back there."

"Show us," Devlin urged him.

Scott got to his feet and led the way to a large receptacle situated just outside the apartment's back door. Raising the metal lid, he hauled two grocery bags out of the half-empty container. Both of them were crammed with trash.

Scott took one of the bulging paper sacks and Devlin the other. Squatting on the pavement, the men burrowed down into the bags while Karen watched, impatient for results.

"Here it is!" Devlin announced, producing a crumpled newspaper from the depths of the bag and then frowning as he examined it. "No, you said Wednesday, didn't you? This is the wrong date. It's an earlier *Bugle*."

They resumed their search, and a moment later Scott slid a folded newspaper out of the bottom of his sack. "Got it!"

Sharing their eagerness now without comprehending it, he spread the newspaper on the ground and rapidly turned the pages until he reached the middle of the news section. "This is it," he said, indicating the spot where Bonnie had removed the story, leaving no trace of it behind.

Karen looked over his shoulder at the hole in the paper, murmuring, "Page 9."

Devlin at her side nodded, both of them committing the number to memory.

Scott glanced at their faces. "Oh, I get it," he said. "If you can find another Wednesday *Bugle,* you'll know what Bonnie cut out of the paper."

"That's it, Scotty, and you have our gratitude."

"But you won't tell the cops?" he asked anxiously. "I just don't wanna take any chances of their being interested in me again, you know?"

"We won't mention you," Devlin promised him.

They helped him to pile the trash back into the bin and then walked with him to his car. The front fender was crumpled, but the wagon was otherwise unharmed.

"Do you have family or friends to go to?" Karen asked, concerned about the forlorn young man.

Scott nodded. "My buddy said I could stay with him until I get back on my feet."

They watched the battered station wagon bump out of the lot and disappear up the street. Then Karen turned to Devlin. "What do you think? Call the *Bugle* offices in Green Bay?"

He considered that idea before shaking his head. "On a Saturday of a holiday weekend the chance of getting anyone there to fax that article to us, or even to locate and read it to us over the phone, isn't very likely."

"Then our best hope is the public library. I know that the main branch in St. Paul carries all kinds of out-of-town newspapers, especially from neighboring cities of any size.

Let's pray that Green Bay qualifies.'' She glanced at her watch. ''But they won't be open yet.''

''So we get ourselves some breakfast while we wait.''

She nodded, but she was too distracted to care about eating. Aware of her tension, Devlin found her hand and squeezed it.

''Hang on, Karen. We're not there yet, but we do have a glimmer of light now at the end of the tunnel.''

THE MAIN LIBRARY in St. Paul, a massive, classic building from another era, was situated near the river. Karen was familiar with the multi-storied structure. She and Livie had paid frequent visits here to select books from the children's department.

With no hesitation, she led Devlin up the handsome marble staircase to the second level where the magazine room was located. Once inside this section, they found the library's sizable collection of newspapers arranged alphabetically by city on long racks. Rapidly consulting the letters, they made their way down the row until they reached the G's.

Karen held her breath. What if the library didn't carry the *Green Bay Bugle?* What if—

''It's here,'' Devlin announced to her relief, tapping the *Bugle* on its rack.

''That would be the latest edition, not Wednesday's,'' she said. ''But I think they keep a week's worth of issues in this spot, so the one we want should be...''

She bent down to the shelf under the rack, searching through the pile stored there. Her eyes met Devlin's in frustration. ''It's not here. Wednesday is missing.''

''Check again.''

She looked again carefully, then shook her head. ''It's gone. Oh, Devlin—''

"Hang on."

He turned around, surveying the room. Parked in an easy chair several yards away was a figure buried behind an open newspaper. Devlin headed for the chair, Karen at his heels. Leaning over, he peered at the paper's front page heading. It identified itself as Wednesday's *Green Bay Bugle*.

Sensing their presence, the occupant of the chair lowered the paper, revealing herself as an elderly woman with a pinched face. She glared at them disapprovingly. "I beg your pardon."

"Uh, would you mind if we borrowed that?" Devlin asked, indicating the newspaper she clutched. "It's important."

"When I'm through with it," she informed him severely, snapping the paper so that it rattled.

"We only need it for a quick minute or two, and then we'll give it right back."

Her reply was to stubbornly lift the newspaper in front of her face again, pointedly hiding him from view. Devlin looked like he was prepared to snatch it from her angrily, which Karen knew would only result in their eviction from the library. Tugging at his arm, she drew him away.

They settled down to wait on a nearby sofa. Devlin fumed. "Look at the old bat. She's carefully reading every word, probably cackling over the obituaries."

"It's a public library," she reminded him. "She's entitled."

But Karen's own patience was strained as the minutes passed, and the woman showed no signs of surrendering the newspaper.

Devlin could take no more. "This is deliberate. I'm going over there and—"

"No, you won't," she said, restraining him as he started

to get to his feet. "You'll just make a scene. You stay right here and let me handle it."

Karen rose from the sofa, went to the chair and politely cleared her throat. The newspaper was lowered again, the woman behind it offering a sharp, "Well?"

"I'm sorry," Karen said. "We should have explained it's an emergency. Look, I know it sounds fantastic, but the simple fact is my little girl has been abducted, and there's something in that paper that could help us to get her back."

The woman stared at her for a few seconds and then laughed rudely. "You must think I was born yesterday."

"Why, you—"

Karen was saved from the furious response she would have regretted afterwards by Devlin's sudden appearance at her side. Sliding an arm around Karen's waist, he favored the old woman with a persuasive smile.

"Now, dear, why don't we just tell the lady the truth? It's like this," he explained to the woman. "My wife went and bought an expensive pair of Italian shoes from a store here in St. Paul. Then when she talks to her family back home—we're visiting from Wisconsin, see—her sister thinks she remembers an ad in Wednesday's *Bugle* saying the same shoes are going on sale in Green Bay. Only she's not positive, and she can't check because her paper got thrown out. So we need to see if it's true, and if it is we're going to get a refund on the shoes here and buy them when we get home to Green Bay. Could mean big savings," he finished, recovering himself with a deep breath.

Karen stared at him, impressed. He had spun his elaborate lie in beaming innocence.

"Well, why didn't you just say so in the first place instead of telling me some silly lie?"

It was apparently a story the woman could appreciate.

She handed over the newspaper without hesitation. Pouncing on it, they retreated to the sofa.

"So P.I.s aren't always ethical," Devlin excused himself as they sat side by side. "Can't afford to be." She didn't argue with him. "Page 9," he reminded her as Karen took possession of the paper, rapidly turning its pages.

"Found it!" she said, and she began to read the story in a low, intense voice.

"The crowds in Door County will have a choice when it comes to next Monday's annual Fourth of July celebrations. And what a choice it is!"

Devlin stopped her. "Wait a minute. Door County?"

Karen had forgotten that Door County had become a well-known tourist destination after he'd left the Midwest and moved to Colorado. She explained it to him. "It's a vacation peninsula in Lake Michigan. All kinds of visitors in the summer. Green Bay is the gateway for it, which I guess is why they report the activities up there."

"Go on."

Karen continued with the article.

"Both Ephraim and Gills Rock are hosting galas. Each village guarantees the usual parade, popular rock bands, refreshment stands and evening fireworks. So what's the tough choice? It comes down to the speakers who will be on hand to address the crowds that afternoon. Gills Rock promises presidential hopeful Hayden Collier on its platform, while Ephraim wants to woo you with our own Governor Vernon Andersen. Quite a decision, huh? Guess for a lot of folks it will depend on which political party they favor. Or maybe the brands of beer they're serving."

Karen looked up from the article, her wide eyes meeting Devlin's gaze.

"Looks like there's no question of it," he said grimly. "One of those speakers is Michael Ramey's target. Only which one? Without Bonnie or that file, we can't know."

"I think I do know," Karen said slowly. "In fact, I'm certain of it. It's Hayden Collier."

"How do you figure that?"

"Andersen has never been a controversial politician, but Collier with his liberal views is. He's also very popular. Popular enough to have serious enemies."

"Meaning one of those enemies wants him permanently eliminated?" Devlin shook his head. "I admit I'm not up on my politics, Karen, but that doesn't sound like a strong enough argument to me to convince any law enforcement agency that Collier is definitely marked for assassination."

"Not by itself, but there's more. Hayden Collier hasn't declared himself an official candidate yet, but when he does he intends running on a health care platform. That's not surprising since he was a pediatrician before he went into politics."

"You still haven't convinced me."

"Devlin," she said quietly, "I've read all about Hayden Collier because he specialized in treating childhood asthma. It was a subject of vital interest to him, and still is."

He stared at her, then nodded slowly. "Now you've convinced me. It makes perfect sense all right. Ramey intends to somehow use Livie and her asthma condition to get close to Collier at that rally. Close enough to kill him."

"Now will the police take us seriously?" she asked him anxiously.

"Armed with what we've learned this morning? Oh, yeah, I think there's no question of it."

NOR WAS THERE any hesitation when they met again with the detective handling the case a short while later. The results they brought him were supported by the phone company's information just minutes earlier that Livie's call had been made from somewhere in Wisconsin's Door County. No exact location was possible since the evidence indicated it had originated from some type of mobile phone.

But to Karen's relief, all of it was enough to galvanize the Minneapolis police department into immediate action. Both the FBI and the Door County Sheriff's Department were alerted. Karen and Devlin came away from the old stone building with the promise that, before he could strike, everything possible would be done to find Michael Ramey and safely rescue Livie.

They paused on the steps outside in the glare of the noonday sun. Karen said nothing. She didn't have to. She knew that Devlin could read it all in her face.

"It's not enough, is it?" he said softly.

She shook her head. No, it wasn't enough. Because if Livie was in Door County, she had to be there, too. She had to go to Livie. Nothing could keep her away.

"Yeah, I figured as much." He glanced at his watch. "Over on the other side of Wisconsin, huh? Well, traffic permitting, we should be able to make it before dark. Guess we'd better run by my hotel and your house first. We'll need some clothes and I have to stop and buy a new cell phone."

Less than an hour later they were headed east on the

expressway. Devlin was at the wheel of the blue car. Karen, beside him, spoke silently, urgently to her daughter.

I'm coming, Livie. Mama is on her way. Just be there for me.

Chapter Ten

If the circumstances had been different he would have enjoyed this place, Devlin thought as he followed the winding highway north out of the city of Green Bay.

Door County had a lot to recommend it, which explained the heavy holiday traffic on its roads. For one thing, it was pleasantly cool, a welcome relief after the swelter elsewhere in the Midwest. The surrounding waters of Lake Michigan and Green Bay accounted for that.

But even without nature's air-conditioning, the county was appealing with its wooded limestone bluffs hugging the shoreline, ripening cherry orchards framed by fieldstone fences, and picturesque villages nestled along the bays.

Yeah, he could have properly appreciated the peninsula—if it hadn't been for the woman at his side counting on him. Even when she was asleep, she filled his thoughts, leaving room for little else.

He glanced down at her, struggling with an unfamiliar feeling of deep tenderness. Exhausted by her prolonged desperation, she had drifted off to the voice of Patsy Cline. The sight of her, face flushed, breasts slowly rising and falling, tugged at his senses. Made him remember all too vividly last night's fantastic lovemaking.

Devlin longed to repeat that sweet session with her. But he feared that, after asking him this morning to be what he couldn't be, Karen now regarded last night as a serious mistake. Maybe she was right. Maybe, with what they had staring them in the face, it was better forgotten.

Livie, he thought. She was somewhere on this peninsula, and he had to use every resource at his command to recover her. She was precious. He knew that, even though he was still unable to think of her as belonging to him. Fear, he supposed. A fear he wondered if he would ever overcome. Or, for that matter, even wanted to conquer.

But there was no use wondering what the future had in store for them. It was better to concentrate on the here and now. Trouble was, he couldn't stop thinking about last night.

EVEN WITH THE slow traffic, they reached the county seat of Sturgeon Bay well before sundown.

Before leaving Minneapolis, they had asked the police department to inform the Door County sheriff to expect them. When they had later checked with his office from the road, they'd been assured that, late though the hour was, he was prepared to see them. Devlin suspected the sheriff's willingness might have more to do with his father than any influence from the Twin Cities.

Casey Hawke had known Sheriff Holland when he'd been on the police force back in Chicago. And since Devlin had called his parents while Karen hurriedly packed a bag, updating them on the situation, there was every likelihood that his father had afterwards contacted his old friend.

Why the granting of such a favor on his behalf should irritate Devlin was something he didn't try to explain to himself. It was another example of the difficult relationship he had with his family.

They met with Neil Holland at his office in the nondescript brick building that housed the sheriff's department. He was a large man with a luxuriant ginger mustache and a bluff manner.

"Talked to your dad," he admitted to Devlin. "Told him he'd have to come up here sometime and go fishing with me."

Karen, from her chair in front of his desk, leaned toward him impatiently. "Is there any word yet on my daughter?"

"Folks, I wish I could tell you we've recovered your little girl. We haven't. Not yet. But we're working on it. There are officers and agents scouring the county for them."

Devlin, seated beside Karen, perceived a problem. "What's the trouble?"

The sheriff hesitated, and then he must have realized he could be direct with them. "It's like this. We're a rural area, and most of the year my department is more than adequate. But on summer weekends, and especially a holiday weekend like this one, we're overburdened."

"Meaning," Devlin said, "you don't have enough people to handle this search."

"It isn't just that. We've added officers, and the FBI has come in from the outside to work with us. But I think you could see for yourself that the county is choked with tourists."

Devlin nodded. "In other words, among all these crowds of strangers, you've got to locate one man and one little girl who could be anywhere."

"That's right. The needle in the haystack. On top of which, we've got to maintain law and order as usual."

Devlin could see that Karen was disheartened. "Then what's the solution?"

"We keep on checking every resort, motel, condo and cottage. If Ramey is here, we'll find him."

Devlin wished he could believe that, but he didn't express his concern. He knew that the sheriff and his force were making every effort possible. But would it be enough to stop Ramey?

"In the meantime," Holland continued, "we're being careful not to let the media get wind of this. So far we've been lucky, and we aim to keep it that way until it's all over. Because if Ramey should hear on the news that he's wanted, he'll just vanish again and maybe take your little girl with him."

Devlin saw Karen shudder over that possibility, and he quickly changed the subject. "What about Hayden Collier?" he asked the sheriff. "Has he been told he's marked for assassination?"

"Informed and urged to cancel his appearance. He refuses. Says he's been threatened before and won't let terrorist tactics stop him. Too bad he's not an official candidate yet. Then he'd qualify for Secret Service protection. But don't worry. Ramey won't get near him. We'll see to it that security is swarming around him Monday afternoon. I could almost wish, though, that Governor Andersen was the target."

"Why?"

"Because he's always protected in his public appearances by the state patrol. Doesn't involve us. Well, things like this are never easy, are they?"

"No," Devlin agreed, "which is why…"

The perceptive sheriff gazed at him sharply. "What is it?"

"Any objection to my lending a hand in this search?"

Holland's gaze turned severe. "You have a right to be here, both of you, but I don't want either one of you involved in this."

Devlin didn't argue with his warning, but he couldn't see himself holed up somewhere with Karen uselessly waiting for results. It wasn't in his nature.

The sheriff turned to Karen. "Mrs. Ramey, it's particularly important for you to keep a low profile. If the man who called himself your husband should spot you somewhere around the peninsula…well, you can see the risk in that."

Karen nodded reluctantly.

Holland got heavily to his feet, his round face brightening. "At least there's one nice little surprise I have for you."

"We could use one, Sheriff," Devlin said.

"I have an accommodation for you, and believe me nothing is scarcer this weekend. A last minute cancellation on one of the cottages at the Nordic Inn. They're holding it for you. Interested?"

AFTER THEIR long drive, the Nordic Inn was a welcome haven. They reached the resort in the last lingering light of day. When Devlin saw the place, tucked away in the deep woods on the Lake Michigan side of the peninsula, he reminded himself to express an extra measure of gratitude to Sheriff Holland the next time they met.

The inn was a sprawling operation close to the sandy shore of a wide, curving bay. It was dominated by the main lodge, which was Scandinavian in character with log walls, carved dragons on its eaves and window boxes filled with bright blooms. They registered here before being directed to the separate cottage they had been assigned. There were several of these scattered under the cool pines a short distance from the lodge.

Devlin parked the car, and they followed a flagged path to the front porch. Letting themselves into the cottage with the key they had been provided, they switched on a lamp and inspected their surroundings. The place was cozy, scrupulously clean and like the main lodge, Scandinavian in flavor with a stone fireplace and rosemaling on its cupboards. A bath and two bedrooms opened off the rear of the sitting room.

"Which one do you want?" Karen asked him.

Devlin noticed that she avoided his gaze, but her meaning couldn't be plainer. She didn't plan for them to share a bedroom. All right, he wasn't going to argue about that. But his mood suddenly turned sour.

"Doesn't matter."

"Then I'll take the one on the left."

"Fine."

He left her abruptly and went out to the car to bring in their cases. She was in the bedroom she'd chosen when he returned. He started to take her bag to her when he heard her gasp in something like alarm. Dropping both cases on the floor, he forgot his bad mood and sped into the bedroom.

He found Karen standing in the gloom at the window on the back wall. "Look!" she said, excitement in her voice.

Devlin joined her at the window. There was another cottage behind theirs. Parked in front of it was a van. Even in the thickening twilight he could make out its color. Burgundy. And he could see the jagged gap in its left headlight cover. But logic denied its existence.

"Karen, it isn't the same van. Not here."

"Why not? It could have followed us."

''All the way from Minnesota without our once spotting it?''

''But it can't be another burgundy van with a broken headlight cover. That would make it too much of a coincidence.''

''There's one way of finding out, and it's time we did just that.''

Turning on his heel, he strode with determination into the sitting room where he recovered his suitcase. Unlocking it, he extracted the Colt revolver he rarely carried.

Karen, who had followed him, expressed her anxiety. ''Maybe a confrontation wouldn't be wise.''

''You forget it's my business to get answers, and sometimes that involves risk. Don't worry, I know how to take care of myself.''

He could see she wasn't convinced of that, but she offered no further objection. Loading the gun, he got to his feet and moved toward the front door. Karen was right behind him.

''You stay here and let me handle this,'' he cautioned her.

Leaving her behind in the sitting room, he went outside and crept around the side of the cottage. He had the revolver in his hand, but he kept his arm down close against his side where the weapon wouldn't be easily visible in the fading light.

When he came in sight of the van, he stopped. The vehicle was no longer deserted. Its front passenger door was open, the light inside revealing the figure of a woman. Her back was to him as she leaned into the van, searching for something on the floor.

Devlin started forward, prepared to challenge her. At that moment she backed out of the vehicle, closed the door and turned around. He stopped, his grip tightening on the revolver. But he could see she wasn't armed with anything more dangerous than a lost earring she must have recovered from the floor. It glinted in the light that continued to burn inside the van as she reached up to fasten the gold hoop in her ear. That was when she saw him.

Startled, she went very still. They gazed at each other in a long silence. The sky was almost completely dark by now, and the delayed light inside the van had blinked off. But Devlin realized it didn't matter. Now that he was this close to her, there was enough illumination from the security lamps scattered around the grounds, and the glow spilling from the windows of the cottages, to disclose everything but the details. Probably in her early thirties, she was tall, brunette and strikingly attractive.

There was something else that the shadows couldn't conceal. Her whole attitude registered recognition.

"You've found me," she said in a husky voice. "Both of you," she added, looking over his shoulder.

Devlin glanced around. Karen stood there at the corner of the cottage. Damn her for not listening to him. Exposing herself like this.

"What did you do?" the woman asked, directing her question at Karen. "Trace me here all the way from Minnesota?"

Karen came forward to join them. "Yes," she lied to Devlin's amazement, "that's just what we did. Ironic, isn't it, after the way you stalked us?"

Devlin didn't contradict her. He quickly realized that Karen was shrewdly protecting their actual purpose in being here and at the same time creating a believable reason to expect answers.

The woman nodded. "I don't know how you managed it, but I'm impressed." She seemed to realize then that Devlin was clutching a revolver. "You don't need that, you know. In spite of what it may have looked like back in Minnesota, I'm not the enemy.''

"Convince us," Devlin said. "What are you doing here?"

"Working." She gestured toward the lighted cottage behind theirs.

Devlin followed her gaze. He thought he could hear the sound of a TV somewhere inside. Who else occupied that cottage?

"You don't have to worry," she said, reading his concern. "I promise you there's no one in there but my employer. He's elderly and frail and, if you don't mind, I'd just as soon he wasn't disturbed. Look, could we sit down out here, and I'll tell you everything you want to know." She indicated a rustic picnic table several yards away under the pines.

Deciding to trust her for the moment, Devlin tucked the Colt in his belt where it would be less threatening but still within reach. "All right, let's hear what you have to say."

The brunette, leading the way, seated herself at the table. Karen settled opposite her, and Devlin selected the same bench, straddling it at an angle that permitted him to keep an eye on the lighted cottage.

The woman folded her hands on the tabletop, introducing herself in a low voice. "If you haven't already learned it, my name is Veronica Delgado. I live in San Francisco. Or, anyway, I did live there before—"

"Is all of this necessary?" Devlin interrupted her impatiently.

"I'll try to be brief, but just bear with me and you'll understand."

"Go on," Karen urged her more kindly.

"I'm a private nurse," Veronica continued, "which is how I met Fletcher Stowe. I was hired to take care of him after a car accident that confined him to a wheelchair. There was a considerable age difference between us, and when Fletcher and I became engaged everyone thought I must be marrying him for his money. It was true I wanted the security he offered, but I genuinely loved Fletcher, and when I lost him…''

"How?" Karen asked her sympathetically.

"He was brutally murdered aboard his yacht. Even though they had solid alibis, I was convinced his sons were responsible, that they must have hired a professional assassin. The police thought so, too, but they couldn't prove it. That's when I decided to find his killer myself and see all of them punished."

"When did all of this happen?" Devlin wanted to know.

"Several years ago."

"And all this time you've been hunting his killer?"

"Not me personally. I'm not trained for that, and I had my living to earn. All of Fletcher's wealth went to his two sons, you see. But he'd given me some very valuable jewelry. I sold the pieces and hired a private investigator. It took him months and months between other cases to finally track the man he believed was Fletcher's killer to the Twin Cities."

"Where he was living as my husband, Michael Ramey," Karen murmured.

"Yes," Veronica said softly, "I'm sorry."

"And then?" Devlin asked.

"Nothing. I was out of funds by then, and the investigator refused to go on with my case. I was able to beg a few days off from my current job, which is caring for the old gentleman in the cottage there, and drive to the Twin Cities where the investigator agreed to meet with me."

"And by that time," Devlin guessed, "Ramey had disappeared again."

"That's right. It was so frustrating to get that close and then have him slip away again. I pleaded with the investigator, but he wouldn't go on hunting for Ramey without the fee I could no longer afford. He did tell me, though, before he walked away that he'd learned another P.I. had been hired to go after Michael Ramey. He even shared your names and Mrs. Ramey's address." Pausing, Veronica leaned toward them appealingly. "I was desperate. That's why I began following you. I hoped you'd lead me to Michael Ramey."

"It sounds good," Devlin said. "Except for one thing. Why didn't you just come to us with your story?"

"Because," Veronica said calmly, "you would have stopped me from doing what I swore to do when I caught up with Fletcher's killer." She sat back, and even in the weak light Devlin could see her wry smile. "You aren't the only one who owns a gun, Mr. Hawke. I meant to use mine to send Michael Ramey to hell."

"Is that so? And would that be the same gun that killed Bonnie Wodeski on a Minneapolis skywalk the night before last?"

She stared at him, appalled. "What are you talking about?"

"Okay, I'll play along with that." He briefly explained about Bonnie's murder and the missing file.

"And you think that I—" She shook her head vehemently. "I thought you knew. I thought you would have learned it when you traced me here."

"What?"

"I left the Twin Cities before noon on Friday and was back here at work by Friday night when you tell me this Bonnie was murdered. I could no longer afford to be away from my job, and also…"

"Yes?" Karen prompted her.

"I came to my senses. I realized my intention to stalk and kill Michael Ramey was a madness. I—I just simply had to let it go."

Before they could react to Veronica's story, the front door of the cottage she occupied opened. A thin, silver-haired man appeared on the porch. Though he moved slowly with the aid of a cane, he carried himself with an innate dignity as he made his way to the rail.

"Veronica," he called into the gloom, "are you there?"

"Coming," she answered, rising from the table and moving toward the cottage.

"You were gone so long I was beginning to worry," the old man said as she reached the area just below the porch. Then he noticed Karen and Devlin trailing behind her. "You have company, I see." And before Veronica could explain, he went on cheerfully, "I'm Cassius Bennett. Are you folks staying here, too? It's an excellent resort."

"We're just here temporarily," Devlin said. "It's business, not a vacation."

"Oh?" The old man's seamed face looked puzzled as he peered down at them from the porch.

"Mr. Bennett, I wonder if you'd mind telling us whether Ms. Delgado was here with you Friday evening. It's important."

"Is there something wrong?"

"It's all right, Cassius," Veronica assured him. "You can tell them."

The old man, leaning on his cane, didn't hesitate. "Of course Veronica was here with me all of Friday night. Where else would she be?"

"Thank you, Mr. Bennett."

"You go on inside now, Cassius," Veronica urged him gently, "before you get chilled. I'll be there in a minute and explain everything.'' She turned to Karen and Devlin after the door had closed behind her patient. ''Unless there's anything else you need to know, I'd better go to him. He frets when I stay away too long. I don't think he cared for my replacement while I was gone.''

''I wish there *was* more you could tell us,'' Devlin said, ''but I guess that's everything.''

''I'm sorry you came all this way for nothing. Just exactly how did you trace me here, anyway?''

''My agency networks with contacts throughout the country. Your car and license plate were reported.'' He was not about to confide that it was Michael Ramey they'd tracked to the peninsula, not her.

''I see. Well, I wish I could have been the one to lead you to Michael Ramey. I just pray you catch up with him. What will you do now?''

Devlin shrugged. ''Go back to Minnesota and try again to pick up his trail. At least the police there are working with us now.''

They parted from her and went back to their own cottage, waiting until they were inside the sitting room to compare impressions.

''Do we believe it?'' Devlin asked.

''What part of her story are you referring to?'' Karen wondered.

''Not her story, her hair color.''

She stared at him for a few seconds, confused. Then she understood. ''Meaning, can she possibly be Michael's secret accomplice? The blonde he was seen with on several occasions in that cafe. Well, hair color can be changed.''

''Exactly. Which leaves us with nothing but her word for it that she is who and what she says she is.''

''Not just hers,'' Karen reminded him. ''The old gentleman swore she was here Friday night. He seemed so genuine I can't think of a reason not to believe him. For that matter, she struck me as genuine herself.''

"I'll go along with that, except I am wondering now just how this P.I. she hired learned I was working on your case.''

"*Seriously* wondering?''

"Not enough to change my mind about her innocence but enough to say we need to keep an eye on Veronica Delgado. Just in case.''

Karen nodded. "There's only one thing that bothers me. It does seem to be an awfully big coincidence to find her here.''

"Yeah. On the other hand, maybe not. Half the damn country seems to have collected on the peninsula for this holiday weekend.''

THAT WASN'T as much of an exaggeration as it seemed, Karen decided early the next morning when an unexpected visitor arrived at their cottage. Roused from her bed by an insistent knocking on the front door, she slipped into her robe and slippers and went to answer it. Devlin's bedroom door remained closed, so she assumed he was still asleep and hadn't heard the knocking.

She supposed she should have checked on the identity of their caller before she unlocked and opened the door, but her only anxious thought was that someone from the sheriff's department had arrived with news for them. No one else knew they were here.

However, it was neither the sheriff nor one of his uniformed officers who stood there on the porch. The man was somewhere in his mid-fifties, with liberal amounts of gray in his dark hair, an easy smile on his wide mouth, and strong features that were vaguely familiar to her. Did she know him?

Before Karen could place him, or either one of them could exchange greetings, Devlin's voice from the sitting room behind her rumbled a surprised, and not altogether happy, "Pop! What are you doing here?"

"Invite me in, and maybe I'll tell you."

Karen's gaze flew from Devlin, who stood there in nothing but a pair of jeans he'd hastily dragged on, to the man in the doorway. His father? No wonder he had looked familiar to her. Did all the Hawke men have these same compelling blue eyes and bold features?

Since Devlin had yet to welcome his father, Karen stood aside, offering him a warm, "Come in, please."

When she turned from closing the door behind him, Devlin performed a hasty introduction. "My dad, Casey Hawke. Pop, this is Karen."

He shook hands with her, and she noticed there was one thing he didn't share with his sons. Devlin and Roark were over six feet tall. Casey Hawke, though as compact in build, couldn't be more than five-three.

Karen and Casey expressed their pleasure in meeting, and then there was an awkward moment as father and son turned to each other. Karen, sensing Devlin's reluctance as he went on standing there, his naked chest evoking disturbing memories for her, thought unhappily: Oh, no, not again. First he resents his brother turning up in St. Paul, now his father. What *is* wrong with him?

Casey finally spoke, his tone affectionate but his reproach clear. "I left your mother back in Chicago holding the fort, and she's very well and sends her love, thank you for asking."

Devlin shook his head, as if to clear it. "Sorry, Pop. Uh, what did you do? Drive all night to get here at this hour?"

"No, I pulled in last night. Too late to come calling.

Thanks to Neil's influence," he said, referring to his friend, Sheriff Holland, who must have kept him informed, "the main lodge managed to squeeze me in with a spare room."

"You're staying here?"

"And where else would I be now that we know my granddaughter is somewhere in this county?"

"Pop—"

"Don't say it. I know that everything is being done to find her, and maybe my help isn't needed. But I'm offering it just the same. Besides, your mother would never have forgiven me if I hadn't come."

"I'm glad you're here to lend your support, Mr. Hawke," Karen thanked him.

"Casey," he corrected her automatically, his gaze never leaving his son's face. "But Devlin isn't glad about it. Are you, Dev?"

For a moment Devlin had no response, and then his feelings surfaced in an uncontrolled anger that shocked Karen. "I wish you'd let me alone, all of you! I can't turn around that someone in the family isn't calling to check on me or showing up at the door without warning! I don't need any of you worrying about me! I'm handling my branch of the agency just fine, aren't I? And, for that matter, my private life as well!"

"You can't let it go, can you, Dev?" his father said sadly.

Karen had no idea what Casey was referring to, but Devlin did. "Sure I can," he said bitterly. "It's all in the past, isn't it? All you and the rest of the family have to do is to stay away and stop reminding me."

"It wasn't your fault, son," Casey said, his voice gentle but insistent. "It wasn't your fault."

Karen, staring at Devlin, caught her breath. His features

had twisted in an expression of anguish. She had seen this haunted look on his face before. That night in the motel in Rocklyn when she had caught him gazing at Livie's photograph. But she understood it now no better than she had then.

"Excuse me," he muttered to his father. With no other explanation, he turned around and left the sitting room, closing his bedroom door behind him.

There was another awkward silence, and then Karen said helplessly, "I'd offer you some breakfast, Casey, but I'm afraid we didn't stop to buy any supplies. There isn't even coffee in the cottage."

"It's all right. They're serving breakfast in the dining room at the lodge. I thought the three of us could go over there and eat. Maybe discuss a strategy for today."

But Devlin had something else in mind when he returned to the sitting room a few minutes later. He was fully dressed now and carrying a guidebook of Door County he had picked up at the desk last night when they'd registered. Karen recognized in his other hand copies of the photographs of Livie and Michael that were being used in the search.

"Sorry, Pop," he apologized to his father, apparently regretting his earlier outburst. "Look, I appreciate your help, but right now I'm better on my own."

His father didn't argue with him. "What do you intend?"

"Neil Holland probably told you they've got a tough job covering the peninsula this weekend. The county is loaded with accommodations for tourists, some of them small out-of-the-way bed and breakfast houses his people wouldn't have gotten around to yet. Whether the sheriff likes it or not, I'm going to check on those places. Ramey could be holed up in any one of them."

"Be careful," his father cautioned him.

"Right." Devlin eyed Karen in concern. "She needs to stay here where the sheriff can contact her and where she can keep a low profile. It's going to be a long day for her. Keep her company, will you, Pop?"

He was gone before Karen could object. She was furious with him. He was employing the same avoidance tactic with his father as he had used with Roark back in St. Paul. And, to her further frustration, both men forgave his action.

Casey regarded her thoughtfully. Then he asked her abruptly, "Are you in love with my son?"

Karen didn't see any point in denying it when she knew that, as usual, her traitorous face must be an open book. "Yes, but right now I could cheerfully push him off one of his Colorado mountains."

Casey nodded with understanding. "I have something less drastic to suggest. Let's go for a walk on the beach out there."

"I thought you were interested in breakfast."

"Breakfast can wait. Right now I think there's a story you need to hear."

Chapter Eleven

Devlin's secret, Karen thought as she put on shorts, a T-shirt and a pair of tennis shoes. The thing that Roark said she should wait for Devlin himself to reveal. That's what their father, who apparently didn't share Roark's hesitation, was going to tell her. She was sure of it.

Karen had longed to hear this story, had prayed to hear it. Now she was suddenly fearful. What if it was something so terrible it destroyed all hope of Devlin loving her and Livie, of ever wanting to be a part of their lives? On the other hand, it was better to learn the worst than to live with uncertainty.

Casey was waiting for her on the porch. She saw Veronica Delgado out by her van as they headed toward the shore. The brunette smiled and waved, but Karen knew Veronica must be wondering why she was still here at the resort. Why she and Devlin were not on their way back to Minnesota, as they had led her to believe they would be by now.

She forgot about Veronica, though, when they reached the beach. There was something more important to think about. But Casey wasn't in any hurry to open doors. They strolled in silence for a few minutes along the hard-packed sand near the water's edge.

It was a peaceful morning, warm and clear, the sun spangling the inky blue waters of the lake. Gentle waves folded on the shore while scolding gulls circled overhead. Karen, in her tenseness, could appreciate none of it.

To her relief, Casey finally spoke, though it was a puzzling beginning. "Families are funny things," he said. "That can be true physically as well as emotionally. For instance, Moura and me. My wife is a petite woman, and I'm barely five-three. But our kids, all except Christy, anyway, are tall."

He turned his head and smiled at her. "And you're wondering what this has got to do with anything. It has, though. You see, Karen, if I'd been anywhere near as tall as my three boys, I could have been the cop I'd always wanted to be. But in my day police departments had requirements about things like that. None of them would take me. That's when I decided I'd start my own police department."

"The Hawke Detective Agency," Karen said.

"Well, it was as near as I could get to being a cop. It was tough, though. My folks weren't in any position to help us and Moura's family didn't approve of our marriage, so we were on our own."

"But you did make a great success of the agency," Karen pointed out.

"Yes, but at a cost that we failed to realize until the damage was done."

"Devlin?"

He nodded. "Trouble is, Moura and I loved kids, and the babies just seemed to come along. That would have been fine if we hadn't both been so busy struggling to establish the agency. And with limited funds in those years, that meant too much of the time the care of the youngest children became the responsibility of the eldest."

"Which would have been Devlin."

"He never complained. I wish he had. Then maybe we'd have understood sooner how unfair it was of us to depend on him like that."

"In other words," Karen said, "he ended up resenting his family because they smothered him with expectations."

"It was partly that, but there's much more." Casey paused, gazing out over the expanse of Lake Michigan where a distant sailboat glided through the waters. Karen sensed that what he was about to tell her next was extremely difficult for him.

"Christy is our youngest now," he went on softly, "but there was a sixth child. A little girl named Jenny. We all adored her, but she was Devlin's special pet."

Oh, no, thought Karen, knowing that what she was about to hear would be heartbreaking.

"When Jenny was five and Devlin was in his late teens, Moura and I became involved in this important case that demanded a great deal of our time. We were in the middle of it when Jenny came down with the chicken pox. Just a light case, nothing serious. She didn't seem to need or want anyone but Devlin with her." He paused again and then continued abruptly, "Reye syndrome. You've heard of it, haven't you?"

"Dear God," Karen whispered.

Casey nodded. "Yeah, most informed parents today understand the danger of it with a condition like Jenny's. But we didn't know about Reye syndrome back then. Devlin certainly didn't when he gave Jenny that aspirin. He thought he was helping her."

"And the aspirin triggered convulsions," Karen murmured.

"It was already too late by the time she was rushed to

the hospital,'' Casey said. ''It was a bad time for all of us. But Devlin—well, he never stopped blaming himself or us. That's when he started to withdraw from the family. Oh, we know that underneath his pain he still loves all of us. He can't help that, and he'd be there for any of us if we needed him, but he keeps his distance.''

''Because,'' Karen said, understanding it, ''you can't be seriously hurt if you should lose what you're not close to. No wonder he doesn't want a family of his own. But why didn't he just tell me about Jenny? Why did he keep it hidden?''

''If you were him, would you have talked about the loss of your little sister when he knew you've been sick with worry about Livie?''

''No,'' Karen said, shaking her head, ''no, I guess I wouldn't.''

Livie and her asthma, she thought. Is that why his daughter's existence troubles Devlin, and has from the start? Does he fear caring about her, as he once cared so deeply about another little girl who suffered an ailment?

She isn't Jenny, Devlin. Livie isn't Jenny.

SUNDAY, KAREN kept thinking as the day wore on. This was Sunday, and tomorrow was the Fourth of July. Time was running out, and there was still no word about Michael and Livie.

Even with Casey to keep her company, as he faithfully did, the useless waiting unnerved her. Someone came by from the FBI and questioned her extensively and then went away without anything more encouraging than an impassive, ''We're still searching.'' They were all searching, Karen thought frantically, police and FBI alike, but as yet there was no result. They heard nothing from Devlin, not a word.

It was late, and at her insistence Casey had gone back to his room in the lodge, when the Camry finally returned to the cottage. Karen was waiting for Devlin when he came into the sitting room. He looked tired and discouraged.

"There was no one in the places I tried, and I think I must have visited every bed and breakfast in the county, who has had so much as a glimpse of either one of them. Anything been happening with Veronica Delgado while I was gone?"

"I've tried to keep an eye on her as we agreed, and as far as I can tell she and her employer never left the resort." She told him about her visit from the FBI agent. "They haven't had any luck finding Michael and Livie, nor have the sheriff's people. Devlin, where can they be?"

He shook his head. "I'm beginning to wonder if they're here at all. Maybe we're wrong about his target and this peninsula."

She knew he was in a low mood when he began to doubt his careful detective work. "We're not wrong," she insisted. "All the pieces fit. They have to be holed up here somewhere."

He didn't argue with her. She went on to tell him, "Your father and I found a little grocery store down the road where I was able to stock up on essentials. Can I fix you something to eat?"

"Thanks, but I had something on the road. All I want is a shower and a bed."

He disappeared into the bathroom. Knowing she had to keep busy, Karen did up the dishes from the supper she and Casey had shared. She was storing the last pot under the counter when Devlin emerged from the bathroom. He wore nothing but a towel wrapped around his waist.

She had seen him like this so often in the past several days that the situation was beginning to seem familiar. And so did her breathless reaction, she thought, taking in his hard masculine form and the appealing way his damp hair stood up in dark, glistening spikes.

They gazed at each other in a long silence. Then in a low, raspy voice he said, ''Pop told you all about Jenny, didn't he?''

He must have figured this out before he went into the bathroom. He would have realized she was no longer angry with him and that there was a reason for both this and the sympathy that had to be evident on her face. But he hadn't found the courage until now to mention it.

''Don't be angry with him, Devlin. He wanted me to understand.''

He didn't say anything. He just stood there, looking so heartbreakingly vulnerable that she couldn't prevent herself from going to him. From putting her arms around him and holding him close.

He groaned, a ragged, wild sound wrenched from deep inside him. And then he began to kiss her with a feverish urgency. Karen, knowing how much he needed her in this moment, and that her own desperation was equal to his, returned his kisses with the same hungry recklessness.

Within minutes they were stretched across her bed, her clothes shed, his towel abandoned. Their bodies close, they offered themselves to each other with stroking hands and an exchange of kisses punctuated by breathless, murmured endearments. She embraced him with both arms and legs when, unable to wait, he joined with her. Their lovemaking that followed was intense and explosive, culminating in a blinding release.

Afterwards, Devlin slept with his head pillowed on her breasts. She held him, tenderly caressing his broad shoulders and fighting the despair that threatened her.

Their intimacy had been wonderful, but the love she was

prepared to offer him made no difference. Nor her knowledge now of the demon that haunted him. Before he had drifted off, she'd tried to discuss it with him. He had refused. And unless he overcame this barrier that continued to separate them, stopped running away from himself, she would lose him.

Devlin was still asleep beside her when Karen awakened sometime later. She glanced at the clock on the bedside table. It was after midnight. Sunday had gone. This was Monday, the Fourth of July. Time was running out. The realization chilled her.

Livie, where are you?

THE MAN who had called himself Michael Ramey for the past two and a half years stood on the beach, hands shoved into the pockets of his slacks, cold gray eyes hidden behind a pair of sunglasses as he watched the child. Kneeling in the sand, her mop of dark curls stirring in the breeze, she tugged at a half-buried shell.

For the moment she was content, but he didn't know how long that would last. She missed her mother and had grown increasingly fretful over the past twenty-four hours, repeating questions that drove him crazy. Not satisfied with his answers, she'd managed the other morning to get hold of his phone while he was still sleeping. Had actually succeeded in calling her mother. He had severed the connection in time, but it had been a bad moment.

"Look, Poppy!" Freeing the shell, she trotted back to where he stood and held it up for his approval.

"Very pretty. You can add it to the others." She was as bad as her mother about collecting useless junk. "Why don't you see if you can find one of those shiny black pebbles we spotted yesterday? Then you can start a new collection."

Restlessly combing his fingers through his fair hair, he watched her go off again to hunt for new treasures. He wished he didn't need the damn kid. She was a burden. But a necessary one.

Finding ways to entertain her, with just the two of them cooped up on a small boat, had been a challenge. But the powerful little cabin cruiser, bobbing at anchor in the shallows just behind them, was also a necessity.

Thinking about the boat, he smiled with satisfaction. They were looking for him. He knew all about the intensive search from his contact who phoned him regularly. But they wouldn't find him. Not out here on these unoccupied wilderness islands that were scattered everywhere among the upper waters of Green Bay. As an added precaution, he moved the cruiser to new locations on a regular basis.

"Another shell, Poppy!"

"That's fine, but keep on looking for one of those pebbles."

Just hours to go now, he thought, squinting at the position of the morning sun. Then it would be all over. His last hit, and his most lucrative one. Added to what he already had hidden away in that secret account, it was going to make him a rich man, able to retire in style. And this time he would vanish for good.

Only hours away, he thought again, and then he could proceed on schedule. No need to abandon or alter his original plan either, even if they were looking for him, even if Hayden Collier was surrounded by an alert security force. Because they didn't *know*.

THE HEAT WAVE had finally penetrated the peninsula, accompanied by an uncomfortable humidity. There was no air-conditioning in the cottage. That's why Karen had every window wide open. Not that it helped much. The breeze off the lake had failed over an hour ago. The air was thick and still.

Karen stood at the screen door, staring out at the pines beyond the porch, hating the suspense that was clawing at her as she kept her lonely vigil. Devlin and his father had driven off together in Casey's car shortly before noon, headed for the Independence Day celebration in Gills Rock at the tip of the peninsula. She had been left behind after fighting a losing battle with them.

"Karen, I know it's killing you," Devlin had argued, "but you can't be there. Ramey doesn't know Pop and me, but he does know you. He'll be armed and dangerous, and if he should spot you in the crowd—"

"Do you think I'd let that stop me?" she had cried.

"No, but what about the risk to Livie? She'll be with him, remember, and if she should glimpse you and cry out, he won't hesitate to use her as a shield. The security force there has to prevent that. They have to surprise and disarm him before he can hurt anyone. It's the only choice now."

Casey had sided with his son, using Sheriff Holland to support their objections. "Neil feels the same way. He's asked that you stay here. In his opinion, he's already made a big enough concession by permitting Dev and me to be on the scene."

In the end, it was the danger to her daughter that her presence might produce, and nothing else, that convinced Karen to remain behind. But she didn't know how she was going to endure the waiting. Four o'clock. That's when Hayden Collier was scheduled to speak. And until then…

Oh, why couldn't they have found and apprehended Michael before it came to this? But, in spite of all the efforts, he hadn't been discovered. Now they had to take him at the gala itself, and if anything went wrong—

No, don't permit yourself to think it.

She went on standing there at the screen door. The minutes crawled by, long, empty minutes that emphasized her frustration. The air was so muggy that it was difficult to breathe. Or was her tension responsible for that? She couldn't stop wondering what might be happening at Gills Rock and where Livie was at this moment. And she longed to be there for her, not waiting uselessly in this cottage.

The phone shrilled on the table behind her. Devlin? He had promised to call the minute there was any news. Four o'clock was still a long way off, but maybe—

She rushed to the table, snatching up the phone with a breathless, "Karen Ramey!"

"It's Moura down in Chicago, Karen."

Karen tried to conceal her disappointment. "I guess you know just what's happening here, Moura. Casey said he called you first thing this morning with all the latest."

"Are either he or Devlin there?"

"No, they left sometime ago for Gills Rock."

"Damn, I hate calling that cell phone of his, but looks like I don't have a choice."

For the first time Karen realized there was concern in her voice. More than concern, in fact. Her tone expressed urgency. "Moura, what is it? What's wrong?"

She hesitated only briefly. "I suppose you'd better know. Someone up there needs to contact the sheriff immediately. I tried, but with everything going on their line seems to be all tied up, so I thought if I could reach Devlin or Casey—"

"Moura, tell me!"

"It's about Livie. You remember that I posted a description of her, along with her photo, on the Internet, asking for information on her whereabouts. Well, I had this long e-mail response just a short while ago. It was from a woman in Madison,'' she said, referring to Wisconsin's state capital.

''Are you saying—''

''No, she doesn't know anything about Livie,'' Moura went on quickly. ''But, Karen, what she had to tell me was pretty startling. It seems that this woman worked for Vernon Andersen and his family about twenty years ago, long before he was ever the governor or even involved in politics. He and his wife had a little girl who was abducted when she was three years old. She was never recovered.''

''But what has Governor Andersen's lost child got to do with Livie?''

''Karen, the woman swears that Livie is the spitting image of that daughter when she disappeared. She says the resemblance is uncanny, and she wonders if there can possibly be some connection. She asked me all about Livie's mother. Do you see what this means?''

''Oh, dear Lord!'' Karen said, her stomach lurching sickeningly as she understood the implication. ''We've made a terrible mistake, haven't we? Hayden Collier isn't Michael's target! It's Vernon Andersen in Ephraim! And the governor has only a few of his state patrol to protect him because every available officer is up in Gills Rock guarding the wrong man!''

''Karen, we can't be certain of that. Collier could still be—''

''No,'' Karen insisted, ''I can *feel* it! This was never about Livie's asthma! It's about her close resemblance to that vanished daughter! Michael is going to use Livie as the irresistible lure that will let him get close enough to the governor to— Moura, I have to go!''

''Do you want me to—''

''No,'' Karen cut her off, ''I'll take care of it! I'll stop at the front desk here on my way out! I'll have them phone the sheriff's office until they get through, and I'll have them contact Devlin and Casey as well! I'm not going to lose time making those calls myself because I have to get to Ephraim! I won't risk a phone call there going wrong! Somehow I have to reach the governor's people in person and make them understand that he mustn't appear on that platform this afternoon!''

"Be careful, Karen," Moura cautioned her.

Careful? Karen thought as she rang off. She'd had enough of being careful, of hiding out in this cottage. She was going to Ephraim. This time, whatever it took, she would be there for Livie.

Her purse was on the table behind the phone. She grabbed it up, fishing in it for the keys to her car out front. She had them in hand when the screen door squeaked open behind her.

"You won't need those," said a low, throaty voice.

Karen whirled around. Veronica Delgado stood there inside the cottage, a venomous little smile on her lovely face. Karen didn't have to wonder how long she had been on the porch just outside the screen door. The revolver the brunette had silently removed from her shoulder bag, and which was now pointed at Karen, told her that the woman had managed to overhear everything.

"That's right," Veronica said, "I'm the second terrible mistake you made."

It's true, Karen thought with shock and anger. How could Devlin and I have been such fools? How could we have believed that pack of lies she told us, convinced ourselves of her innocence when all along—

Veronica was Michael's accomplice, of course. That much was obvious now. She had been monitoring their actions from the start. Had probably stopped by the cottage this afternoon to pay a friendly visit, using it as an excuse to subtly question Karen about their latest efforts.

Oh, but what difference did it make why Veronica had appeared on her porch? She was here, holding Karen with that deadly gun, keeping her from going to Livie. Karen had to find a way to outwit her. Exactly how much *had* Veronica heard of her conversation with Moura? Maybe not quite all she feared.

"Veronica, listen to me," she appealed to the woman as she made an effort not to tremble, to control her voice. "If Michael is important to you, and I know he must be, and if you have the means to contact him, then do it now. Have him call off this assassination attempt before it's too late. He'll never get anywhere near the governor. They're not taking any chances. They have security swarming all over Ephraim as well as Gills Rock."

Veronica laughed. "I'm not as gullible as you and your P.I. were. Even the tourists aren't blind to what's been happening on this peninsula in the last twenty-four hours. I've heard them talking about it in the lodge here and on the beach. How every cop and agent that can be spared have been setting up at Gills Rock to protect Hayden Collier. That leaves Vernon Andersen vulnerable, and Michael knows that. No, I don't think he'll have any trouble getting close to the governor."

"But members of the state patrol are with him," Karen pleaded. "And with Collier threatened, they'll be alert for trouble. If Michael tries anything, they'll kill him."

"How touching. You're worried about Michael."

"He was my husband. Naturally, I care," Karen lied.

"Why should you when he never cared about you? He never loved any of his wives. None of you were anything but a temporary necessity. It was always me that he loved," she gloated, her green eyes blazing. "Always me who was there for him. I helped him in San Francisco to get Fletcher Stowe, just as I'm helping him here.''

"Yes," Karen said, losing her self-control in her impotent rage, "by murdering for him! By killing helpless people who get in your way, like Bonnie Wodeski back in Minneapolis!''

Veronica must have been watching Bonnie and her brother like she watched us, Karen thought. Probably instructed by Michael to keep a close eye on the assistant he didn't trust after Bonnie had caught him with that file. The file he'd prepared, not on Hayden Collier, but on Vernon Andersen. The incriminating file Bonnie had copied and which Scott had later secured for her. The file that Bonnie had carried with her to the skywalks. Veronica must have seen it all and, suspecting the contents of the file, had followed Bonnie. When she had confronted her on the skywalk, and Bonnie had refused to part with the file, Veronica had cold-bloodedly eliminated her.

Veronica confirmed as much now with a furious, "She would have destroyed us! Just like you will if I let you! But that isn't going to happen, is it? This will make certain it won't.''

She gestured threateningly with the lethal weapon in her hand, and Karen thought desperately: Livie! If I don't find a way out of this, Livie may die! I have to go to her, and I have to let Devlin know he's needed in Ephraim! That his daughter is going to be there, not in Gills Rock, and that her life depends on us reaching her in time!

Frantic thoughts. Thoughts born out of a wild panic. They swooped in and out of her head, and none of them were of any use to her. Only action could help, and this wasn't possible with that revolver trained on her.

Like a cornered animal, Karen cast her gaze rapidly from side to side. Searching for a means of escape, even the remote possibility of rescue. Veronica, watching her, understanding her fear and frustration, wore the malicious smile on her mouth again.

"I'd forget any miracles if I were you," Veronica advised her. "The lodge is too far away, and all of the cottages are empty. They've all gone off to the beaches and the celebrations. We're alone here, isolated."

She was deliberately prolonging this moment, enjoying Karen's torment. So busy, in fact, with her vile pleasure that she failed to be aware of the scene behind her.

But Karen, facing the screen door, was suddenly conscious of a movement off through the pines beyond the porch. Hardly daring to breathe for fear of alerting Veronica, she watched a figure emerge from the trees. With the aid of his cane, he moved slowly, quietly toward the cottage. Was it possible that her prayer was about to be answered in the form of Cassius Bennett?

Oh, but how could Veronica's patient possibly help her? He was elderly and frail, powerless against the revolver in Veronica's hand. The gun! If only the old gentleman managed to glimpse that gun through the screen door before he got too close, realized that Veronica had it leveled at her, there was the chance that he would retreat in time, go back to his cottage and phone the lodge.

Karen realized she had to keep Veronica from learning that Cassius Bennett was approaching the cottage. Had to cover any sound he might make as he neared the porch. And at the same time she had to try to let him know what was happening in here.

Fearing her gaze would give her away, she looked directly into Veronica's face. She began to speak rapidly, lifting her voice in what she hoped would be regarded as hysteria.

"They'll find out you're holding me here at gunpoint!

Devlin and his father left instructions at the lodge that I was to be checked on at regular intervals! Someone will be around again any minute now!''

Her lies must have sounded very pitiful. Veronica was nothing but amused. Karen concentrated on her face and not the sight over her shoulder. Cassius Bennett had reached the porch, was climbing the steps. Karen sent a silent plea to him.

Go back! Don't come to the door!

The steps didn't creak under the old man's weight. He never made a sound. It was Karen who betrayed his presence. Karen, with that treacherous face of hers that could never manage to conceal any intense emotion, who warned Veronica. She could see the sudden awareness in the woman's eyes that were pinned on her, and her heart sank.

Veronica glanced briefly over her shoulder. Cassius Bennett had arrived at the door. "I thought I told you to stay in the cottage." There was no alarm in her voice, nothing but mild exasperation.

"You've been gone so long I wondered if you'd run into trouble over here."

"Nothing I can't handle." There was scorn on Veronica's face as she swiftly returned her attention to Karen.

The screen door squeaked again as the old man opened it. He limped into the sitting room, a grin on his face as he took in the situation. "On to us, is she?"

Karen stared at the thin, silver-haired figure and wondered how she could ever have deceived herself that there was genuine dignity and kindness in that seamed face. Cassius Bennett was not her potential ally. He was another ruthless enemy.

"She had a phone call from Chicago," Veronica explained. "You don't need to hear the details. It's enough for you to know she's not going to be warning anyone that Andersen is the mark.''

Though he leaned on his cane, perhaps even depended on it, Bennett was neither frail nor gentle. Karen could see that in the tough way he looked at Veronica, hear it in the sudden harshness of his voice.

''If I want those details, you'll give them to me without an argument. Or do I have to remind you again it's my money that's paying for those unscheduled Fourth of July fireworks over in Ephraim?''

Karen's face must have expressed her surprise and sudden understanding because Bennett peered at her, cackling in amusement.

''Look at her. She's just figured it out.'' He moved toward Karen a few steps, his pleasure in her helplessness every bit as vicious as Veronica's. ''That's right, Mrs. Ramey. I'm the one who hired your husband to put a bullet in Vernon Andersen. And with good reason. There's only one being I've ever cared about, and they put him in prison for life. Said my grandson committed a brutal murder, which is a lie. Jason killed the bastard in self-defense.

''I fought to get him out of that place and ended up with only one hope. Governor Andersen could pardon Jason, but he refuses. That'll change when Andersen is dead, and the lieutenant governor takes his place. He's a man who can be persuaded for the right price to sign—''

Veronica stopped him with a sharp, ''Why are you telling her all this? She doesn't need to know.''

Cassius shrugged. ''What difference does it make? She isn't going to live long enough to tell anyone.''

''Until we hear from Michael and know it's done and that he's in the clear, we keep her healthy. Because if anything should go wrong, we may need her to get safely away from here.''

"And what are we going to do with her until then?"

"Why, entertain her, of course."

She gestured with the gun for Karen to sit down on the sofa. Feeling her legs could no longer support her, Karen collapsed on the cushions. After shutting and locking the inner front door to be sure there were no more surprises from that direction, Veronica settled on a chair facing Karen. Cassius Bennett took another chair beside her. With her free hand, the brunette produced a cell phone from her bag and placed it on the table between them. Then, the revolver still firm in her grip, she leaned toward Karen, her lips curled in a taunting little smile.

"Cassius is right. I don't think there's any real risk in sharing a few tidbits with you. And you would like to hear about Michael and me while we wait for his call, wouldn't you, Karen?"

"I don't want to hear," Karen said. "I don't care."

Veronica ignored her objection. "Of course, Michael isn't his real name, but then after that visit to Rocklyn you know that. No need to go into actual identities. All that matters is how he feels about me and how I feel about him. From the moment I met him I sensed there was something different about him, something extraordinary. And when I learned what it was, when he finally trusted me to know, I found it exciting. Can you understand that, Karen?"

Hands tightly linked together under her breasts, Karen stared at her. There was a glow in Veronica's green eyes, passion in her voice. It sickened her to realize that this woman could actually be thrilled by a man because he was a hired killer.

"He never had anything but contempt for you and the others," Veronica said. "I'm the only woman who understands him, the only woman he wants. We were secret lovers the whole time he lived that lie with you. And when all this is finished, we're going away together...."

She's as twisted as Michael, Karen thought. Convinced she's tormenting me by boasting of her intimacy with him.

And all the while the only thing tormenting Karen was the gun in Veronica Delgado's hand that kept her from going to her daughter.

Chapter Twelve

Maybe the crowds weren't minding the heat, Devlin thought as he mopped at his perspiring brow, but he sure as heck was. He thought longingly of his cool Colorado mountains as he surveyed the shifting masses of people that had congregated here at Gills Rock.

He'd been told by Sheriff Holland, who was also on the scene, that for most of the year the tiny village with its picturesque fishing sheds huddled on the shore was quiet, practically deserted. But this afternoon it was choked with humanity.

Devlin supposed that all of these people were having too much fun to complain about the temperature. There had been a water parade a little while ago, a flotilla of fishing boats decked out in Fourth of July colors. They had circled through the harbor, tooting their whistles to the cheers and applause of the onlookers packed along the docks. Tonight the sky above that same harbor would blaze with fireworks, but right now there were other forms of entertainment. A rock band played while vendors in their booths sold a variety of refreshments, and strolling clowns performed for children and adults alike.

The milling crowds could afford to have fun. Devlin couldn't. It had nothing to do with the broiling sun or the throbbing music either. It was this mounting tension he suffered as he moved restlessly through the swarms, anxiously searching the sea of faces. But nowhere in the noisy throngs did he spot a man and a little girl who resembled the photographs he carried in his pocket.

There were others armed with the same photographs. A multitude of officers in plain clothes who circulated through the mobs, watching, checking with each other on their two-ways. Squinting against the glare of the sun, Devlin glanced in the direction of the speakers' platform draped in holiday bunting. The security was already heavy there, even though Hayden Collier wasn't scheduled to appear for at least another hour.

And where were Ramey and Livie, and how much more of this suspense would Devlin be able to stand? He thought of the child who was his and of the woman who was her mother keeping her lonely vigil back at the cottage and of his conflicted feelings for them. He would do everything in his power to protect them, bear any sacrifice that was necessary to make certain that Livie survived this afternoon and that she was reunited with her mother. And what then? Would he be able to just walk away as he had promised himself? Devlin didn't know. He was no longer sure of anything except that he had to somehow keep his daughter safe.

It was in this seething state of indecision that his father found him several minutes later.

"I've just been talking to Neil," Casey reported as he joined him. "He assured me they'll be taking every precaution. They intend to disarm Ramey before anyone is hurt."

"That's good, Pop."

"No sign of him yet, though."

"No." *Where was the bastard?*

He could feel his father gazing at him with concern. And that was something else that troubled Devlin. His relationship with his family. Could he resolve the problems there? Did he even want to?

"Look, I've been thinking," Casey said. "You don't really need me here."

He thinks his presence is only making me more nervous, Devlin thought. And maybe he's right. But it was a realization that added to the guilt Devlin already felt in connection with his father.

"What are you saying, Pop?"

"That there is someone who can use me. We shouldn't have left Karen waiting all alone. I'm going back there to wait with her. Maybe it will help."

"I guess you're right, Pop."

"I'll leave the car for you. One of Neil's fishing buddies is headed down the peninsula. He'll drop me off at the resort."

A few minutes later his father was gone, on his way back to the Nordic Inn. Devlin made his rounds again through the crowds, whistling softly, tautly to himself.

MILES AWAY, in another part of the county, Michael Ramey was on the move.

He stood at the wheel of the tiny cabin cruiser, guiding the craft toward the wooded shores of the peninsula. The waters of the bay were slightly choppy under a stiffening wind, making the boat bounce, but he scarcely noticed. His thoughts were occupied with his objective.

He was relieved that the waiting was over. It was time to undertake what he'd carefully and patiently planned for all these weeks. He was ready. A baseball cap covered his light hair, and sunglasses hid his sharp gray eyes. Not that he needed a disguise. There was no one in all those crowds who could possibly be interested in trying to identify him. They weren't looking for him where he was headed, because he was expected elsewhere.

It was probably too warm for the lightweight jacket he wore, but it was a necessity. The jacket covered his Smith and Wesson semiautomatic.

His mind and body were also ready for action. As always just before a hit, he felt alive and stimulated with anticipation. But underneath, where it counted, he was in control, his nerves cool and steady.

As he neared his destination, the massive shoulder of a limestone bluff loomed off to the right. He spared it a glance. He knew that out of sight around the far side of that sheer bluff was a sheltered little cove. He'd land the cruiser in that deserted spot after he fulfilled his contract. Hidden on a fire lane in the deep woods behind the cove he would find the fast car Veronica had left for him. By tonight they would be together and far away from here.

But right now he needed to concentrate on his mission. Passing a tiny island on the left, he crawled into the broad blue harbor of Ephraim. The place was busy with boat traffic. He maneuvered a passage through the other vessels and found a spot to anchor out in the harbor. It was too soon to tie up at one of the docks.

Cutting the engines, he lifted a pair of binoculars and gazed at the town with its white buildings spread out on the hills. Down near the shore he could see the platform where the governor would appear. The crowds were already thick in that area.

Lowering the binoculars, he checked on the small figure curled up on a deck mat near his feet. Livie was still napping, the fingers of one upraised hand wrapped around her dark curls as she slept.

She was going to give him Vernon Andersen.

He smiled to himself, thinking of the results his thorough research on his target had provided. Andersen would be excited when he saw Livie, would have to wonder if she could possibly be his granddaughter. He'd tell Andersen that Livie looked just like her mother. That her mother, who was feeling unwell, had remained aboard the cabin cruiser. Andersen could be enticed to the boat with a father's desperate hope that Livie's mother might prove to be his long-missing daughter.

The man who called himself Michael Ramey was convinced his plan would work.

KAREN DIDN'T KNOW how long she sat there rigidly on the sofa listening to the nonsense that poured out of Veronica. It seemed forever. An eternity in which the woman's harsh voice clawed at her nerves while the room grew so stifling that she could feel the sweat trickling down her sides.

And all the time Karen could think of nothing but her mounting fear for Livie and her need to reach her. But how? With that gun pointed at her, there was no way she could leave this cottage.

The sofa faced the open windows at the front of the sitting room. Karen's position afforded her a glimpse of the distant lodge through the evergreens. Every so often a car would arrive at the main entrance and discharge its passengers. But those people were too far away to help her, and none of them wandered in this direction.

That was why Karen failed to be aroused by the sight of the figure that alighted from a battered pickup truck. It wasn't until the pickup pulled away, and the man it had left behind started toward the cottages in the pine grove, that she permitted herself to be interested.

She almost gasped aloud when he got close enough that she was able to recognize him. Casey! Questions swarmed rapidly through her mind. What was Casey doing back here at the resort? Who had dropped him off, and where was his own car?

But just as suddenly she realized that none of this was important. In this particular crucial moment only one thing mattered. Her face! The traitorous face that was her perpetual curse! It had already betrayed her earlier! She mustn't permit it to give her away again! Not now, when hiding her excitement was so vital!

Her captors knew she couldn't help seeing the view that the windows framed, but they mustn't learn there was anything in that scene to raise her hopes. With every effort she could summon, Karen concentrated on maintaining a look on her face that expressed nothing but a dull defeat.

And all the while, as Casey advanced toward the cottage, she prayed that Veronica, who continued to watch her closely, would keep her back to the windows. That a restless Cassius Bennett beside her wouldn't leave his chair as he did from time to time, checking the other cottages from the windows to make sure they remained silent and unoccupied for the rest of the afternoon.

Seconds later, when Casey neared the cottage, a new fear seized Karen. He didn't know Veronica and Cassius Bennett were holding her in here, that the instant his step sounded on the porch Veronica would be alerted and meet him at the door with her gun. Casey would be walking into a trap!

How could she warn him?

But it wasn't necessary. At some point on the path Casey came to a halt, staring at the cottage. He was close enough now that Karen could make out the puzzled look on his face. Just what was it that had caught his attention? And then she thought she knew. The door! The front door that Veronica had shut and locked! Casey must be wondering why, with this heat, that door was tightly closed?

Devlin's father was too good a detective not to guess that something might be wrong. He went on gazing speculatively at the cottage, and Karen went on striving to keep her features composed. A miracle, because for once in her life she must have managed to keep a blank expression on her face. Neither Veronica nor Cassius showed any sign of suspicion.

The old man, who'd apparently had enough of Veronica's rantings about Michael and her, finally lost his patience. In a loud voice that had to have carried clearly through the open windows, he turned on her with exasperation.

"Oh, for God's sakes, will you give it a rest! Can't you see she doesn't give a damn? If we have to wait it out with her, then let's do it in silence!"

It was all Casey needed. He was suddenly a P.I. ready for action. From somewhere under the baggy shirt he wore, he whipped out the compact little handgun he'd carried with him to Gills Rock. Then, crouched over, he sprinted off through the trees.

Karen's struggle to keep relief and anticipation from flickering across her face probably failed in that moment, because Veronica glanced at her sharply, green eyes narrowed. Quickly turning her head, the brunette checked the scene outside the window. But Devlin's father had vanished by then. Satisfied, Veronica relaxed and went back to guarding her captive.

Casey, Karen wondered. Where was he?

She found out just seconds later. From an open window at the side of the sitting room came a burst of gunfire. The bullet, expertly delivered, tore through the screen and struck the back of Veronica's extended hand. The revolver she was holding seemed to jump out of her hand and went clattering across the floor.

With a cry of pain and rage, Veronica started to surge to her feet. A stunned Cassius Bennett also struggled to rise from his chair.

"Sit back, both of you, and stay there," Casey ordered calmly from his position just outside the window. With his revolver directed at them, they had no choice but to obey. "Karen, get that gun of hers and then open the door for me."

Careful to stay out of his line of fire, Karen recovered the weapon from the floor, edged her way around the room, and unlocked the door. Only when he was satisfied that she was able to cover Veronica and Bennett with the revolver did he back away from the window.

Karen was shaking by the time Casey joined them inside the cottage. She was more than happy to turn Veronica's weapon over to him. By now blood was oozing from the brunette's hand, dripping onto the floor. Casey took charge.

"Karen, have you got something she can wrap around that?"

Karen sped into the tiny kitchen and returned with a clean dish towel which she placed in front of the woman. Veronica, glaring at them murderously, twisted the cloth around her wounded hand. Cassius sat there, silent and white.

"That'll do until we can get some medical attention for her," Casey said. "Now tell me what's going on here."

Karen filled him in on the essentials, ending her hurried account with an urgent, "Casey, I have to get to Ephraim! This time I have to be there for Livie!"

Casey didn't hesitate. "Go. I'll deal with these two."

Karen grabbed up her purse and then stopped on her

way to the door. "The governor and his people need to be warned! And there's Devlin! Devlin should know!"

Casey was already moving in the direction of the phone. "I'll manage to reach them. You just worry about being careful when you get there."

Karen spared a last glance in the direction of Veronica and Cassius Bennett. The old man sagged in his chair, looking sick and beaten and every bit as feeble as he'd first appeared to be. But there was still a defiant fire in Veronica's green eyes.

"We might be finished," she said in her husky voice, "but you won't get Michael. He'll kill Andersen, and he'll use your precious Livie to do it."

Casey smiled at her grimly. "Lady, you don't know my son. He'll stop Ramey all right, and if that bastard hurts his kid…well, there won't be anything left of him but the pieces."

Holding onto that promise as though it were a lifeline in a violent sea, Karen rushed from the cottage. Once inside the car, she paused only long enough to put on sunglasses and a head scarf in an effort to keep Michael from immediately recognizing her.

Moments later, with the Nordic Inn behind her, she was tearing across the peninsula in the direction of Ephraim.

Hang on, Livie. Hang on until Mama gets there.

DEVLIN'S HANDS gripped the wheel of his father's white sedan as he dealt with the frustrating traffic on the highway. Once clear of Gills Rock, he had hoped to find an open road to Ephraim. But there was no chance of that.

What tourists weren't gathered for the celebrations in either Ephraim or Gills Rock seemed to be crawling in convoys in both directions along the only route between the two villages. It was the Fourth of July, and they were enjoying the holiday. They weren't interested in hurrying.

There were few opportunities for passing, but Devlin seized them whenever they occurred. More than once he risked a collision as he raced around a slow vehicle, only to find himself caught behind another parade of cars. And all the while he seethed with impatience and his urgent need to join Karen in Ephraim.

Ephraim. Ephraim and Governor Vernon Andersen. He still had trouble believing it, but he didn't doubt his father's startling story. They had been protecting the wrong man in the wrong place! The question now was, would there be enough time to intercept Ramey before he struck?

Devlin could only pray that his father, after reaching him on his cell phone, had been able to contact Sheriff Holland and the state patrol as well. He hadn't hung around Gills Rock long enough to find out.

These were the thoughts chasing through his mind as he tried to hurry, *hurry* along a highway that seemed endless. But they were fleeting thoughts. For the most part he found himself concentrating fiercely on Karen and an awesome self-revelation.

When his father had told him that Karen had faced death at the hands of Veronica Delgado and Cassius Bennett, his brain had exploded. That was when Devlin had realized that he couldn't live without Karen. He was in love with her, and if they ever managed to survive this nightmare he would tell her so and beg her to marry him.

He didn't think he'd have much trouble making her understand just how precious she'd become to him. The problem was in convincing her, after denying it for so long, that he was ready for the responsibilities of such a commitment. And that meant fatherhood as well as marriage, because he knew he couldn't have one without the other.

It was a risk that still unnerved him, but he would have to confront that challenge. He would have to put the tragedy of Jenny behind him and learn to be a caring father to Livie. How hard could it be?

But underneath his determination the fear still nagged at him. Only it wasn't important. Not now, when the only real fear that counted was wondering if Karen was at this very moment in danger. He had to get to her.

But there was all this maddening traffic between them and the delays he encountered as he fought his way through two other busy villages along the highway. And then, reaching the edge of Ephraim at last, he met another maddening obstacle. The road had been blocked to all vehicles in order to permit the highway itself down in the village to be used as a setting for the celebration. A sheriff's deputy rerouted the traffic around the back side of the town, which meant another agonizing crawl.

Devlin's jaw ached with tension by the time he found a spot to park the car along a busy street above the center of the village. He was out of the sedan in a flash and flying down the hill to the highway that rimmed the expansive harbor.

When he emerged from the tree-shaded lane where it joined the highway, he came to a halt, dismayed by the scene that met his eyes. The road was jammed with people, a river of bodies that made Gills Rock seem tame by comparison.

There were noise and activity everywhere along the curving shoreline. An outdoor art fair, carnival rides, horses drawing open buggies filled with tourists, refreshment booths and a country and western band. How would he ever connect with Karen in all this frenzy?

The speakers' elevated platform they had erected next to the stone-walled village hall seemed the likeliest place

for him to start. Karen would be drawn to the spot where
Governor Andersen was scheduled to appear, because
that's where Ramey expected to find his target.

Devlin began to weave his way through the throngs,
working toward the platform whose decorated railings he
could see above the bobbing heads in front of him. He
could smell popcorn and beer and feel the heat from the
fires where they were cooking bratwurst. He was perspiring freely by the time he squeezed through the worst of
the crush and reached the area near the platform. The sun
was blistering.

Devlin scanned the faces around him and almost missed
her. She wasn't immediately recognizable with a scarf
wound around her auburn hair and dark glasses covering
her hazel eyes. It was a uniformed member of the state
patrol who first caught his attention. Karen was engaged
in an earnest argument with the young officer.

Her relief was evident when Devlin managed to join
them. "Thank God you're here!" she cried, turning to him
for support. "Devlin, he won't let me through to speak to
anyone in charge!"

Devlin faced the officer. "That's crazy! Hasn't anyone
alerted you yet?"

The officer was stubborn and suspicious. "There's been
no word about a problem here, not to me, and until this is
sorted out I have no choice but to hold the lady. You, too,
if you're involved."

Karen was frantic. "I've been trying to explain, but he's
not listening! Your father promised he'd get through to the
sheriff and the state patrol! What happened?"

"Some snag in communication, I suppose," Devlin
said. "Not surprising with all the confusion."

He was about to insist that a delay could be fatal when

a long black limousine nosed its way slowly through the crowd.

"Stay back," the officer ordered.

Prevented from any action, they watched as the limousine arrived in front of the village hall. The crowd applauded when a smiling, waving figure emerged from the vehicle. Devlin knew this had to be Vernon Andersen.

The governor was immediately surrounded by sober-faced officers who conducted him swiftly up the steps and into the hall. Devlin decided that this meant they now knew of the threat to him.

Within seconds, the two-way carried by the young officer detaining them crackled to life. There was a rapid exchange between the officer and one of his superiors.

And now he knows it, too, Devlin thought.

Lowering his two-way, the officer turned to them, demanding identification. He was satisfied when Karen and Devlin produced it for his inspection. "All right, they know about you, but wait here until I see if the governor's people want to talk to you."

He left them, hurrying into the village hall.

Karen was desperate. "Devlin—"

He understood what she was trying to say. "Yeah, I know. The governor is safe now, but we could be forever answering their questions."

"And in the meantime there's Livie."

Devlin made a decision. "The hell with it. We'll find them ourselves."

"But where do we begin in all this mob?"

He thought about it for a few seconds. Then, turning his head, he eyed the raised platform just behind them. "Up there," he said.

There were steps at the side of the platform. He started

to mount them. Karen was close behind him, but he stopped her.

"You'll have to stay down here. If he's out there and notices me above the crowd, it won't matter. But if he should see *you*— Yeah, I know," he said when she started to object, "but the scarf and glasses aren't enough."

She nodded and reluctantly stayed behind. Reaching the deck of the platform, Devlin crossed to the rail. In order to justify his presence here, he made a pretense of adjusting one of the loudspeakers while he gazed out over the heads of the strolling masses. For long seconds he searched group after group.

Karen stood just below him, her face upturned as she watched him. "Anything?" she asked him anxiously.

He shook his head and continued to look. "No, I don't see anyone who fits—"

He stopped in sudden excitement. From the direction of the boat docks on the waterfront appeared two figures. One of them was a lean man in baseball cap and sunglasses. Walking slowly at his side, hand in his as she gazed with fascination in the direction of the merry-go-round, was a little girl with dark curls. Devlin, his heart doing a strange bump, knew he was seeing his daughter.

"What?" Karen demanded, realizing he had discovered something.

Gripping the rail, he swung himself to the ground beside her. "They're out there," he informed her, "and headed this way."

He could see her draw a steadying breath before she trusted herself to speak. "What do we do? Should we find one of those officers?"

"No time. We could lose them. Anyway, if a uniform gets too near him, he'll just disappear in the crowds."

"What's the answer then?"

"I'm going to slip through the mob and try to work my way behind him. If I can get this into his back—" He patted his waistline where the hanging folds of his loose shirt concealed the Colt revolver he carried at his belt.

Karen, understanding his intention, expressed her alarm. "Livie! You will be careful?"

"I need to make him drop his gun, and then he won't be able to hurt anyone. Karen, it's necessary."

"I know. Let's go."

"Karen, no." He wanted her here and safe.

"I'm coming," she insisted, "because the second you shove your gun into his back, I'll be there to snatch Livie away from him. And don't worry about his spotting me. I'll stay behind you where he can't see who I am."

There was no time to argue with her. They were wasting vital seconds. Devlin began to shoulder his way through the throngs. He could feel Karen, fearful of losing him, pressed close to his back. The pitiless sun beat down on them as he cut a path through the packed bodies.

A moment later, several yards off to their left, he caught a glimpse of Ramey making his cautious way toward the speakers' platform. Devlin was about to circle around and close the distance between them when a loud shout from somewhere behind them sank his hopes.

"Hey, you there! Hawke, Mrs. Ramey! Where do you think you're going? I told you to wait!"

Devlin cursed the young officer hailing them. An alert Michael Ramey froze. In that instant the shifting crowd parted for a few seconds, giving the assassin a clear view of both Devlin and Karen. There was both disbelief and rage on his face.

What happened next was swift and terrifying. From inside his jacket Ramey whipped out a Smith and Wesson, firing it up into the air to clear a path of retreat for himself.

"Out of my way!" he screamed. "Get out of my way, all of you!"

The frightened crowds obediently shrank back, offering him an avenue of escape. Snatching up a howling Livie and tucking her under his arm like a bundle, he fled toward the docks.

Devlin knew there was no way he could bring him down, not without endangering either Livie or one of the innocent onlookers. His only choice was to pursue Ramey and hope he could catch him before they lost him again.

The crowd, nervous and calling out questions, started to flow again, threatening to close the swath Ramey had created for himself. Devlin fought his way through the ranks, demanding a passage for himself and Karen who was clutching at the back of his shirt in order not to be separated from him.

"Livie!" she cried in horror. "He'll hurt Livie!"

"No," he tried to reassure her. "She's his shield now. He'll keep her safe."

Devlin had to believe that. He'd go to pieces otherwise, Karen along with him. Finally breaking free of the bodies squeezed around them, they raced along Ramey's route of escape. Devlin could see him again. The bastard had reached the main dock and was headed for a small cabin cruiser berthed there.

Somewhere behind them the young officer was still yelling. Looking over his shoulder, Devlin caught a glimpse of him trapped in a sea of bodies, trying to restore order before the bewildered, apprehensive crowds worked themselves into a stampede.

We're on our own, Devlin thought grimly, and he intensified the chase, his long legs pumping like pistons.

With a ferocious effort that left Karen behind him, he gained the dock just as the cabin cruiser, coming to life, started to slide away toward the open water. He ran beside it along the length of the dock, but before he could leap into the boat it gathered speed and roared off across the harbor, bearing Ramey and his tiny hostage. A breathless Karen caught up with Devlin, staring in despair after the speeding cruiser.

There were several people on the dock looking at them with startled faces. One of them was a teenager standing by a sign that offered boats for hire.

"You in charge of the rentals here?" Devlin demanded.

"Uh, yes, sir."

"We need your fastest boat!"

"Th-that would be that one there," the young attendant stammered, indicating a small but powerful-looking inboard just below them. "But it's just come in, only half full of gas, and I haven't had a chance yet to—"

"Never mind. We'll take it as it is." Producing his wallet, Devlin slapped a thick wad of bills into the youth's hand. "Don't bother to count it. There should be enough there to practically buy the thing!" He turned to Karen. "We're not giving up. Let's go."

She didn't hesitate. She scrambled after him into the boat, both of them ignoring the teenager's timid objections. The craft was sleek, low, and with open seats.

Devlin started to settle himself at the controls behind the windshield when the young attendant, kneeling on the dock above them, asked with concern, "Uh, sir, you do know how to operate her?"

Devlin had only a vague knowledge of boats, but in his rash desperation he hadn't let that stop him. Now, swearing under his breath as he gazed at the unfamiliar controls, he wished he'd been more interested in waterways than in ski slopes. His frustration must have been obvious because Karen, shedding all traces of helplessness, thrust him out of the way and climbed into the pilot's seat behind the wheel.

"No, but I do," Karen informed them with determination.

Sinking into the seat beside her, Devlin gazed at her, impressed by her sudden confidence.

"I'm a Minnesotan," she said, turning the key and pressing the starter button. "I grew up with lakes and boats." As the twin engines rumbled to life, she called to the attendant, "Cast off those lines, will you?"

Seconds later, clearing the dock, they picked up speed as Karen opened the throttle. The boat responded to her capable handling of gears and levers, leaping forward like a prize thoroughbred.

Through the spray they kicked up, Devlin could make out the cabin cruiser and the figure of Ramey on its flying bridge. The cruiser was slicing steadily toward the bulk of a high bluff that guarded the left side of the enormous harbor. Hard to tell over water, but he judged that the cruiser had to be better than a mile away by now.

Karen sensed his concern. "He's got a head start on us all right, and his boat is fast, but it's also much heavier than we are. I think we stand a good chance of catching up with them. We just *have* to!" she added fiercely.

But could they? Devlin wondered.

There was one thing in their favor. The harbor was studded with crafts of every size and description ranging from tiny foot-propelled paddleboats to cumbersome pontoon boats, all of them on the move. The heavy traffic prevented Ramey from setting a direct course at full speed.

It should have slowed their own boat as well, Devlin thought. But Karen, seemingly oblivious to the traffic, plowed straight ahead, managing somehow to neither swing to the left nor the right.

He supposed she knew what she was doing. Her hands certainly held the wheel with an easy assurance. He didn't worry about it, even when a couple of angry boaters aimed obscene gestures in their direction as they tore past. But Devlin was less ready to forgive her recklessness a moment later when disaster confronted them in the shape of a swift powerboat.

Actually, there was no danger of a collision. Not from the boat itself. There was a considerable distance between them when it cut across their bow. That was before Devlin noticed the lines stretched tautly behind it. Lines that he discovered, when he whipped his gaze to the left, were attached to the figure of a parasailer, his chute blossoming behind him. And they were headed for those lines!

Didn't Karen see the lines and what they meant? Why wasn't she slowing, veering away? Devlin hollered a warning. Then, coward that he was, he shut his eyes.

Seconds passed. Nothing happened. He looked again. There was no sign of the parasailer. Karen calmly pointed back and up. Twisting around and lifting his gaze, he saw the parasailer soaring above them, the lines with him.

All right, so she had correctly judged that the parasailer would be safely aloft when they crossed his path, but Devlin was still shaken. And mad enough to bellow over the roar of the engines an impulsive, "God almighty, are you going to kill us before I ever get the chance to tell you I love you and to ask you to marry me?"

With everything that was happening, he couldn't have picked a worse moment for a confession like that. But then he'd always been lousy with his timing.

She turned her head to stare at him, an expression of shock on her face. "When did all this happen?"

"On the way down from Gills Rock when I realized—" He broke off in a fresh panic when a sailboat loomed in front of them. "No! Don't look at me! Just watch where we're going!"

She did, and they cleared the sailboat.

"Look," he said, his raised voice husky with emotion, "I want you safe and I want Livie safe. I want you where I can *see* both of you safe, and that's with me."

"I thought you told me you weren't a safe kind of guy."

"I was wrong."

She was silent, and for once her face wasn't animated with emotion. He didn't know what she was thinking, but he feared she didn't believe him. And, with his love for her swelling by the moment to new dimensions, he longed for her to believe him, longed to hold her tightly in his arms.

When all this was over, he promised himself, he would do just that, providing she would let him. But not now when overtaking Ramey and rescuing Livie was a priority.

With that aim in mind, Devlin concentrated again on their objective. He was encouraged. Thanks to Karen's skill, he could see that they were gaining on the cabin cruiser. They were near enough now that he could just make out the boat's name on its stern. *Bonanza.* Good fortune. But not for Ramey, Devlin vowed. Not if he could help it.

ON BOARD the cabin cruiser Michael gripped the wheel with a savage anger. A series of quick glances over his shoulder had informed him that the boat bearing Karen and her P.I. threatened to overtake him.

He considered the possibility of stopping them with his semiautomatic, but he abandoned that intention. Not because he had any qualms about killing Karen. Though he had played her loving husband, he had no feelings whatever for her.

The reason for his reluctance was entirely a practical one. Expert shot though he was, with the cruiser repeatedly jouncing across the wakes of other boats, he could never hope to steady the Smith and Wesson long enough to hit them. Livie also would have spoiled his aim. The sniveling kid was huddled on the deck at his feet. She kept pulling on his pants leg, kept pleading, "Mama, I want Mama," until he could have slapped her. If only he didn't need her. But he did.

Besides, he had to stick with the wheel. He had to round the bluff, beach the cruiser in the little cove on the far side. If he could get that far, he would be able to elude them, make good his escape. They'd never find him in the thick woods, not before he reached the car at the side of the fire lane.

He refused to believe the car wouldn't be waiting there for him as he and Veronica had planned. But he couldn't be certain of anything anymore. What had gone wrong? How had Karen and her P.I. learned he was here in Ephraim and not in Gills Rock? Damn them for ruining his last hit!

He was in the channel now between the island and the huge bluff directly off to his left. Not far to go. The kid chose that moment to drag at his leg as she tried to pull herself to her feet.

He looked down, issuing a severe reprimand. "I told you to sit there. Why can't you listen to me? Why can't you—"

The blast of a horn commanded his attention. When he lifted his startled gaze, he discovered a loaded excursion boat bearing down on him. His reaction was quick and automatic, without thought. He swung the wheel, and the cruiser cut sharply to the left. The bluff was straight in front of him now. Not until it was too late did he realize he had crossed the line of the channel markers.

It happened suddenly and without warning. There was a grinding sound under the hull, then the crunch of rended metal. The engines stalled, the boat scraping to a halt with a lurch that almost tossed him to the deck.

When he righted himself and looked over the side, he could see the gleam of white rock just beneath the water. The cruiser had grounded on the flat shelf that formed the roots of the bluff.

No time to curse his luck. No time for anything but to abandon the helpless craft. Scooping up Livie, who was too scared by now to do anything but whimper softly, he lowered himself and his armload into the water.

It was shallow, barely reaching his knees. He was able to wade to dry land within seconds. He found himself on a spit of broken rock at the base of the towering cliff. His intention to gain the cove on foot was, he realized with a desperate glance in both directions, impossible. Water lapped against the sheer walls of the bluff on either side of the narrow spit. *Deep* water. He'd have to swim to reach the cove, and that would make him an easy target, even if there was time for that option. Which there wasn't. He could see Karen and her P.I. already crossing the line of the channel markers, undaunted by the hazard of the shallows. And, if he wasn't mistaken, that was a patrol boat crowded with uniformed officers not all that far behind them.

Trapped! No, he had one choice. He could climb to the top of the bluff, descend through the woods to the fire lane down on the other side.

He lifted his gaze, measuring his chances. How hard could it be when, thanks to his strenuous workouts, he was in great shape? The cliff was high and it was precipitous, but the limestone was so fractured that ledges occurred every few feet. And where they didn't, twisted cedars springing from the rock itself offered dependable handholds.

There was only one difficulty. He would have to take Livie with him. If he didn't, that P.I. or one of the cops could pick him off the bluff face with a single shot. But with the kid in his possession, they wouldn't risk it. Could he manage it?

Livie had been quiet since they'd reached the spit. But when he hefted her higher against his shoulder so that she was half hanging down his back and approached the rock wall, she seemed to sense his intention.

"No, Poppy, no!" she cried, squirming in his arm that pinned her to his shoulder.

"Keep still," he ordered her roughly, and with his free hand he began to scale the bluff, lifting them from ledge to ledge.

The kid shut up after that, hanging against him like a limp rag doll. By now she was probably too scared to struggle. Even so, she was too much of a load. It required all of the strength he could summon to ascend the cliff.

He was gasping and dripping with sweat by the time he dragged them onto a narrow shelf where he had to pause long enough to recover his wind. He judged they were a good seventy-five feet above the shore. Looking up, he realized he still had about a third of the distance to go.

There was something else he understood. He would never make it. Not one-armed and with a weight over his shoulder. He would have to free himself of his load.

Slinging the kid down from his shoulder, he parked her against one of the gnarled cedars. "Stay here," he instructed her. "Don't move."

He ignored her wide, bewildered eyes and the tears trailing down her cheeks. Abandoning her without a shred of guilt, he began to climb again. A quick glance informed him that Karen and the P.I. were now splashing on foot through the shallows. If he hurried, he still had time to avoid being a target.

A slight overhang at this point challenged him. But there was a projecting knob of rock just above his head. He could use that to swing himself up to the next level. But the knob wasn't solid. When he clutched it with both hands, it tore loose, destroying his balance.

He tried to save himself. It seemed like he ought to have been able to save himself. But suddenly there was nothing for his clawing hands and feet. Nothing but air.

His last bitter thought as he plunged to the hard rubble far below was: *It was all for nothing.*

THE BASTARD couldn't have survived a fall like that, Devlin thought. They didn't have to check his broken and twisted body to know it. Besides, there was no time. Livie was up there on that ledge!

Karen's horrified gaze was pinned on the sight of the tiny figure high above them.

"I'm going to her," he said.

Her eyes implored him to hurry. Devlin attacked the bluff in a desperation that had him swarming up the wall of rock. And all the while, as he drew himself from ledge to ledge, his heart pounding, he prayed that Livie wouldn't try to crawl off that shelf.

"Wait for me, Livie!" he called to her. "Just hang on tight and wait for me!"

It was with an immense relief that Devlin finally pulled himself up onto the shelf. But his relief vanished as he crouched there, staring at the small, defenseless child huddled against the cedar. Her face was pale, and she was wheezing, struggling for air.

Dear God, she was going into an asthma attack! This was his child, and stress and terror were triggering one of her asthma attacks!

The tragedy that had haunted him all these years stared him in the face. Jenny suffering those convulsions and dying. He hadn't been able to help her, and so he had lost her. And if he didn't confront that cruel memory and defeat it, he could lose Livie as well. That possibility was too horrible to bear.

It suddenly didn't matter to him anymore that he had avoided fatherhood and family all these years because he had feared them. That fear was no longer real. All that counted now was saving his daughter because, first meeting or not, she was precious to him. She belonged to him, and he wanted to be her father, *needed* to be her father.

He couldn't fail her. Wouldn't permit himself to fail her. He spoke to her carefully, gently.

"Livie, listen to me. Your mama is waiting for you down below. I'm going to bring you to her. But you have to help me to do that."

"H-how?" she whispered between gasps.

"Tell yourself you're going to be all right. You're a brave girl, so I know you can do that. Tell yourself you're going to be all right, and you will be all right."

She searched his face, and Devlin knew she was wondering if she could trust him. He smiled at her, nodding slowly. "It's true," he said.

Watching her, he begged for a miracle, and he got one. Within seconds, she had calmed herself. Her breaths slowed, becoming nothing more alarming than a series of soft hiccoughs. He thanked God.

There was one more difficulty. She'd been through a

frightening episode, and he was a stranger to her. Would she let him touch her, or was he another threat? He held out his arms. "Will you let me take you to your mama now?"

She hesitated only briefly. Then, to his joy, she crawled into his arms.

"Put your arms around my neck, sweetheart, and hold on tight."

The sensation of her arms clasping him with confidence, and her face buried against his shoulder with a small sigh, tugged at him sweetly. Devlin knew that she had just stolen the piece of his heart that didn't belong to Karen.

"Here we go."

With Livie clinging to him, he picked a way for them down the bluff in easy, careful stages. He could hear shouts from below and someone calling to him.

"Do you need help?"

He knew the police had arrived on the scene. He hoped that one of them had covered Ramey's body so that Livie wouldn't have to see it.

"We're okay!" he yelled back.

Karen's anxious arms were waiting to receive Livie when he descended the last few feet to the base of the cliff. Devlin handed her over, and the reunion of mother and daughter hugging each other fiercely brought a silly lump to his throat.

Livie, lifting her head from Karen's breast, pointed at him and demanded, "Who?"

Devlin could see with pleasure that Karen's face had never been plainer to read. There was pure exhilaration there when she answered her daughter.

"His name is Devlin Hawke, darling, and you are absolutely going to love him. I do."

Chapter Thirteen

Not the Twin Cities. Or Denver. Or even Chicago. Devlin wanted them to be married right here in Door County at the Nordic Inn. Nothing else would do.

He had consulted with Karen about it in the cottage the morning after their recovery of Livie. "I've been out exploring the place. Do you know it used to be the summer estate of a family from Milwaukee before it was turned into a resort? And guess what? In a clearing off the other side of the main lodge is this little *stavkirke.*"

"A what?"

"*Stavkirke.* They're traditional Norwegian churches. Looks like something out of a fairy tale. The family built and used it as their chapel. I talked to the management here, and they said a wedding could be arranged for the chapel and they'd handle a reception for us in the lodge afterwards. Karen, it's perfect. So what do you think?"

"Well…"

"Of course," he had added hastily, "if you'd rather not consider the peninsula at all, I'd understand. I guess it does have some pretty unpleasant associations for you."

He had been so boyishly eager about his discovery that she couldn't bear to disappoint him. Besides, he was wrong about her feelings for the peninsula. Hadn't they been reunited with their daughter here and pledged their love to each other? The rest didn't matter.

"Yes, darling," she had agreed, "I think this county is a beautiful place to begin the rest of our lives together."

Devlin had grinned happily and taken her in his arms.

Now, almost two weeks later, on a sunny Saturday morning with a cool breeze blowing off the lake, Karen stood before the full-length mirror in the spacious bedroom of an elegant suite in the main lodge. The Hawke women were with her, helping her to dress for her wedding. There was Moura, energetic and efficient, ready to welcome a new daughter into the family. Standing beside her was the willowy Eden, warm and caring. And on her other side was the youngest, a petite and cheerful Christy.

"Gorgeous!" Moura pronounced, stepping back to admire Karen after adjusting her veil.

Karen, gazing at herself in the mirror, *was* pleased with the result. She wore a white silk suit over a pale yellow shell. On her head was a small matching hat with just a hint of a veil.

Christy nodded her own approval. "And yellow sweetheart roses for the— Hey, where is the bridal bouquet?"

"It's supposed to be in the cooler in the lodge's kitchen," Karen answered.

"Huh, I'd better go see and bring it back to you. Because if it's not there," Christy threatened, "I may have to go out in that field and pick some wild daisies." She left the suite to find her way to the kitchen.

"Speaking of flowers," Karen asked after she'd gone, "does anyone know how Maud is doing with the arrangements in the chapel?"

"Last time I checked," Eden said, "she and your assistant, Robyn, were still fussing over them."

Her friend and business partner was to be Karen's maid

of honor. She and Maud had spent a portion of these past two weeks engaged in several lengthy business discussions back in Minneapolis. A decision had resulted from their meetings. Inspired by the success of the Hawke Detective Agency and its offices all over the country, Karen was going to open a branch of Dream Makers in Denver. Devlin had been willing to relocate to the Twin Cities, but that didn't make sense when his agency was so well established in Colorado. And though Karen would miss Maud, she was eager to manage her own interior design firm.

"It's going to be a lovely ceremony, Karen," Moura assured her. "Maud and Robyn have candles all over the chapel, and when they're lighted…" She sighed wistfully. "Casey and I never had anything so romantic. We were married in a judge's chambers."

"Ma, you know you wouldn't have had the patience for a church wedding."

Eden winked at Karen. It was a sisterly wink, and it went straight to Karen's heart. The Hawkes had already accepted her as one of them. She was realizing at last her lifelong dream of belonging to a big, loving family, of being one of its cherished members. Devlin's family. Nothing could be more satisfying than that.

Which was why, she told herself firmly, she had no right to this thing that had been nagging at her since yesterday when the Hawkes had met them here at the resort. After all, nothing was ever really perfect. Just the same, she couldn't shake her concern. She had promised herself not to mention it to Devlin, to say nothing that would spoil their wedding day, but if only—

The door to the sitting room opened, and Christy reappeared. "Look who I ran into out in the hall!"

The burly figure of the Hawkes' old family friend, Sheriff Neil Holland, appeared behind her in the doorway. "Is it safe to come in?'' he inquired with one of his hearty smiles.

"Oh, yes, please join us," Karen invited him.

"Stopped by to offer my best wishes to the bride," he said, entering the bedroom.

"Aren't you staying for the wedding?"

"Thank you for inviting me, but I can't. The Fourth of July may be behind us, but it's still crazy in the county at this season, and I'm still short of officers. I will spare a few minutes to talk to you, though, if it won't make you late for the ceremony."

"Of course."

"I'd better get on to the kitchen and that bridal bouquet," Christy said.

"And Eden and I need to see what happened to our men," Moura said.

The Hawke women excused themselves, leaving Karen and the sheriff alone in the suite. She offered him a chair, but he declined.

"This won't take long," he said, "but I thought you might appreciate knowing that everything has been cleared up. It took some lengthy persuading, but Veronica Delgado finally agreed to cooperate. I guess she realized it would benefit her when she and Cassius Bennett stand trial."

"She told you the full truth about Michael?"

"As much as she knows, and that's considerable. Michael Ramey wasn't his real name, of course, but then you already learned that. It turns out his real name was an ordinary Roy Jones. Born in poverty in rural Texas and grew up wanting to be anything but ordinary. And because he had a talent with a gun and a willingness to—"

The sheriff broke off, frowning as he stroked his luxuriant ginger mustache. "But maybe you don't want to hear this. Maybe you'd just like to forget about it."

"No, I want to know. I think that's the only way I can put it all behind me for good. What else did Veronica tell you?"

"How she and Jones met in San Francisco. She caught him when he was researching Fletcher Stowe, preparing for his latest hit, and instead of exposing him she fell for him."

"I know. She boasted to me how in the end she actually helped him to kill Fletcher Stowe."

"That's right. She managed to get him aboard Stowe's yacht and then enticed the old man's bodyguard to a place where Jones could eliminate him first."

"It's twisted, isn't it? She would have been a rich woman if Fletcher Stowe hadn't died before they married."

"She expected to be one anyway with the man she really wanted. Jones had accumulated a fortune in a bank in the West Indies. They'd planned to disappear down there after he murdered Vernon Andersen." The sheriff paused, gazing at Karen speculatively. "I don't suppose it's possible, is it?"

"What?"

"That you actually could be Governor Andersen's missing daughter."

Karen smiled and shook her head. "I'm sorry for the governor, but there's not a chance of that. It's Livie who resembles his daughter at the age she disappeared. And Livie looks like her father, not me."

"That's right. But it did occur to me for just a second there, after remembering how Casey told me you grew up an orphan—"

"Not anymore she isn't," Devlin said as he strode through the open door. "She's got me now."

Neil Holland rounded on him. "Hey, are you supposed

to be in here? It's bad luck for the groom to see the bride before the wedding, isn't it?''

"Not for us," Devlin insisted.

His words conveyed a promise to Karen: Now that they'd found each other again, nothing really bad would ever touch them. He wouldn't permit it. And his gaze, meeting hers across the room, expressed a love that made her heart skip a beat and her eyes grow moist.

She feared she was in danger of making a fool of herself in front of Sheriff Holland. That Devlin was so breath robbingly handsome in a dark blue suit didn't help her emotional state.

The sheriff must have sensed her vulnerable condition. "Your bride can share with you what I've just been telling her," he said to Devlin. "I've gotta run." He shook their hands, offered them his best wishes, and made his hasty departure.

Devlin came toward her when Neil was gone, but he wasn't interested in the sheriff's news. All he wanted to talk about was Livie, a subject that seemed to occupy his conversations a great deal these days.

"The little stinker," he complained. "I make sure she's looking like a sweet doll in that pink dress she begged for, just like you asked me to, and then she goes and gets herself all grubby."

Karen laughed. "Welcome to the agonies of parenthood. And exactly how did she, uh—''

"Throwing stones on the beach. Now don't look at me like that. She's all excited about the wedding. I had to keep her entertained, didn't I? It was supposed to be nothing but a stroll along the shore. How did I know she'd go and get both of us in trouble.''

"What did you do with her?"

Karen was surprised Livie wasn't with him. She already

adored him and accompanied him everywhere. And Devlin, who had so long denied himself the joys of fatherhood, couldn't seem to get enough of his daughter.

"Turned her over to her grandmother. Ma has her down in her room cleaning her up."

Moura doted on Livie. Karen feared that, between her grandmother and her father, Livie was at risk of being spoiled. But she didn't complain. Livie was going to grow up with all the pleasures and memories of a family that Karen had never experienced.

Devlin took her hands and held them. "Look," he said solemnly, "I sneaked in here hoping to get you alone for a minute before the ceremony. There's something I want to give you."

"You've already given me everything I need." Almost everything, anyway, she thought, but she couldn't bear to tell him that.

"Yeah, well," he said awkwardly, "I still wanted to surprise you with a wedding gift. Something special from me to you. Only I couldn't think of anything that seemed just right. And then it came to me."

"What?"

"The perfect gift. At least I hope you'll think it is. Karen, I know that the father you never knew always left a hole in your life. I'm pledging my P.I. skills to find him for you."

She was touched by his proposal. "Darling, I'm pleased by your offer, and whoever he is, wherever he is, I wish him well. But I don't need to know him, because that hole doesn't exist anymore. I've got the man I love already filling it."

"Yeah?" He smiled down at her. A dazzling, teasing smile that made her weak. "Then why are you looking at me like you're not sure I'm for real?"

"Because I can't believe you're the same man who walked back into my life less than three weeks ago."

"That's easy. I'm not. I never believed it when they said a woman's love can change a man. But it's true. Know something else?"

"What?"

"Our daughter is beautiful, but her mother," he said, his admiring gaze traveling the length of her in her wedding outfit, "is an eyeful."

What she saw in his pure blue eyes stirred her senses like a warm caress. And when he released her hands in order to slide his arms around her waist, pulling her close, she was at risk of losing her self-control.

Molding his body to hers, Devlin growled in her ear a low, sexy, "Why don't we skip the wedding and go straight to the honeymoon?"

"Can't. I promised Livie the first piece of wedding cake. You'll just have to settle for a preview of the honeymoon."

Clasping her hands behind his head, she drew his mouth down to hers. He kissed her eagerly, deeply. A potent kiss that promised a lifetime of commitment.

They were still locked in each other's arms when a crowd consisting of the entire Hawke family and an excited Livie trooped into the suite.

"Hey, you two," Roark called from the doorway, "break it up before you melt the rings in my pocket."

Roark, in charge of the wedding bands, was to be Devlin's best man. His brother, Mitch, who shared the same dark good looks, compelling blue eyes and wicked sense of humor as the other Hawke men, grinned his approval of their intimate embrace.

The room was suddenly all noise and happy confusion. Livie ran to Karen. "Look, Mama, Grandma Moura took a sponge and made me pretty again!'' Christy produced the bridal bouquet for her, and Eden informed her that the minister had arrived.

Karen, surrounded by the family she already loved, glowed. Then her eye fell on Devlin. He stood a little apart from the rest of them, an inscrutable expression on his face. She hated herself for it, but she couldn't stop the yearning she felt.

If only, if only…

"Look," Casey interrupted them impatiently, "if we don't get these two married, I won't get in the fishing I promised myself this afternoon. So let's get on with it, okay?"

They started to stream out of the bedroom, but Devlin stopped them. "Hang on a minute."

They stopped and turned, gazing at him expectantly.

"There's something I need to say before we go."

"What is it, Dev?" his mother encouraged him.

"Just this," he said earnestly. "For a long time now I haven't been a very good son or brother to any of you. I guess it's no secret why."

"We understood, Dev," Eden assured him.

"I know you did, but it doesn't excuse my rotten behavior."

Karen listened to him, her heart swelling with joy and gratitude. This was the thing she had been wishing for, *hoping* for since the Hawkes had arrived at the resort. Devlin was at last making peace with his family.

"I owe you all an apology," he continued humbly, "and I'd like to ask your forgiveness."

"You have it," his mother promised him. "You always did have it."

"Thank you." Devlin hesitated. "There's something else. All those years I was pushing you away, acting like you didn't matter…well, it was a lie. I want you to know that underneath I never stopped loving my family.''

I won't cry, Karen thought fiercely. If I start to cry, I won't stop, so I won't cry.

Casey saved her from that threat by announcing in a booming voice, ''This calls for a Hawke huddle!''

''Hawke huddle,'' they all agreed.

What on earth are they talking about? Karen wondered. Mystified, she watched them close in on Devlin from all sides. She understood what was happening when, arms clasping one another, the seven of them formed a tight circle like a football huddle. She was seeing a moving expression of family love and solidarity.

Casey turned his head, grinning at Karen and Livie. ''What are you two waiting for? You're part of this outfit now, too, so get over here.''

An eager Livie took her mother by the hand and dragged her into the huddle. So that she could be a part of it on their level, Devlin hoisted his squealing daughter onto his shoulders. Then, for the next thirty precious seconds, Karen found herself enveloped in a group hug. And that was when she fully understood what it felt like to be a part of a caring family.

It was Livie this time who rescued her from the tears that were swimming in her eyes when she demanded loudly, ''Am I a real Hawke now?''

''You will be,'' Devlin informed her, ''just as soon as we make it official. Hear that?''

They paused to listen to the bell that had begun to toll in the tiny, pointed belfry atop the roof of the chapel.

''It's calling us out to the chapel where we're going to make it official,'' Devlin explained, lowering her from his shoulders. ''Are you ready?''

Guests staying at the resort lined both sides of the stone

flagged path leading to the chapel. Karen saw their smiling faces and heard their applause when the wedding party emerged from the lodge. Sunlight streamed into the clearing, and as the procession moved toward the wooden chapel, with a proud Livie leading the way, she could see Maud and Robyn and the minister waiting for them on the porch.

The bell continued to peal sweetly, but Karen no longer heard it. All she could suddenly hear, or wanted to hear, was Devlin's voice husky with emotion. Squeezing her hand, he leaned over to whisper at her ear, ''I know now what they mean by a radiant bride. And thank heaven she's all mine.''

HARLEQUIN®
INTRIGUE

**High up in the Rocky Mountains
there is a place where the wind
blows fast and fierce,
where trust is precious
and where everyone has a secret...**

Welcome to

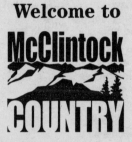

**Join author Sheryl Lynn
as she crosses the fine line
between deception and loyalty
in this brand-new series.**

TO PROTECT THEIR CHILD
Available March 2001

COLORADO'S FINEST
Available April 2001

Wherever Harlequin books are sold.

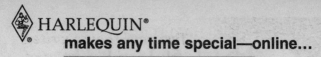

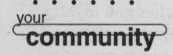

INDULGE IN A QUIET MOMENT
WITH HARLEQUIN

Get a FREE
Quiet Moments Bath Spa

with just two proofs of purchase from
any of our four special collector's editions in May.

**Harlequin® is sure to make your time special this Mother's Day
with four special collector's editions featuring a short story
PLUS a complete novel packaged together in one volume!**

Collection #1   Intrigue abounds in a collection featuring *New York Times*
     bestselling author Barbara Delinsky and Kelsey Roberts.

Collection #2   Relationships? Weddings? Children? = *New York Times*
     bestselling author Debbie Macomber and Tara Taylor Quinn
     at their best!

Collection #3   Escape to the past with *New York Times* bestselling author
     Heather Graham and Gayle Wilson.

Collection #4   Go West! With *New York Times* bestselling author
     Joan Johnston and Vicki Lewis Thompson!

Plus Special Consumer Campaign!
Each of these four collector's editions will feature a
"FREE QUIET MOMENTS BATH SPA" offer.
See inside book in May for details.

Only from

HARLEQUIN®
Makes any time special ®

Don't miss out! Look for this exciting promotion on sale in May 2001,
at your favorite retail outlet.

Visit us at www.eHarlequin.com   PHNCP01

HARLEQUIN®
INTRIGUE
opens the case files on:

TOP SECRET
BABIES

Unwrap the mystery!

January 2001
#597 THE BODYGUARD'S BABY
Debra Webb

February 2001
#601 SAVING HIS SON
Rita Herron

March 2001
#605 THE HUNT FOR HAWKE'S DAUGHTER
Jean Barrett

April 2001
#609 UNDERCOVER BABY
Adrianne Lee

May 2001
#613 CONCEPTION COVER-UP
Karen Lawton Barrett

Follow the clues to your favorite retail outlet.

HARLEQUIN®

Makes any time special ™